To Walter Miller

With thanks for a memorable Summer workshop in Vermont and for the encouragement to shape this thing up and eventually publish it.

And with appreciation for your

BRASS CROSS

considerate way of working with writers — not the easiest bunch to get along with.

You have my prayers and best wishes.

Gene Blackie

BRASS CROSS

Bruce Blackie

Hampshire Books
Akron • Philadelphia
1989

BRASS CROSS. Copyright © 1989 by Bruce Blackie. All rights reserved. No part of this book may be used or reproduced in any manner whatsoever without written permission except in the case of brief quotations embodied in critical articles and reviews. For information, address Hampshire Books, 1300 Weathervane Lane, Suite 221, Akron, Ohio 44313.

Cover Design: John Manko

Library of Congress Cataloging-in-Publication Data

Blackie, Bruce L., 1936-
   Brass cross.

   I. Title
PS3552.L3425B74 1989   813′.54   89-11201
   ISBN 1-877674-00-1

Printed in the United States of America.

To
ROLAND W. TAPP
for encouragement
and
STEPHEN R. DONALDSON
for being tough

He who begins by loving Christianity better than Truth will proceed by loving his own sect or church better than Christianity, and end by loving himself better than all.

Samuel Taylor Coleridge

Part One

1

Peter Campbell glanced up from his roast beef; all eyes were staring at him. The blue eyes of the white-haired lady whose head seemed to levitate several inches above her neck. The green eyes of the lawyer with the pale face and thick, reddish hair, who precisely phrased his questions as if he had worked them out beforehand on a yellow pad. There was the salesman with brown eyes whose voice rose excitedly when he recited the virtues of Good Samaritan Church: as if it were his job to sell the church lock, stock, and barrel to a new minister rather than hire him as pastor. And the heavy-jowled chairman's eyes—red with fatigue, or was it frustration at how long his committee had been looking for a minister?

As Peter met their gazes, their eyes glanced elsewhere. He breathed more easily. If he were surrounded by unblinking stares of possession, he wasn't sure how he would respond.

What did they see in him, he wondered? His tall, lanky frame clad in a brown suit with last year's wide lapels that must shout he's not in their class. His wife, Brenda, sitting opposite him, had said with his curly hair and square jaw he looked like a movie star. Others said, "You certainly don't look like a *minister*." If homeliness were a necessary quality of ecclesiastical promise, apparently he didn't have it. But surely the committee would base its decision on something of more theological importance than jaw set and hairline. But what was it?

He recalled the last meeting of the board at his ailing

downtown church. The members were scattered about in the sanctuary dimly lit because the property committee chairman said the church could not afford electricity. The sanctuary was further dimmed by its aging mahogany pews and brown carpet worn down to the backing. The subject of the meeting was the orange stain in the ceiling above the pulpit which expanded with each rainstorm like an ever-growing toxic cloud.

"It'll cost at least fifty thou to fix it right," said the wiry roofer in blue jeans and a red flannel shirt. His shrill voice sounded like John the Baptist warning the Pharisees of impending judgment.

"We don't have it," said a Board member out of the darkness.

"We don't have *five* thousand," said another.

"Then we'll just get it patched," said a third. "A few buckets of tar won't cost much."

Peter felt himself sinking. "But it's been patched," he said. "It's the patches that are leaking. Someday the plaster's going to fall in." He envisioned it occurring while he was preaching—an avalanche of shards and dust and whatever else had accumulated up there for a hundred years hurling him to the chancel floor and burying him. The headline would read: CHURCH KILLS MINISTER.

Brenda smiled sweetly at the salesman buzzing in her ear. She had dressed for the role of the pastor's wife—red hair tied back in a ponytail, slight tint on her smooth cheeks, just a hint of blue eyeshadow—nothing on the lashes. Her dark blue suit looked matronly. She ate with small bites and chewed each one thoroughly, her face a lineless mask of neutrality.

On the drive to the meeting, he had asked her what he should do. "It's up to you," she said. "You're the one who does the work."

"But they'll expect something of you," he replied.

"They'll get something, you know that."

He did. She would show up at some of their meetings

and always smile. The smile, with her eyes sparkling, that was what did it.

"As long as there's a ballet class in the town, I'm happy. And things for the kids to do."

"Well, it's a good-sized city," he said. "I'm sure that won't be a problem."

But thus far, Brenda had not mentioned ballet to the committee. And the committee had not asked if either of them or Jackie or Jeff had any interests other than Good Samaritan Church.

The door of the private dining room swung open, and the black waiter entered and planted himself at the end of the table. "Dessert?" he asked. All the waiters were black, and all the members of the Delaware Club visible in the leather-chaired lounge and chandeliered dining room white. By some baffling stroke, the tidal wave of the sixties that had swept over Peter's city parish had ebbed before reaching the island shores of Oakdale. Hard to believe.

Or maybe not so hard when he considered that the eyes observing him had probably not been in the city in the sixties, or early on they had joined the exodus to the suburbs. Could he challenge these people to follow Jesus? Could he himself follow Jesus in their church? He searched the eyes scrutinizing menus as if the choice between cheesecake and chocolate mousse were weightier than the decision that had sunk like a cold stone to the pit of his stomach and saw no answer.

The waiter took a step backward and blended into the background of a large painting—illuminated by the glare of an indirect light—of one of the Delaware Club's former presidents. Enshrinement in oil apparently signified ascent to the apex of Oakdale's social pyramid. Framed in ornate gold and clad in a double-breasted blazer, with a monogrammed handkerchief peeking from the pocket, the subject wore beneath his thatch of white hair a mask of stern respectability. More on the side of Pilate, Peter thought, than of the Apostle Paul.

On the far side of the room, the waiter fell under the gaze of another past president. This one wore a striped suit and vest. Fat cheeks puffed around a small mouth, the wrinkled forehead was framed on either side by a puff of gray hair and capped by a bald dome. His name inscrutable on a small plaque on the lower part of the frame, he reminded Peter, especially in the glaring eyes, of a stained glass rendering he had once seen of Caiaphas, the high priest who had voted for Jesus' crucifixion.

To an unnerving degree, he also resembled the chairman of Good Samaritan's committee seated directly below. Having delivered his order to the waiter, the chairman slid a hand into his coat pocket, drew out a cigar, nodded about as if requesting permission to enjoy his repast, and lit up. Clouds of smoke billowed out over the table. Two other members of the committee rummaged for cigarettes, and soon the oil paint witnesses were wizened by the thickening air.

"And you, sir?" The words stabbed from behind Peter's left ear. He rubbed his chin in nervous discomfort, resisting an urge to disavow to the waiter any affinity with the Delaware Club's social stratification. His eyes dutifully scanned the menu of offerings far too sumptuous after the slab of roast beef. On top of that, the question of whether he could take on Good Samaritan had detached his stomach from the rest of him.

He glanced up and asked for a small piece of cake. The corners of the waiter's mouth drooped with irritation. Peter added coffee, and then he was alone with the committee and the decision.

Finally the chairman sighed, leaned back, and leveled his gaze at Peter. "Well, we've covered everything. Too bad with the lousy weather we couldn't show you more of the town. But the tour should've given you a good idea of what Oakdale is like. Great place to live, really." He glanced about as members of his committee nodded in agreement. "The air's clean. People get along well. None of the problems they're having in the city." He paused, then added, "Not that we don't have an obligation there. We do, and we take it seriously. But it's just that people here tend to be more hard working. They know what they want out of life."

Through the rain-blurred windows of the chairman's speeding Cadillac, Peter had not been able to detect what the citizens wanted out of life. He did know Oakdale had a business district of renovated brick and new steel and glass buildings and sprawling suburbs with curved streets, cul-de-sacs, and gray, white, and green colonial aluminum houses guarded by black eagles above their doors. If there were older, non-colonial neighborhoods, or slums, they had been skirted.

The chairman launched another cloud of smoke and shifted his gaze to Brenda. "Sorry we couldn't get you into the parsonage, Mrs. Campbell. We know that should be part of your decision, but the Strongs are out, and we don't know where to find a key."

From the car, Peter had glimpsed the house—an adequate looking split-level. Brick below, aluminum above, a detached two car garage.

The lady with the sky colored eyes and floating head stirred. "It's a beautiful home. Good Samaritan would have nothing else. I've been in it many times. There's plenty of space for your children. The family room makes it nice when you've got someone over. There's a fireplace there too. It's so cozy."

Brenda's eyes rested on the table. In their walnut depths, Peter still could detect no leaning. "Well, if the church requires us to live there," she replied in a monotone. "I guess it really doesn't make any difference . . ."

The chairman leaned forward with the amiability of a well-sauced Santa Claus. "I'm certain you'd be happy with it. Fine house. Old enough to have quality workmanship. New enough so you won't have to worry about repairs."

Peter groaned inwardly. Having been ankle-deep in water while fixing a toilet and having once grabbed a hot wire on a ceiling fixture, he had learned to leave the upper reaches of house repairs to professionals.

The stock broker's thick eyebrows rose. "What did you have in mind, Mrs. Campbell? There could always be some alterations."

Brenda's eyes rested on Peter. "We were thinking of a house in the country," she said. "Nothing fancy. Maybe something with an old barn. Our son's a sculptor. He needs lots of space for his work."

Peter had promised Jeff. They were in the cellar discussing what to do with 'Neanderthal' if they moved. Neanderthal, a nine foot man Jeff had shaped from hundreds of pounds of plaster of Paris, lay on his back on a thick-legged work table. Between his size and weight, there was simply no way they could get him out of the cellar. Peter had thought of a heavy hammer, but Jeff always became strangely attached to his creations.

"It would be easier to go if I was getting a better place to work," Jeff said. He was tall, studious, a bit on the awkward side when it came to running or playing ball. Behind his thick glasses loomed dreams of huge sculptures.

"We'll get a better place," Peter said.

"Who will?" Jeff retorted.

"We . . . we will," Peter repeated.

"But there never is a *we*. It's *them*, the church, or some goshawful committee. *They* decide where we'll live."

"Well, even then we can make a place for your sculpture. We can do with the house what we want."

Jeff turned away and his eyes gazed at Neanderthal. Peter wished they could take him with them. But how would they get him out? And even in the best of parsonages, where would they put him?

The chairman puffed more smoke out over the table and knocked a cylinder of ash into the tray. "Well, the parsonage goes with the job. So there's not much room for discussion." His voice took on a dulcet tone. "Look at it this way. No mortgage. No taxes. No maintenance. You'll find it's a real saving."

"We'll fix it up however you want," the blue-eyed lady added. Her smile seemed fired in glaze. "That's what we did for the Strongs. Our property committee is very good at things like that."

"Well, do you want the job?" The question, lobbed by the dour man with penetrating eyes who seldom spoke, whistled in like a mortar shell. The chairman's head jerked up as if he were about to swat down the query in mid-flight, but then he sagged back awaiting Peter's reply.

A bubble of gas burned in Peter's stomach. If he told them "yes," what would he say to Jeff? And to Jackie, his daughter?

She had sat him down for a daughter-father talk. Sweat beaded on her red face, welled in her dark eyes. She was tall, lean; when she ran, her long legs slid smoothly, her arms pulled her along, her body leaned strongly into the wind.

"I'm tired of broken sidewalks and broken bottles and traffic and traffic lights and exhaust," she said with an unblinking gaze. "Mom said we would move to the country."

"We're trying," Peter said. "You know I don't have full control . . ."

"But you don't *have* to take whatever house they give you. Mom says they can sell the house, give us the money, and let us buy our own."

"Some churches do that," he conceded.

"Dad, I want you to promise. It doesn't cost any more to live in the country than it does in one of those suburban developments."

"Maybe less," Peter allowed.

"Then you'll promise?"

"I'll try," Peter said.

"That isn't the same as a promise."

"I know."

"Mom says."

"I know what mom says. If it's up to us, the country is what we'll have."

"I can see it now," Jackie said. She gazed off. "Narrow lanes across fields, through forests. Hardly any cars or trucks. I can't wait."

"You've got an impressive church," Peter stammered. The eyes of the committee members softened. "Of course it's not buildings that are important." His observation left a hole of awkward silence.

Heads nodded, thin smiles appeared. Brenda studied the white tablecloth and refused to look at him.

The door burst open, and the waiter careened in with a large tray. He banged it down onto the stand and motioned the waitress behind to put hers beneath the bald dome cast in oil. Peter breathed more easily.

But he couldn't rid his mind of Good Samaritan's buildings seen on the tour: glass domes, glass walls, glass doors, glass corridors, glass roofs, glass ceilings, glass partitions, glass offices. Even restrooms of glass — opaque, thankfully, in the walls. He had let on to the chairman that he thought the structures a bit strange, but the chairman hadn't taken to that. "Unique," he said, and then the term kept surfacing like the response to a litany.

"My only hesitation is whether we truly fit here," Peter said. "Am I the man for you?" He had an impulse to reflect aloud whether Good Samaritan was the church for him, but he resisted. In the eyes glowing around him, refusing Good Samaritan might be tantamount to refusing the Creator himself.

The waiter struck a match and ignited a chafing dish. Flame whooshed, fruit sizzled, the pungence of brandy mingled with tobacco smoke.

The chairman leaned forward. "What do you mean?" Erratic motions of his cigar-bearing hand sent the blue-eyed levitator shrinking back in her chair. "We've examined all your papers. We've talked to your references. We're more than satisfied with what we've heard today. You're a hard worker. Your people are with you. You may not realize it, but you don't find that very often nowadays." He nodded to the rest of the committee. "Make no bones about it. We're impressed with your record . . . or we wouldn't have invited you here today."

Peter flinched from peaches flambé crackling at his elbow. "It's the way I view the church. I don't see it as a corporation . . . . It's people."

One day when he was thirteen, his Aunt Katherine, who had raised him, came home from church, thumped her Bible down on the coffee table in her modestly furnished living room, and sat shaking her head. "They're on the preacher again," she said. "Last time they said the church doesn't do enough for old people. Now they say it ignores the kids." She shook her head in disgust. "If it isn't one thing, it's another. The preacher this. The preacher that. Why don't *they* do something? After all, they're the church. They don't seem to see that, though. They hired the minister to do their religion for them, and by George, the only responsibility under heaven they think they've got is to make sure he does it right. How misguided can they be? The sick go unvisited, the grieving sit alone, kids who need help in this town are just stared at like they were rodents — and what do they care? The problem is people. Never forget that, Peter. It's people and nothing more. Christ knew that, but they don't want to take it from him. Sometimes I wonder if they know anything about him. It's just the church they want—their church, a church that satisfies all their quirks."

She stirred about in the shapeless easy chair and fanned her sweating face. "'Course I'm just as bad. That's the trouble with Christianity. As soon as you see something wrong in other people and get down on it, you see all your own faults too. Yes, Peter, it's people, including you and me. If this Christian faith would work with just a few of us, things in this world would be a lot better."

The man with thick glasses leaned forward, his hands tightly clasped. "Don't you see that's precisely what we're looking for? We *want* ministry to people. Let the Council and the Board of Trustees run the business part."

"Coffee?" the waiter asked tonelessly. Steaming cups were poured and passed.

"There's the fight of faith," Peter went on. He felt as if he were blundering through a forest. "Self-denial. We may suffer for doing what's right. If we do, we're to count it a blessing." He paused. So much more pushed into his mind than he could shape into words.

The blue-eyed lady's lips moved. "What makes you think that's not what we want? We've seen what you believe in. We're impressed. That's why we've kept after you."

"But all that glass . . ." Peter was hardly conscious he had blurted it. Rectangles, squares, trapezoids, triangles, flat pieces, curved pieces, walls, doors, domes – all glass.

"My God, is that what's holding you back?" the chairman roared. The lines in his forehead softened. "*We* didn't design those buildings. They were *given* to the church by a member who died several years ago. They aren't us. Oh no!" He unleashed a deep guttural laugh. "No, not at all." He glanced about for confirming glances from the committee.

"What we *want* is the good old rugged Christian faith – like 'the old rugged cross' we don't sing about any more. We've been slipping. We're soft, lazy. We need to get back to those old disciples. They were determined sons of guns. Independent. Self-reliant. We need to be like them." He leaned forward and pressed his arms on the table. "I'll tell you, if you can produce people in Good Samaritan like those characters in the Bible, you'll be worth your weight in gold. Not that we don't have some real saints now. We do. Make no bones about it. But with your hard work, there'll be hundreds more. We're convinced you're our man."

Peter scanned their faces. Every orb stared with possessiveness. Brenda looked up at the ceiling as if tracing the path of an errant spider.

Behind her hung another oil painting – different from the others. It portrayed a large city lying in a valley as seen from a rounded bluff. On the edge of the bluff stood a lonely figure with his head pressed forward as if he were bent on going to the city—perhaps to deliver an urgent message. The man reminded Peter of Jesus, staring down at Jerusalem from the Mount of Olives prior to the Triumphal Entry.

He recalled the glass structures he had seen on the tour. Only now he saw faces pressed to the windows, glad faces of men, women, and children. Glass doors sprang open, and out they came—to sell their luxurious homes and give the proceeds to the poor. In a hospital ward, they bent over sick bodies and whispered words of comfort. A craggy man sounding like Elijah denounced the stolid Board of Directors of the Delaware Club: "It's a travesty this Club has no black members and yet hires only blacks to wait on tables and work in the kitchen!"

A piece of cake popped off Peter's fork and disintegrated on his lap. His face burned with embarrassment at his old nemesis—main motor dysfunction. During his growing up years, his nervous system had always lagged behind his tall body, and there still had been no coming together. As he came up from searching for crumbs, his head was nodding.

"You'll take it?" the chairman asked. "Are you agreeing to come?"

"Yes . . . yes," Peter stammered. He didn't know what else to say.

With a wheeze the chairman rose to his feet. His face broadened into a grin of triumph. "You've made the right decision. You're exactly the man Good Samaritan needs."

Peter stood and hung out a tentative hand. The members, one by one, clutched it confidently.

2

Brenda said, "I think it's what they call a 'splanch.'" She was behind Peter as he stood at the open door directing the moving men where to place the Campbell's earthly possessions. "Do you notice how you can see every part of the house from the other parts? You can look from the kitchen, through the living room, down into the family room. You can also look through the living room up into the bedrooms. It's a house built for people who can't stand privacy."

Peter directed another box of miscellaneous — he had lost track of how many there were — to the cellar. "Doors," he said.

"Doors?"

"We'll have the church install doors between the family room and the living room and between the living room and the kitchen."

"Walls, you mean."

"Walls?"

"Why, yes. Look at the size of the openings."

Peter looked. Brenda was right. The opening between the kitchen and living room was large enough to drive a car through. And next to the stairs descending to the family room you could fit a sofa. "Walls then," he said.

"Do you think they'll do it?"

"The committee said they'd do anything we asked."

"Yes," Brenda replied without conviction.

"You're thinking of the problems we had before?" It had taken so long to get repairs done on the parsonage in the city, Peter had hired someone from the outside on his own.

"Yes," she replied.

"This'll be different. This is a large church with a lot of wealthy people. Our days of scrimping are over."

"Oh," Brenda replied. "And the decor?" she asked.

Peter glanced at the white walls and the albino carpet and the living room ceiling someone had tried to make look colonial with raised plaster circles — they looked as if they'd been made with a plumber's helper — and at Brenda's pine chairs and cabinets and tables adrift on the white sea.

"They'll paint it," Peter said confidently.

"And put down carpet?"

"And put down carpet," he added. Although when he bent down and ran his fingers through the pile, it appeared the carpet was quite new.

"And the circles?"

He looked up. How someone would get them off, he could not imagine. Perhaps a chisel. Then could they ever get the ceiling smooth? "And the circles," he said hopefully.

Brenda kept staring up. "They're like eyes. It's as if someone is looking at us all the time."

They didn't look like eyes to Peter. Just circles made with a rubber ring. Tacky.

"We get watched enough in the church without having a ceiling full of eyes."

"We'll have them fix it," Peter said. "They said they would."

"They'd better," Brenda added, her voice trailing off. She headed toward the stairs.

"Where are you going?"

"I'm cold. I want to lie down."

"On what?"

"I'll pull a mattress out of one of the boxes and use Jeff's sleeping bag."

"That's not comfortable."

"I'm cold, Peter. And tired. I just need a half hour or so." She disappeared up the stairs.

The movers took a break, so Peter went to the thermostat in the living area and slid the lever to a higher temperature. There was no noise of a furnace starting down below. He descended to the cellar, picked his way past stacks of boxes, and bent down to the furnace controls. He turned several knobs, pushed a button marked 'pilot,' and lit a match. A whoosh of orange flame leaped out and enveloped his face.

"What was that?" came Brenda's faraway voice.

"The furnace."

"Are you all right?"

Peter felt his eyebrows — they were slightly singed. And his hairline — his hair was there, but the ends were fluffy. "Yes," he shouted up. He put the matches away and climbed to the family room.

The logs he had asked the movers to put on the truck were stacked on the hearth. He wadded newspaper into balls, tucked them into the grate, covered them with small sticks, and laid on several logs. He struck a match and lit the paper. It caught easily, and then smoke poured out into the room. He groped up the chimney for the damper—a cold iron plate that wouldn't budge. He picked up a log and hammered on it. Stuck tight. Then he noticed the electrical socket at the back of the firebox: the bricks had never been charred.

"Peter, do you smell something burning?" came Brenda's plaintive voice.

"I've got it under control," he shouted. He was running from the kitchen with a pan of water, which he poured on the flames. They sizzled out, and a gray stream of water coursed out onto the hearth. He grabbed papers to stanch the flow. "Everything's fine," he added. His hands were coated with newsprint which he had to wash off in the kitchen.

He went up to the master bedroom. Brenda lay curled up in Jeff's long khaki sleeping bag on a mattress still in its cardboard carton. Only her nose and eyes were visible. "Do you really think they'll fix it up?" she asked. "I don't want to be unreasonable. I was content with the old house. It was such a comfortable place for our antiques."

"Sure they will," Peter replied. "They were very emphatic that they would do what we asked."

3

The doorbell rang. On the front step stood a brunette with sparkling eyes and a freckled face wearing a tan coat. She balanced in one hand a tray covered with a red and white checkered cloth. "Hi, I'm Marge," came her melodious greeting. "Okay if I come in?"

Peter had to resist an urge to embrace her, not because of any drive in himself, but because Marge looked like the kind of person who could pull Brenda out of the Slough of Despond. He motioned her in.

"I'm a member of the church. I thought with moving in and all you might not have time to fix dinner." She set the tray down on a carton and lifted off the cover.

Just then Brenda drifted down the stairs like Lady Macbeth after a sleepless night. She had pulled a bathrobe over her jeans, her face was lined with sleep grooves. But when she beheld spaghetti and hot Italian bread and salad and bottles of milk and red wine and pecan pie, she looked like a female counterpart to Lazarus. There was even silverware and napkins. "What a godsend," she said with more energy than she had mustered all day. "How thoughtful."

Marge's smile brought dimples to her smooth cheeks. She surveyed the chairs and tables and boxes floating on the opaque sea and shook her head. "Ugh."

Brenda laughed. "You can say that again."

"All this white fits the Strongs. But it sure doesn't fit you. I can't imagine why they redecorated the place a year ago when they knew Strong was going to retire."

"Well, the committee promised the church would fix it up the way we wanted it," Brenda said.

"I hope so," Marge replied. "I'd hold them to it."

"We will," Peter added. "They said all we had to do was ask."

Marge eyed the two of them closely. "You're a lot younger than I thought you'd be. I'm relieved. I was afraid they were going to bring in another old geezer — just to please the senior members. Strong did that plenty — pleased them, I mean. What we need now is new blood."

Peter smiled with a twinge of embarrassment that he had not shared the committee's confidence.

"Do they have ballet?" Brenda asked. She sounded like a drowning person shouting for help.

"Ballet?" Marge's brow wrinkled. "There's no one who just does dance. Only if it's needed in a play."

Brenda looked crestfallen. "But look," Marge continued.

"With my husband Byron at the U, we get all the notices of what's coming up. I'll keep my eyes open and let you know. There's bound to be something." Peter and Brenda thanked Marge profusely, and then she was gone. Peter's mouth watered from the aroma rising from the spaghetti. "Things are looking up," he said.

Brenda smiled. "The day's ending better than it began."

"See, I told you it wouldn't be too bad. It's just that we haven't moved for a long time and haven't had to make new friends."

Brenda reached up to Peter and kissed him. "I should trust you more. And the church. I apologize for being such a grouch."

Peter squeezed her tight. "That's all right," he said. "In the end everything will work out."

4

Before Peter and Brenda could sit down to eat, the doorbell rang again. Jackie was out running, and Jeff was unloading his sculpture tools into the garage. He was not happy.

"But the basement here won't work," Peter had said. The two of them were standing in the cramped cinderblock room jammed with boxes. "Like with Neanderthal, there's no way we can get finished pieces out."

Jeff stared at the narrow stairs and shrugged his shoulders. "And Trojan will be larger than Neanderthal."

"Trojan?"

"The Trojan horse. Greek legends."

"Yes, I know," Peter said. "But the original Trojan horse could hold an army."

"A few soldiers. Don't worry. I won't do it to scale."

"Plaster? Trojan's going to be plaster?"

Jeff smiled. "Dad, don't you know? Plaster isn't strong enough."

"Then what?"

"Iron, Dad. All iron. I can see him now."

"I'm Miss Hensley, the church secretary," came the toneless announcement from the lady who had entered the living room without waiting for the Campbells to open the door. Her black eyes peered through dark rimmed glasses perched on a nose that resembled a shark's fin. Her dark hair was short, with bangs cut in a straight line as if the hairdresser had employed a straight-edge and X-acto knife. She wore a black coat, and under one arm she bore a gray cardboard portfolio.

Peter identified himself and reached out to take her coat.

She took a step backward, placing herself just beyond his reach. "No, thanks. I only stopped by to drop off these records. I was on my way home and saw the lights in the back window." She nodded toward the large window behind the dining table.

Peter introduced Brenda. Miss Hensley carefully studied the sneakers, the jeans protruding from beneath the old bathrobe, Brenda's face—uncosmeticized from her nap— and released a lifeless greeting. "How's the house?" she added.

"A little cold," Brenda put in quickly.

"The decor?"

"No," Brenda replied diplomatically. "The furnace—we can't get it to work."

Miss Hensley strode to the thermostat and moved the lever.

"We tried that," Brenda said kindly.

"That's strange." Miss Hensley's cold stare hinted at sabotage. "The property committee was supposed to have everything ready. I'll call Mr. Shanklet. He's the chairman." She took in the wingback sofa and chairs, the pine coffee table and doughbox, the rocker with the print cushions Brenda had made, her nose elevated slightly as if to avoid some unpleasant odor that had stowed away in the Campbell's possessions. "Dr. Strong's furniture was modern. His wife had the carpets put down. Real taste that woman had."

Taste reminded Peter he had not eaten. The steam rising from the spaghetti had grown thin. "We were just going to sit down to dinner," he said. "Would you like to join us?"

Miss Hensley apparently didn't hear. She jerked herself to the back window and gasped. "What a view. Imagine. Every evening, seeing the sun set on Good Samaritan. Do you know it's a landmark? Architecture students come from everywhere to study its construction."

Peter dragged his hungry stomach over and followed Miss Hensley's gaze. In spite of the committee's protestations, the church's buildings still looked strange. The four glass domes and their glass interconnecting walkways formed a crystal diamond on the opposite slope of the valley. The buildings themselves looked as if a flight of flying saucers had landed on the broad expanse of grass. Each was circular, with the lower wall leaning out and the upper slanting in to form support rings on which reposed one piece glass bubbles. Peter recalled from the tour with the committee that the big one at the top was the sanctuary. The one at the bottom, the narthex, housed the church offices. Between it and Valley Road lay a rectangle of blacktop for parking. The two middle domes, Assisi and Benedict, were used for education and group activities. Strange, Peter said to himself. Very strange.

Miss Hensley's eyes shone as if she were in the clutches of a beatific vision. "You can see the garden. At least where it *will* be when they get it finished. Around the fountain."

Peter spied an undulating plume of water at the center of a yellow scarp. That too was strange. As was the cobalt light flickering at the top of the ridge to which he called Miss Hensley's attention.

"Didn't anyone tell you?" she exclaimed. Her voice quivered. "That's Hermann Gottschalk's grave. He's the one who donated the land and the buildings."

Peter could think of nothing profound to say but, "Oh."

"The glow?" Brenda asked. "I noticed it shines in daylight." Peter had noticed it too. It looked as if someone were shining a mirror from the peak of the ridge. Miss Hensley's eyes glowed. "He designed it before his death. He wanted Good Samaritan to be a light to the community. 'The light of the world,' you recall – from the Bible." Peter did recall, only it was those who did good works that were light, not twinkling gravemarkers. "The sphere always shines," Miss Hensley went on. "I understand airline pilots use it as a beacon when they're heading for the airport."

"Well, that's a help," Peter said half-facetiously. Beneath his hand Brenda's shoulder felt cold. She too must be hungry. Lights turning on in Good Samaritan's saucers cast a yellow glow into the night air.

Suddenly the front door banged open. Miss Hensley jerked about and stared up in wonderment at Jackie. Thin, tall, clad in gray sweatpants and a baggy sweater, she paced among the pieces of furniture and boxes gasping for breath. Her chest heaved, her skin glowed red, tiny beads of sweat glistened around her mouth. Peter introduced her to Miss Hensley. Jackie's hand shot forward in greeting. Miss Hensley seemed immobile, then hung out a hand like a limp flag of surrender.

"She's a jogger," Peter said.

"A runner," Jackie corrected tersely.

Miss Hensley squinted as if her vision were impaired. "The Strongs didn't have any children." She lunged toward the door and stopped. "I almost forgot. Those are Dr. Strong's records." She nodded toward the portfolio. "He had a sheet of information for each member of the congregation."

"That's amazing," Peter said in a lackluster tone that thinly disguised his disdain for detailed record-keeping.

Miss Hensley held him in her gaze. "Dr. Strong was an amazing man. He gave his life to Good Samaritan. In all the time he was here, there wasn't one need a member had that Dr. Strong didn't attend to. No matter what the inconvenience." She paused. "I understand from the committee you'll keep up that tradition."

"Well, that's not quite what I was called here to do," Peter said jovially.

"You mean the committee didn't tell you about Dr. Strong?"

"They didn't say very much." In retrospect, Peter thought, the committee had avoided him.

Miss Hensley's eyes glowed with determination. "Then what did they tell you?"

Peter told her about the early disciples and the old rugged cross.

Miss Hensley's cheeks quivered. "Disciples!" she scoffed. "How could that committee be so out of touch? It didn't know what it was talking about." She glanced at the files. "Forget what the committee said. Everything you need is right there. If you want to succeed as pastor of this church, then memorize those files. Disciples!" She repeated the word as if she'd eaten rotten fruit and couldn't get the taste out of her mouth. With a jerk of her head, she turned and was gone.

Peter picked up the gray portfolio, removed the rubber band, and drew out several sheets. Only one caught his attention: it had several names typed, crossed out, written over. He saved it, thrust the rest back in the portfolio, and dropped the portfolio into the box of miscellaneous it had been resting on.

5

They ate the cold spaghetti in silence. At one point, Jeff said, "I'll have to have the whole garage — both stalls."

"Why?" Peter asked.

"In order to have enough room. Even then I won't have enough."

"So you can make Trojan smaller."

Jeff stared hard. "You promised."

Peter sighed. "We can leave both cars out. You'll shovel

them out in the winter?"

Jeff nodded.

Unable to endure Jackie's muteness any longer, Peter said, "What's wrong?"

She held back with a pout, then said, "There are no open places."

"Streets," Peter replied. "They're everywhere."

"Yes. And all with houses. This isn't what you promised."

Peter tried to be consoling. "You're right. But I have to go where I'm called. And for now, this is the church."

"That?" Jackie asked, with a glance at the saucers glowing on the other side of the valley.

Peter looked at the buildings. Yes, they were strange. "Well, not that exactly," he said. "The congregation—the people."

"Oh," Jackie said with sarcastic politeness.

Peter felt himself sinking. "The high school will have a track team. That'll give you all the chance to run you need. You could . . ."

A knock at the front door cut him off.

"Krohn's the name," announced a short man standing on the stoop. He wore a gray coat over gray trousers, a gray hat, and black shoes. "Chairman of the Trustees."

Peter invited him in and introduced himself. "May I take your coat?"

"No, no thanks. I'll only stay a minute. Trustees are meeting tonight. I've got to get on down. Just thought I'd drop off some papers for you to look at. Want you to be up to date on what's going on." Words shot from his mouth like bursts from a machine gun.

He lunged to the window overlooking the valley. "Gottschalk was a great guy. Generous as hell." Mr. Krohn seemed enraptured by the glowing domes and the fountain, the pinpoint of light at the top of the ridge. "Too bad the old buzzard didn't live to see it. This church was his dream. Strange man in some ways. He was on the Board of Trustees, but never came to meetings. Preferred working behind the scenes, so to speak. Single-minded son of a gun, but right about most things. Built that glass factory from an old garage to our strongest industry. Employs more than anybody around." Mr. Krohn turned to look Peter in the eye. "Just one mistake. He never saw the energy crunch coming. The church was dedicated a month before the Arabs shut off the oil back in '73. It's a bear to heat. All that glass — single pane. Utility bills have gone through the roof. We try to cut down on people using the place, but what can you do?"

Peter retreated under a gaze that suggested his seminary training might have included a course in energy conservation. All he knew about energy was turning a thermostat up or down, which, he reminded himself, in the parsonage had produced nothing.

"Don't want to lay it on you," Mr. Krohn went on, as if Peter's modest talents were transparent. "But with winter coming, something's got to be done. Rates are higher than last year, and you know people with their giving. Inflation's got 'em. But it's got the church too. They don't seem to realize that." He paused and looked again at the glowing buildings. "Well, we'll see what we can come up with tonight."

Brenda drew up. Mr. Krohn jerked his hat off in introduction, then returned to the window. "Didn't know you could see Hermann's light from here. Well, I guess I should have. The church bought this house because it's in line with the axis running from the light down through the fountain and the narthex. Hermann wanted it that way." He paused. "Isn't that light the damnedest thing? Kennedy's got his flame and Hermann that ball. Not that there's power on in the daytime. It's a prism. Some people say his mind was going, but I say it was his love for the church. Wouldn't have himself buried anyplace else."

Mr. Krohn started for the door and paused. "Garden's on the agenda again. Those women. They're a pain in the you know where. Wouldn't bother us, except most of 'em are wives of trustees. 'Course we can't do anything with winter coming. Do you know about the garden?" He stared inquiringly as if he might just have awakened Peter from a nap.

Peter knew no more about horticulture than he did about energy. The diversity of concerns in the church seemed broad indeed. "Miss Hensley mentioned it," he replied.

"Another donation," Mr. Krohn continued as if his supply of ammunition were inexhaustible. "Miss Hayes. Lifetime member of the church. Fought moving it out from the center of town, but in her will she provided for a rose garden to fill in between the buildings and walkways. Do you know what roses cost?" Mr. Krohn's eyes alternated between Peter and Brenda. "A fortune. Damn things die just for looking at 'em. Don't know what's wrong. There used to be salt mines under this part of the county, but the State Aggie boys say there's no salt on the surface. They found traces of chemicals in the samples, so we stripped off all the topsoil and put down new. Roses went like crazy and then fell apart. Leaves turned yellow, petals fell off. They looked like a pack of dogs had peed on 'em. Well, I won't bother you with that now, but come spring the women will be on us. They demand it be finished next year."

Mr. Krohn turned as if to leave. "By the way, do you need anything?"

"The heat," Peter replied. "It doesn't work."

Mr. Krohn glanced at the thermostat. "I thought it was kind of cold in here. I'll see what I can do. Anything else?"

Peter gestured toward the white walls. "The committee said the church would redecorate. Did you get the word?"

Mr. Krohn's brow wrinkled. "No. I can't imagine they'd promise you that when everything was done last year." He turned the doorhandle and jerked back. His head was nodding slowly. "I think you'll do the job."

"The job?" Peter replied.

"Get this church off dead center. Bring in new members. Raise the level of giving so we've got some cash to spend.

We've been sliding backwards the last few years. Strong was a good minister, but this was too much church for an old man. The committee said you're the one to get us back on the track."

"Track?" Peter asked. "What track?"

Mr. Krohn's eyes brightened. "Why Good Samaritan used to be *the* church in town. No doubt with the right leadership it will be again."

Peter stepped toward Mr. Krohn. His head was beginning to throb. "The committee told you I was called to restore Good Samaritan's prestige?"

"Of course. They said you've done a damn good job in a very difficult situation. Given all Good Samaritan has going for it, you should get us in the black and growing in no time."

The throbbing in Peter's head leaped down the back of his neck. "That isn't what the committee told me. I was to help people become disciples. There was something about the old rugged cross . . ."

Mr. Krohn pursed his lips. "Well, that's important. But if you do things right, people will come." He looked Peter over again. "You're much younger. A lot more energy. Your appearance is much different from Strong's." Peter did not know if these were compliments he should respond to, so he kept his mouth shut.

Mr. Krohn stepped through the door. His breath vaporized in the night air. Again he halted. "Oh, by the way, the neighbors over there." He nodded to the house next to the driveway. "They've got some strange quirks. Don't like it when cars are left out overnight. Strong always put his car away. It's a small thing, I know, but just to keep peace in the neighborhood."

Peter lunged through the door and was about to shout to the retreating gray figure that the cars would be left out because his son was a sculptor and the committee had promised. But Mr. Krohn was already in his car with the engine running.

Reentering the house, Peter found himself confronted by Brenda, Jeff, and Jackie. They stood among the boxes — staring.

"Well, the secretary and chairman of the Trustees aren't everyone," Peter said. "There's Marge, who brought us the dinner. There'll be others like her." Brenda and Jeff and Jackie did not move. Their expressions did not change.

"You'll see," Peter said. "You'll see."

6

Peter pulled his car through the line of evergreens along Valley Road into the church parking lot, shielding his eyes from the morning sun glaring off the dome of the sanctuary. Cars were drawn up near the narthex. He searched about for his name, but, not finding it, sighed with resignation and steered into the place marked, 'Dr. Strong.'

From recollections of Synod meetings, he tried to picture Dr. Strong as Good Samaritan's pastor. Furtive, short, eager, always anxious to agree with an opinion before he heard it, he seemed dreadfully concerned that he be liked and that everyone around him get on well. For thirty-five years, he was all Good Samaritan had known as a pastor. Striding toward the narthex, Peter felt as if he were about to intrude into someone else's house.

The narthex was just a slate floor, clear glass outside walls and darkened wood coat racks — probably a vestige of the old church downtown. On the other side of the opaque glass dividing wall lay the offices: Miss Hensley sitting erect at her vacant desk commanding the central portion of the half-moon space, her assistant off to the left amidst work tables and copy machines. On the outside wall were four doors leading to other offices, the one to the right marked, 'Dr. Strong.'

Miss Hensley's cold gaze settled on Peter. In the same toneless voice she had used at the parsonage, she introduced Mrs. Peck. A frail, diminutive woman with mouse-colored hair, Mrs. Peck grinned meekly and whispered, "Hello."

Peter smiled. "I'm glad to meet you. I'm looking forward to working with you." He turned toward the office marked, 'Dr. Strong.'

"Mr. Krohn was in," Miss Hensley continued. "He brought a copy of the new heating policy for this winter. I've instructed the custodian in his duties." Her lips pursed in satisfaction. "Heating bills have been going through the roof,"

"Yes, I've heard," Peter said.

"This should be a great saving."

Peter took another step toward the mistitled office.

"Did you get a chance to go through those papers?" Miss Hensley's voice had the buzzsaw tone of a schoolteacher quizzing a student on his homework. "A few," Peter replied, recalling that he had no idea in which box he had placed the portfolio.

"Good. If you need anything explained, just let me know."

Peter forced a smile of gratitude onto his face and closed the office door behind him. Beyond the glass outside wall lay the famous rose garden—a circle of gullied yellow clay surrounding a swaying fountain. Tiny stalks stuck up here and there like pencils driven into the clay. There wasn't a leaf on any of them. Above the garden loomed the sanctuary. Visible through it was Gottschalk's ball, obviously situated so the old boy's final resting place would be seen from everywhere in the church buildings.

Peter drew from his briefcase the sheet of names he had discovered in the portfolio, laid it aside, and started on the packet Mr. Krohn had left. Organizational charts, budgets, minutes of dozens of board and committee meetings. His mind wandered. Beneath his ceiling of sky, and with the garden ruin his outside wall, he felt more like a plant basking in a greenhouse than he did a minister. If he could so easily look out, what privacy did the arrangement afford those who came for counseling? Something the late Mr. Gottschalk-buried-above-the-sanctuary apparently had never thought of.

Lines of print on Mr. Krohn's pages mingled with muffled voices in the outer office until the lines vanished under Miss Hensley's shrill cackle mounting like an overture to violence. It was not the kind of sound to which Peter was accustomed in a church office.

He went to the door and looked out. Miss Hensley stood at her desk, her eyes impaling a bearded young man. Black leotards covered his bony frame, dark hair falling almost to his shoulders made his face long and narrow. From behind his glasses radiated a fierce glare.

He wheeled toward Peter. "Are you the new pastor?"

Peter opened his mouth to reply, but Miss Hensley cut in. "I'm sorry, Mr. Drissle, but *I* take care of all arrangements for the use of the buildings."

The man refused to take his eyes off Peter. "Chuck Drissle's the name."

Peter reached out, shook hands, and introduced himself. Miss Hensley wrenched herself from behind her desk and glowered at the two of them.

Drissle's forehead wrinkled as if he were beseeching. "You're the one I'd like to talk to," he said to Peter.

Miss Hensley's head shot forward. "Mr. Drissle, I handle these matters." She cast Peter a warning glance. "You needn't bother yourself." Peter refused to retreat.

Mr. Drissle held his ground. "You mean I can't appeal?"

"I'd like to hear what the problem is," Peter said. Several women in thin tights crept through the door and huddled behind Mr. Drissle like a colony of leprechauns. Bulging bosoms, bellies, and bottoms proved a mild distraction.

Mr. Drissle pleaded. "I lead the Holiness and Health Club. We've been assigned to Assisi three times a week. Most of the members belong to the church." He nodded toward his silent disciples. "We do yoga, talk about diet, and meditate. Soul and body. Both together — nirvana."

The ladies smiled. Dark energy radiated from Miss Hensley, which Peter ignored.

"Things have been going well," Drissle continued. "We don't mess up the building. Because we meet in the daytime, we don't use the lights. But this new heating regulation is an insult. The custodian refuses to turn up the thermostat. Forty degrees." His eyes grew large. "Pastor, have you ever tried to meditate in leotards at forty degrees?"

Meditation was not one of Peter's strong points, no matter what the temperature. Silence gave him an overpowering urge to gather wool. When he was in seminary, he had vowed he would arise at 4 a.m. to meditate and pray. He had gotten the idea from a 9th century monk who had had a vision of angels. But no vision of angels came. By 5 a.m., he was invariably sound asleep, slumped in a chair and freezing. If he did manage to stay awake, he dozed off during theology lecture and had to be awakened by a classmate so at the end of the period he would not fail to stand up and carry his exhausted body into ecclesiastical history.

Miss Hensley's head shot forward like a hammer. "That's not the point. We'll gladly supply heat. All you have to do is meet when other groups are in the building. We can't turn up the heat for every jock who wants to come in here and do pushups."

"Pushups!" Mr. Drissle writhed like an insect that had crawled too close to a fire. "You think we're just a bunch of fitness freaks coming in here for exercise? Yoga isn't pushups. Maybe you don't know that." His face broke into a smug sneer as if Miss Hensley were a jungle pagan beyond the reach of his skintight gospel.

Not a muscle in Miss Hensley's body moved. "The Board of Trustees has decided," she shouted with a tone of finality. *"They determine who will use the buildings and when. If you want the policy changed, talk to them."*

"All right, we will," Mr. Drissle said. His cohorts nodded in approval. "But in the meantime, tell that custodian to turn up the heat."

Miss Hensley slapped her hand down on the desk. "No! We cannot change the policy without authorization from the trustees."

Peter took another step forward. "Now wait a minute. Wait a minute. For today, let's find a middle ground." He turned to Miss Hensley. "These people didn't dress for forty degrees."

Miss Hensley glared at Peter as if he were Judas Iscariot. "Dr. Strong never allowed policy to be changed without Trustee approval. Once you let the cat out of the bag, there's . . ."

Peter raised his voice. "Miss Hensley!" She stopped dead and mumbled under her breath. Peter turned back to Mr. Drissle. "Mr. Krohn is the chairman of the Board of Trustees. Address your appeal to him."

Mr. Drissle reached for Peter's hand. "Thanks." His eyes softened. He turned and led his silent group out into the entry, and then they could be seen padding through the glass tube leading to Assisi.

"Vile man," Miss Hensley snorted. "Temperamental. Always complaining." She glared at Peter. "You'll learn about him. Give him an inch, and he'll take over the whole church. I'll make sure those trustees stand up to him."

Peter retreated toward his office. "You'll instruct the custodian to turn up the heat?"

Miss Hensley sat down at her desk and refused to look at him. Her stone face did not reveal whether she had even heard what he said.

7

Miss Hensley buzzed to announce she was going out to lunch. A few moments later, John Rhodes, the church custodian, came knocking on Peter's door. A grizzled man of about fifty, with thin gray hair, clad in a faded red flannel shirt and brown work pants, he sized Peter up as if he were a statue Mr. Rhodes might be interested in buying. "You're younger than I thought you'd be," he said. "This is a big congregation. Sure kept Dr. Strong on the run all the time."

Peter knew nothing about Mr. Rhodes, so he nodded toward Mr. Krohn's papers piled on his desk. "I've been going through the reports of the boards. I guess you've got quite a lot to do around here."

Mr. Rhodes clapped his coarse hands on his knees and sighed. "Too much. They keep addin' on, but they don't get me no help. I told 'em. Told those trustees. They always say they'll do somethin', but they don't. I'll tell you right off, I ain't gonna take it much longer. They want those floors to shine. No fingermarks on the windows — and the place is nothin' but windows!" His voice rose emphatically. "Set up this room . . . do this . . . do that." He shook his head. "I ain't no slave. I been here fifteen years, and ever' year it gets worse. And with what they pay. No, sir. I've had 'bout all I can stand."

His eyes searched Peter's face while Peter groped for a response. The papers gave no clue as to whether Mr. Rhodes did his work well or not.

"And that out there." Mr. Rhodes sneered at the clay scarp. "They try to hang that on me. Those women tellin' me what to do. 'Pick the buds off.' 'Prune the dying branches.' 'Cultivate.' Well, I wasn't hired as no gardener, and I ain't startin' now. I told 'em that, but don't faze 'em at all. 'Just do us a favor,' they tell me. Some day I'll do 'em a favor — a favor for me and them both. Just burn them roses outta there, put grass back in, and be done with it. Grass I don't mind. We got a big mower with a seat. But since they started on those roses, nothin' but trouble."

Again Peter groped for something to say. He felt an impulse to extend sympathy, but what if he were being manipulated? Mr. Rhodes would always count on him to take his side. "Too many people are telling you what to do?" he asked, conscious that he was hiding behind a non-directive counseling technique.

Mr. Rhodes' eyes lit up. "You betcha'. Ever'body 'round here's my boss. Why, when they come with their old clothes or those wretched cass'roles, it's always, 'John, will you do this?' I thought women was s'pposed to be lib'rated these days. A lotta the stuff ain't even heavy."

"Who is your boss?" Peter asked.

Mr. Rhodes sighed as if on the verge of terminal exhaustion. "Krohn. But he ain't here much. So if I got a question, Miss Hensley use-ly gets involved." His visage twisted into a sneer of contempt. He paused, leaned back, groped at his shirt pocket, and drew out a pack of cigarettes. "D'ya mind?"

Peter loathed cigarette smoke. His eyes burned, his throat constricted, but it was a concession he could offer without committing himself to Mr. Rhodes' cause. "Go ahead," he said.

"Like this morning. Krohn gives her that order on the heat. She tells me to turn down the thermostat. I do it, and then I get it from that fruitcake up there. It ain't fair. She isn't supposed to be tellin' me what to do. She thinks she runs everything. And Krohn lets her get away with it."

Mr. Rhodes crossed his legs and dragged on his cigarette as if chatting about his tribulations were a chief form of relaxation.

"Did you ever try to work these things out in a staff meeting?" Peter asked.

Mr. Rhodes' head jerked up. "Staff meeting? What's that?"

"Everybody getting together to work out problems."

Mr. Rhodes shook his head gravely. "Never heard of it. Dr. Strong never had 'em."

"Then how did all of you coordinate your work?"

"Didn't need to. Krohn gives me my orders. Hensley and that Mrs. Peck know what they're supposed to do. And the choir director . . . well, he's on his own wavelength." Mr. Rhodes' eyes grew wide. "You mean you'd get us all together to work everything out? Hensley too?"

Peter nodded. "Certainly. What's so strange about that?"

Mr. Rhodes shook his head vigorously. "It'll never work. You don't know Hensley. Dr. Strong was so disorganized she got to running everything. Most people in the church don't know that. You put her in a room with the rest of us, and she'll take over. You too. You've never seen a woman like her. No way. You'll be just like me—run to death."

Peter sighed. There was no way he would turn Good Samaritan over to Miss Hensley. "I think you're overstating what would happen. She knows I'm the pastor. That means head of staff too."

Mr. Rhodes' head was still shaking. "Yeah. So was Strong. But he didn't try no meetin's. He was smart. He knew how to stay out of trouble before it happened."

Peter felt himself wearying under Mr. Rhodes' obstinacy. He stood up. "There will be meetings. I can't imagine the staff of a Christian church not getting together. After all, we are a family . . ."

Mr. Rhodes squashed out his cigarette on the bottom of his boot and lurched to his feet. "Okay. Go ahead. But if it don't work, don't say John Rhodes didn't warn you. You got a few things to learn about this church."

With that, he turned and wandered out to the outside office. Through the door, Peter could see that Miss Hensley had returned. She was sitting erect at her desk. Mr. Rhodes paused long enough to hurl her a contemptuous look and shuffled away.

8

Late afternoon sun cast long shadows across the office floor. Peter stood before Miss Hensley. "Miss Hensley, there are some things I'd like to go over with you."

Miss Hensley shoved her chair back and crossed her arms across her chest. "Certainly. Go ahead." Mrs. Peck was hunched over a pile of cards, ignoring them.

Peter gestured toward his open door. "I'd like us to use my office."

Miss Hensley hesitated, then rose and marched stiffly ahead of him. She perched herself on the front edge of his spartan fiberglass chair. Not a trace of emotion showed on her face.

Peter picked up the list of names he had set aside and placed it on his desk where she could see it. "This paper has no notation. Do you know what it is?"

Miss Hensley nodded in recognition.

"Who are these people?" Peter asked.

"Key members," she replied.

"Chairmen of committees? Board members?"

"No." Miss Henlsey let him spin in silence.

"Well, key? What does that mean?"

"Influential."

Peter found his nerves bristling at Miss Hensley's grudging tone. "What makes them influential?"

Her eyes fixed on his without a blink. "Money."

"Money?" Peter smothered a gasp. "And the ones crossed off?"

Miss Hensley picked up the list and pointed to various names. "Bad luck. Investments didn't work out. Market conditions changed. Ran off with some fool woman and moved to California."

"And this one?" Peter indicated a name Miss Hensley had passed over.

"Stanley Jeffers?" She paused. "Well, he's got a good business, but . . ." She paused, and Peter waited.

"I don't know. Dr. Strong didn't tell me about these things. I don't think Jeffers was giving much to the church. Maybe he cut his pledge."

Peter pursed his lips to suppress the revulsion rising in his throat. Miss Hensley had to be distorting, exaggerating. Surely Strong hadn't stooped so low.

"The ones not crossed off are the big givers," Miss Hensley continued. "In case you haven't discovered it yet, it costs a lot to run this church. Dr. Strong saw to it that the people on this list were well satisfied. They put a lot of themselves into Good Samaritan."

Peter envisioned Dr. Strong each Sunday morning rushing up to wealthy members with his effusive greeting and rodent smile. A twinge of nausea swept across his stomach.

"Dr. Strong put his soul into keeping this church solvent," Miss Hensley said. "I hope the committee told you you're to do the same. This church may look wealthy, but it isn't. We always have trouble meeting the budget. Costs keep going up . . ."

The steely voice droned on, but Peter ignored it to look out the window. A strange figure had come into the garden. Finally Miss Hensley clattered to a halt and glared at him.

He brought his attention back to her. "I want to have a meeting of the staff," he said firmly.

The color drained from Miss Hensley's face. "Meeting of the staff?"

"Yes."

"Well, who would that be?"

"All of us." The figure in heavy garden clothes bent down to trim rose bush pencils. When it stood up, he realized he was looking at an elderly woman with a red, wrinkled face.

Miss Hensley looked out, but her visage registered nothing. "Well, there's just you and me in charge. I'm willing to meet anytime."

"No, I mean *everyone*—you, Mrs. Peck, the choir director, the custodian."

The lines in Miss Hensley's face hardened. "We've never had any before. There's no need for it. If you'd read Mr. Krohn's papers, you'd know there are policies for everything. You handle the congregation, I run the church. There are no problems. Why, if you have a meeting with everybody—think of the time it'll waste. Everybody knows what he's supposed to do."

Peter bent toward her with exaggerated politeness. "There's more to working in a church than our duties." The gardener was hunched over just beyond where he was sitting. "The staff of a church is like a family. We need to support one another. How do we do that if we never meet?"

Miss Hensley's lips curled in disdain. "I've never heard of such a thing. Dr. Strong never called us a family. We just work here. Our responsibilities are in those papers." She held Peter in a piercing gaze. "Why do you want to change everything when the church has run perfectly for thirty-five years?"

Peter fought the stiffening in his muscles. It was as if Dr. Strong's ghost was in the room. "A new man brings a new style," he said.

Not a muscle in Miss Hensley's face registered that she heard what he said.

"I have the right to conduct the life of the staff as I see fit."

Miss Hensley's head arched forward. "Staff meetings are totally unnecessary. Here's how the church works. You and I carry out . . ."

Peter cut her off. "Miss Hensley, I know how the church works."

Miss Hensley's mouth slacked open as if she were debating whether to continue her speech or unleash a tirade.

"Meeting together won't change our responsibilities," he continued. "We need a sense that we're a team—like the early disciples." An image imprinted itself on his mind—Jesus and the twelve seated around a campfire. "Family is the closest thing I can think of. We're Christians. We're supposed to love each other, and that means . . ."

Miss Hensley stood up abruptly and turned her attention to a second woman limping about the garden.

Peter jerked in irritation toward the window. "Pray tell, what are they doing?"

"Pruning," Miss Hensley said in a sacrosanct tone. "They're members of the garden club trying to save the roses that are left. They hope to get more in before winter. It's been a heartbreaker with all those bushes dying."

"I'm sure it has," Peter observed, aware that his voice was devoid of sympathy. He turned back to face Miss Hensley. "On this staff meeting . . ."

She refused to look at him. "I'll think about it."

"Next week . . ."

Quick steps carried her to the door. "I must go. This church doesn't pay me for working overtime."

Peter raised his voice. "The service this Sunday. What do you need for the bulletin?"

Miss Hensley paused. "Whatever you want."

"There's no meeting with Mr. Straphe to plan the service?"

"Never has been. He never comes here in the daytime. He teaches."

"But he has an office in the church."

"He's here about fifteen minutes before rehearsals."

"Then how does he know what the choir should sing? And the hymns—how does he get them to fit the rest of the service?"

Miss Hensley shrugged her shoulders. "You can leave hymn numbers in his mailbox if you want. He won't care."

"But there's no coordination?"

"No." Miss Hensley said it with a tone of finality, turned, and was gone.

Peter went to the window and looked out on the rose garden. His stomach was churning. One of the gardeners stood up next to the glass and stared in with a hand shielding her eyes. When she saw Peter staring at her, she quickly bent down and lopped off another two inches of dead rose pencil.

9

Peter's first Sunday at Good Samaritan dawned with the distant rumble of thunder. He dragged himself out of bed, stumbled down to the kitchen to put coffee on, and paused to get his mind churning toward his sermon. He was suddenly aware that up until now the congregation was a faceless unknown—that amorphous crowd the calling committee had described as a band of stalwarts ready to be led as Jesus' disciples.

Pulling on his best suit and jerking snug the tie that Brenda said went well with his pulpit robe, he jousted with the guilty suggestion that fine dress was incongruous with the call to discipleship. But stylish conformity was a small concession to make in order to be given a hearing. People with money placed a high premium on appearances. His fulfilling their ecclesiastical expectations would not hinder his call for them to be like Peter and Andrew, James and John. They could still see the rugged cross, the way of self-denial and service to the poor and oppressed.

Before leaving the house, he glanced out the back window. Good Samaritan lay at his feet, glistening under black storm clouds, shimmering with each flash of lightning. Cars streamed into the parking lot. Tiny figures could be seen crawling like insects through the glass tubes leading to Assisi and Benedict and on up to the sanctuary. He recalled the odd painting in the Delaware Club—Jesus poised on the Mount of Olives about to lead his followers into Jerusalem. Pulling himself away from the view and going out to his car, his step was lighter.

10

He stood at the back of the full sanctuary waiting for the processional hymn to begin, lifted by the authority that had been placed in his hands. Even the concussion of discordant Prelude notes bouncing off the surrounding glass like cannonshots could not diminish the anticipation welling up in his chest. Mr. Straphe's semi-bald head could be seen bobbing and weaving behind the organ console as if he were wrestling for control of the instrument. It was the kind of melodramatic show Peter had seen performed by other church musicians. Most church members would recognize the egocentric antics for what they were and keep their minds on the essential purpose for which they came to worship.

But as Peter's eyes swept the rest of the front of the sanctuary, he felt a sudden ebbing of power. It came not from the massive oak pulpit on the left or the more diminished lectern to the right. Not from the naked pipes and tubes and cables of the organ. Not from Gottschalk's twinkling tombstone visible from every seat in the sanctuary, nor from the wooden cross suspended above the chancel, its crossarm spread like the wings of an enormous eagle.

On the blond communion table stood another cross — not of wood, but of brass. Shiny brass, mounted on a pyramid of brass, its arms swept back as if it had been molded by a hundred mile an hour wind. It looked like the hood ornament on a luxury automobile. A cross on which nobody ever got crucified, it mocked the rugged cross about which he was to preach.

Marching up the aisle, he tried to strike it from his mind. But its silent taunt did not diminish; it stood above Straphe's wild gyrations, the choir jockeying for seats in the choir loft, and then, after Peter turned to face the congregation, tweeds, plaids, and pinstripes, and brown and silver furs encircling thin, corded necks.

Stepping into the pulpit to preach his sermon, Peter had to force himself to envision the cross on which Jesus had died. Wood — coarse, dark, heavy. The pathetic figure dragging it up a steep, pebbled road toward Calvary. Sweat pouring off the bleeding brow, coursing down cheeks beaten raw by the lash. Eyes rolling, guttural sounds escaping cracked lips. Knees trembling, muscles twitching, fingers grasping splintered wood, slipping, tearing at the wood to regain a grip. A leg buckling, straightening, another agonizing step. The leg buckling again. The wide-eyed crowd lining the narrow street cheering. The leg giving way, Jesus slumping to the street with the cross landing heavily across his chest. The air filled with taunts. A boy with hate in his eyes running out from the crowd, kicking dirt into Jesus' face.

From the crowd steps the black man, Simon of Cyrene. Shy at first, big eyes glancing warily at the shouting mob, he approaches the prone figure. He stops. Compassion wets his eyes. His mouth moves as if he is about to speak, but words will not come.

Behind Simon struts a centurion, his jaw set. He brings his lash down on Simon's back. "You carry it." The centurion points at the cross. Simon bends down. He steals a glance at Jesus glistening with sweat. He applies his strength to the thick pole, and the cross rises.

"No!" the thirsty crowd shouts.

Simon hoists the timbers to his broad back, leans forward, his feet begin to churn. The centurion's whip cracks across Jesus' back. Blood seeps through torn flesh. Jesus draws himself to his knees, staggers to his feet. His eyes are fixed on Simon as if the black man is all he can see. His path is irregular, a series of lurches. His arms hang down, his head rolls as if his neck has lost its febrile strength.

The eyes in the faces of the tweeds, plaids, pinstripes, and furs are not on the road winding up Golgotha. Peter has seen the same look on the faces of a movie audience dully waiting for a film to begin. Watching faces — faces inured to feeling. The images flooding his mind are not penetrating theirs. What do they see?

He glanced over at the cross on the communion table. It shouted down Peter's words, sucked them out of the air, swallowed them before they could reach the ears before him. The nails he pounded into Jesus' cross would not pound into brass. Blood oozed down Jesus' cross, slaked into crevices and cracks, thirsty fibers and cells. But blood on brass ran quickly; it could be wiped away by the mere twitch of a tissue. Pain throbbed through Jesus' hands and feet, but there was no pain on a brass cross. It was sacrifice without blood, without pain, without shame. While Peter declared that as Jesus had sacrificed and suffered, so should Christians, the brass cross smirked with its silent shimmer and rallied the feelingless faces to believe suffering belonged to Jesus once, but now it had nothing to do with the fight of faith.

When he was finished, Peter's shirt clung to him heavy with perspiration. Every muscle in his body ached. Turning and dragging himself back to his chair, he felt as if *he* had dragged the cross, and not Simon of Cyrene.

The recessional hymn extolled the virtues of a rose e'er blooming. Peter noticed women in the congregation glancing at one another and then back at the clay scarp of the rose garden. He had to hand it to Straphe for his political acumen.

Suddenly thunder boomed without lightning. Peter looked up. A swept wing jet fighter flashed just above the sanctuary dome. Then came another, and another. He looked down, only to be drawn back to the gray sky by the tardy arrival of a fourth. The rose hymn vanished in the rattle of thousands of glass panes, and the service was over.

People stood in line to greet Peter at the door. Hands reached for his, faces smiled, heads nodded. There were compliments. "It's so nice to have a young minister again." "You look handsome up there. You'd better watch out for the females in this congregation." "You have a wonderful preaching voice. I could hear every word. That hasn't happened for a long time." "At last, someone who doesn't read his sermons."

Smooth faces and fine threads passed by. Amiability surrounded them like an aura. They were pleased. But when the glass tube had finally swallowed up the last of them, it dawned on Peter—no one had mentioned his cross. He could have gotten the same response if he had just stepped out and modeled his pulpit robe.

He glanced back at the enemy reposing on the communion table. His hands clenched involuntarily into tight fists. "I won't compete with you again," he snarled.

11

Peter stood at Miss Hensley's desk. Rays of late-day sun cast a red glow in the secretary's eyes. In a few minutes, they would head for home. "Do you know anything about the brass cross?" he asked calmly.

Miss Hensley cast him a blank look. "Brass cross?"

"The one that was on the communion table Sunday. You were here, weren't you?"

"No," she replied quickly. "Alice wasn't feeling well. I couldn't leave her."

"Alice?"

"My terrier. She's getting old." Miss Hensley checked to see that her desk drawers were locked.

"It's shiny, about a foot and a half high," Peter continued.

Miss Hensley shoved her chair back and stood up with a jerk. "There's a brass cross that was given anonymously. Maybe that's it."

"But why is it put out when we already have the hanging cross?"

She picked up her purse. "It must mean a great deal to someone."

Peter's face burned. "But who? And who puts it out? Who prepares the sanctuary for worship?"

Miss Hensley's shoulders shrugged in disregard. "There's a committee. Different people each week." She wrenched her coat from the rack and put it on. She stopped and stared at him. "Does it bother you?"

Peter held back the revulsion he had felt on Sunday. "It's too much," he replied.

Miss Hensley snapped her purse open, rummaged down into its depths, jangled out her car keys.

"I don't like brass crosses," he went on. Miss Hensley's long look at the clock above Mrs. Peck's desk let him know he was keeping her after hours.

"The cross Jesus died on was made of wood, a couple of rough-hewn logs fastened together. Roman execution was a horrible deed." Again he saw the emaciated body, the blood. "Brass doesn't fit. It's too clean. It turns the symbol of sacrifice into an ornament. It denies suffering." He heard his voice rising, but he could not help it. "Does that make sense to you?"

Miss Hensley's eyes remained fixed on the clock. Her tightly sealed lips showed no sign of replying.

Peter leaned toward her. "I want you to instruct whoever is responsible for the chancel never to put the brass cross out. Tell them the hanging cross is plenty."

Miss Hensley started for the door.

Peter followed her. "Do you hear me?"

She turned and glared. "There are people in this congregation who could not live without that brass cross."

"It's a sacrilege," he shouted. "Blasphemy."

Miss Hensley eyed him uneasily, as if he were raving. "Dr. Strong was sensitive to people's feelings. He would never remove something they cherished."

Peter took a lunging step toward her. "Miss Hensley, I am not Dr. Strong. I am the new pastor of this church and the head of its staff. I am telling you I want that cross never again to stand on that communion table. Do you understand?"

Miss Hensley looked at him coldly. "I don't know who puts it out. I don't work here on Sundays. If you want it changed, then you do it." With that, she spun toward the door, opened it, and was gone.

Her sharp heel-steps faded across the stone floor of the entry. Peter's fists clenched and unclenched. The glass around him shimmered with hostility. He felt like an alien. Finally he turned toward his office to get his coat. From the door leered Dr. Strong's name, its letters larger than they had appeared at first.

12

The blue welding torch flickered inside the garage, melted metal spattered on the floor, acrid fumes wafted across the yard. Jeff, clad in a blue union suit, helmet pulled down over his face, hunched over a barrel-shaped maze of rails. Rails he was welding into place hung from ceiling joists with rope.

Seeing Peter come in, Jeff popped the torch off and pushed the helmet onto the top of his head. Sweat streaked his dirty face. "The frame's going real well," he said, standing back so he could take it in. "I'm doing the body now. When I've got it pretty much done, I'll raise it and do the legs."

"How high?" Peter asked.

"Don't worry, Dad. It won't be as big as the original Trojan horse. Besides, it has to fit in here." There was a twinge of disappointment in his voice.

Peter spied more rails piled against the garage wall. "The head too?"

Jeff paused. "Well, I'm not sure about that. I might have to pull the body onto the driveway and do the head there."

The sheer curtain in a window of the neighboring house parted and twitched as if held by a palsied hand. "Do they look out often?" Peter asked.

Jeff stared at the offending window. "All the time. I just wave and the curtain closes for a while." He turned back to Trojan. "It gets on my nerves. Them looking at me. Can something be done?"

Peter thought, but nothing came to mind. He had never set eyes on the neighbors. He recalled Mr. Krohn saying they had quirks. "Maybe they'll get tired of it. Surely they have something better to do than gawk out the window."

13

The parsonage was filled with the aroma of roast beef and what Peter tried to call silence, even though the house wasn't actually silent. It was an indistinguishable sound, like waves dying at the base of a cliff, floating up out of the family room from the high school students Jackie was recruiting for a track team. Those who weren't up to exercise waited while Jackie ran the recruits through the neighborhood.

"They're not your type," Peter had said the first time he saw them camped in the family room. They had long, unkempt hair, scraggly beards, worn-out jeans. Their shirts and jackets the Salvation Army would have turned into rags. They wore combat boots and sandals, as if anything resembling regular shoes would doom them to the curse of normality.

They sat with occasional mumbles of conversation, ensconced in a womb of perpetual hard rock music. Their bodies slumped as if they were exhausted, used up. On their faces they wore resignation as if it were the hope of the future. "Burn-outs," Jackie called them, and hulks of something that might have been was what Peter deemed they were.

"This school doesn't have my type—if there is such a thing," she said coldly later that evening. She sat on her bed in her pajamas while Peter stood like an intruder in the doorway.

"None at all?" he asked.

"None at all," came the reply.

"But the committee told us people here were hard working and knew what they wanted out of life."

Jackie laughed. "And you bought that?"

"I didn't have anything else to go on." Surely the committee was telling the truth. Why wouldn't it? "How are you going to get a track team?"

"We have to apply to the school for certification. In order to do that, I've got to submit the names of kids who will run. Right now, there are only three. I need fifteen. I'm going to get them from the ones I bring home." She eyed Peter sternly. "Does that bother you?"

Peter retreated under her fierce gaze. "Well, I would like to see more of your type, but . . ."

"Dad, you preach that we should love people who aren't like us."

Peter heard the echo of his own voice, but he envisioned a more sanitized reaching out—sending boxes of food or clothing to people in Africa or Asia. He wasn't suggesting the recipients take up residence in his own home.

"So I'm doing it, and I'd think you'd be proud," she said.

He didn't feel proud. The mumbling group posed some unnamed threat. They were more foreign than foreigners. He couldn't communicate with them. Maybe they were on dope, and the parsonage would gain the reputation as a haven for drug users. How would that go over with the plaids and pinstripes and furs?

Jackie's unwavering gaze saw right through him. Without saying anything more, he went over and gave her a hug. She hugged him back, with a touch of moistness in her eyes.

"Good luck," he said.

"Thanks," he heard in a low voice as he left the room.

14

Sue Ritter drove up to give Peter and Brenda a ride to the meeting. Sue was in her early thirties, a striking shorthaired blond with smooth skin and a look of confidence. In her Burberry coat and high leather Gucci boots (Brenda provided Peter the brand names afterward), she looked like a model from a fashion magazine. She smiled with friendly reserve as Brenda and Peter got into the car. It was long, low, and silver with a leather top. Peter sank into the back seat and marvelled at the smooth ride.

After exchanging greetings, Sue seemed at a loss for words. Brenda broke the silence: "And what does your husband do?"

"Ralph's an advertising executive," Sue replied reverently. "He's with Beckwith and Jones. It's an old downtown firm. He's doing very well."

Brenda smiled and cast Sue the nod of admiration expected in most social contexts. Peter knew Brenda didn't care much for ad executives, but after he had told her there were several in the congregation, she declared she would make an attempt to overcome her prejudice.

"And how do you like Good Samaritan?" Sue asked. Sue's face was well tanned for the cloudy fall weather they'd been having. Her lips and eyes were meticulously done with make-up.

"Fine," Brenda blurted. There wasn't much enthusiasm in her voice. The word hung in the air as if demanding further explanation, but Peter heard nothing from Brenda's lips.

"It must be hard for you both to get to know so many people," Sue said.

"It takes work," Peter said.

Brenda nodded. "Yes, it does." Brenda had told Peter it was hard to learn names when everyone knew who she was and she only saw people fleetingly on Sundays. "A hazard of being a minister's wife," he had commented. She was not impressed.

"We like it," Sue said. She turned off the main road through brick gates guarding a cluster of homes scattered among groves of bright yellow maples and large oaks with reddish brown leaves. Sculpted evergreens framed the fronts of the massive houses, shielded side yards, bordered long driveways. "The children love Sunday School, and Ralph's on the Council. You get to know the leading people in town there."

Peter smiled limply out of sight of Sue's rearview mirror. The prestige theme was ever recurring.

Amy Sands was hosting the meeting. Clad in a designer wool suit, she met Sue and Brenda and Peter at the door with a fixed smile. In a melodious voice, she exclaimed: "And what an honor to have the pastor and his wife here. It's a special day." They followed her out of the stone entry hall into an expansive sitting room that overlooked a swimming pool and garden. Peter's feet sank into thick, grass-like carpet. Chattering women in their late twenties and thirties sat on folding chairs lined up in rows facing a wooden lectern.

Amy clapped her hands. "I'd like to have your attention, gals." Her appeal had no effect in diminishing the din of conversation. She raised her voice. "I'd like to have your attention."

Heads turned, half curious-half annoyed eyes searched out the source of interruption.

"We're honored this morning to have with us the new pastor and his wife." She waved toward Peter and Brenda and signaled for them to step forward. "This is Peter and Brenda Campbell."

They stood before the lines of chairs and faced faces as tanned and cosmeticized as Sue's. Nothing profound pressed into Peter's mind. He had no idea what the meeting was going to be about, so was wary of endorsement. "We're glad to be here," he said blandly.

Amy grasped Brenda's arm. "Since we're all women, would you like to say something to the group?"

This was not Brenda's line, Peter knew. She had told him, "I'm glad to be your wife, but you're the one who does the talking. I couldn't stand courses in public speaking." He could feel Brenda squirming, the wrinkles in her brow told him she was searching for something, but would she find? "It's nice to meet you," she said. Her voice was flat, noncommittal.

Amy dismissed Brenda with a nod. "We hope you'll come to every meeting."

Peter had already turned away and was following Sue to chairs next to the floor-to-ceiling windows overlooking the garden. The sun was warm on his back. Beyond the swimming pool, an old gardener, hunched, his movements slow and arthritic, raked up errant leaves and loaded them into a wheelbarrow.

Amy stood at the lectern and called for the group's attention. She introduced the leader of the morning devotions — a thin, nervous girl with glasses, who read the Mary and Martha passage from the Gospel according to Luke.

Peter envisioned the two sisters entertaining Jesus. Martha with her hands thrust in dishwater, wiping them dry to carry more food into the living room. Mary sitting at Jesus' feet listening to his teaching. Martha then complaining to Jesus that her sister did nothing to help her with the housework.

As if on cue, a black maid in a black and white uniform entered by a side door, hesitated, and glanced about. Her brown eyes searched out where to place the heavy silver service of coffee and tea, but she didn't know which table to use. Amy jerked to her feet and pointed to a table with a white cloth. The maid bumped the tray down and unloaded it.

Devotions continued. Jesus defended Mary's sitting at his feet and listening to him and chided Martha for fretting about trivial things. Peter knew Brenda would sympathize with Martha. She could not refuse to cook and clean and serve if Jesus came to her house. Of course she could always hire a black maid to bring in the goodies on silver. That would make sitting at Jesus' feet a lot easier.

The point of the lesson was lost on the woman appointed to pray: " . . . and Lord help us to be good Marthas, obeying our husbands and serving our children in the kitchen, and good Marys, sitting at the feet of Jesus, listening to his teaching." Oh well, Peter thought. It wasn't the first time Jesus' radical demands were watered down with a both/and.

Amy introduced the main speaker and stood aside. The woman sliding stealthily to the lectern was huge. Quivering flesh covered her large frame. Above her round tanned face rose a beehive of silver curls. Spectacles hanging from a silver chain bounced against her white cleaved bosom. Her saucy eyes took in the audience with confident possession. As she spoke, her voice wafted about the room like a cloud of soap bubbles. "Before I pick up on Possibility Posturing for today, I have a special treat for you all." She nodded toward the back of the room. "My husband."

Peter turned to see a slender man in a turtleneck sweater and tweed jacket. A reserved smile spread across his face: as deeply tanned as his wife's. Either they were sun parlor addicts or had just returned from a trip to the South.

Sue Ritter leaned over to Brenda and Peter. "She's a fabulous speaker."

Ronalee Rand chortled seductively: "George just can't let me out of his sight. Isn't that wonderful?" The audience smiled. Ronalee encouraged everyone to fill her coffee cup, eat some cake, and get to know one another before she started her talk.

Peter thought a cup of coffee might taste good, but before he and Brenda could leave their chairs, Amy was at their side. "It's too bad we lost so many," she said in a sad voice. "That liberation thing a few years back. This was such a nice group. And then some of the gals thought we were playing doormats to our husbands and wouldn't come anymore.

They got this career thing in their heads. Now careers may be all right for those who want them. Every time someone said something they didn't agree with, they got mad. If they had just given us a chance. They were so short tempered, so caught up."

Sue Ritter's eyes took on a chill glare. "They're gone, Amy, and there's no use worrying about them. As far as I'm concerned, we're better off without them. They just made trouble."

Amy nodded. "I guess you're right." She looked up at Sue. "But I still wish they'd come to hear Ronalee."

Ronalee resumed her pose at the lectern and waited for the room to quiet. The sheen of her silver pantsuit accentuated her enormous breasts, belly, and buttocks. Peter averted his eyes in embarrassment. The woman definitely needed help in choosing clothes. In spite of George's other virtues, apparently that was not one of them. "I'm so glad George is here," Ronalee cooed. Deep dimples mounded the flesh around her jaws. "George loves Possibility Posturing. He's a perfect example of how it works."

The audience applauded enthusiastically and glanced again at George. Peter shifted about for a more comfortable position on the folding chair. He was prone to backaches, and one was working on him now. Outside, the old gardener had put down his rake and held in his hand a white daffodil bulb he had unearthed from beneath a gnarled oak. He held it up like a prize, dropped it into his jacket pocket, and resumed his raking. He kept in the sun, as if it eased the stiffening in his joints and gave him the energy he needed to do his work.

"You wouldn't believe what a change has come over George," Ronalee continued. "Possibility Posturing has revolutionized his life." She paused to suck in a big breath. "You know he once was doing very well in law. Had his own practice and more business than he could handle. But law wasn't his thing. He felt like he was in chains." She paused so the gasp of her audience would be audible. "Not that there's anything wrong with law, but George was made for a different kind of life. And it was Possibility Posturing that brought him to see that difference. How? you ask. Quite simply, George had to imagine himself doing what he wanted to do. And then he had to take the plunge of self-confidence — to set out like a pioneer and make the changes that would put him on a new course. And now he's doing exactly what he wants. He's my full-time manager. He handles all the arrangements for my books, tapes, records, and TV tours. He's lined up two hundred seventy stations for my daily fifteen minute radio program. He's a marvel; because he knew what he wanted, postured himself for possibility, and took the self-confidence plunge."

Sue leaned over to Brenda and Peter and smiled effusively at the Rands' success. Peter found it difficult to smile in response. George's desire could have come just as easily from a realization that the cash to be gained from Ronalee's success could be more easily earned than sweating out clients' cases in courtrooms.

"Ah, girls," Ronalee bubbled on. "Possibility Posturing. It's sweeping the country. It's the new revolution. You'll go home today with a whole new outlook, an outlook that will *change* your life and the lives of your husbands and children — why it has the potential to change the world." Her eyes rimmed large and glassy as if her omniscient gaze beheld the wheels of history jolting forward. "Those who have heard me talk about it have come back to tell me what it's done for their lives. Never has anything made such a difference."

Her voice dropped, and the words came at a measured pace. "Girls, Possibility Posturing is a new way of looking at ourselves, at our families, at our friends, at our communities, at the universe." Her voice rose to a ringing shout that rippled the fat around her chin. "With only one thought in mind: what can *I* do to make everything better?"

Her hands gripped the lectern, her large body leaned forward. "It sees nothing but the possibilities of improving everything we come into contact with." Her voice dropped again. "This may not seem very revolutionary to you, but just think for a moment. Most of our lives, we are burdened with problems: kids' grades, hubby's promotion, the clothes washer breaking down, the neighbor's dog, rising grocery bills—on and on and on. That's the 'despair posture'—defeat, despondency, depression. That's looking at all that's wrong. It crushes the imagination, saps energy. It turns us into dregs who drag through life never knowing the joy, the sheer exuberance of changing the dull and mangy into objects of beauty." She looked up as if transfigured objects hovered above her head.

"Like George." Her voice softened and flowed like suds down a sluice. "I'm not saying his life was poor and dull. When he went off to his law firm, he thought he was really living. And by today's standards, he was. After all, wouldn't most men consider themselves successful if they were in his shoes?" She paused rhetorically. "Oh, but George didn't know what lay in store for him. And now that he's out of that office and doing something he truly *likes* to do, and he's doing it with the one he loves most, well, even he says words fail when he tries to describe the difference."

The sun had swung away from where Peter was sitting. The gardener stared up into the light filtering through the trees as if in a trance of thanksgiving. There was a look of serenity on his withered face. His bent body and the gnarled trunks of the trees and the curled leaves blowing about him blended into one, all fed and sustained by the power of the sun.

Ronalee paraded by a series of stories about husbands and wives whose lives had been revolutionized by Possibility Posturing. Happiness abounded, financial success doubled, tripled, quadrupled, whole cities had been transformed by snooping souls greedy for change.

Finally Ronalee floated to a halt, and the grateful audience applauded generously. Faces gleamed as if they couldn't wait to rush out and spread the revolution.

15

Sue Ritter started the big car and edged it away from the curb. "Isn't she something—that Ronalee?" Sue's eyes glowed as if she were beholding a vision of paradise. "They must have the happiest marriage imaginable. Did you see the way George looked at her?"

Peter had seen, but the expression was puzzling—like that of a mouse who had been spared by the cat. If he and Ronalee were true revolutionaries, they certainly were a new breed. It was hard to see them in the line with Patrick Henry and Robespierre.

Sue turned to glance back at Peter. "I've been thinking. I know it's hard to get Good Samaritan moving. I think Possibility Posturing would be just the thing. It's what the people in our church need—and they would respond to it."

"Well, it obviously appeals to some people," Peter conceded with less energy than he knew Sue was looking for.

"As a matter of fact," she continued, as if she hadn't heard his tepid response, "I'd like to see Ronalee in our pulpit when you're out of town. Why if all of us in that church thought about all we could do, we could remake Oakdale in a matter of weeks."

"It's up to the Council to decide who preaches," Peter said officiously. "If they want Ronalee, it's fine with me." When he was out of town, he didn't care who preached. Even when he was in town, he would relinquish the pulpit, especially if whoever took his place could get rid of the brass cross.

When they arrived at the parsonage, Peter and Brenda thanked Sue for the ride, but Brenda begged off on the offer to be picked up for next month's meeting. Sue's lips curled down in disappointment, but Brenda said, "I'll just have to see what my schedule is."

Opening the door of the house, they were greeted by

silent cold. The thermometer said fifty-five degrees. As he thought about it, Peter chided himself for being so cynical at Ronalee. After all, Ronalee had changed George, and he and Brenda hadn't brought about a single improvement in the parsonage.

16

Heavy pounding aroused Peter from the nap into which he had slipped. When he went downstairs, he saw Brenda's *New Yorker* had slid to the floor, and a shallow puddle of cold coffee lay at the bottom of the cup on the table beside where she had fallen asleep.

The pounding came again, a succession of insistent blows. It occurred to Peter that Jeff's Neanderthal might have escaped from the cellar of the old house and come to exact retribution for their leaving him behind.

Peter went to the door as Brenda stirred. Confronting him was a vaguely familiar wiry man in a stained brown parka. "I'm Mr. Shanklet," the man said. "Chairman of the property committee. I was told there are some things that need fixin'." His eyes darted as if he could not bring himself to look directly into Peter's face. His jaw was sharp, his face flat and featureless, his hair cut short, a crew cut with several weeks' growth.

Peter opened the door wide for him to enter and introduced Brenda, who was rubbing her face to get herself awake.

"I'm a contractor and have a job nearby," Mr. Shanklet said. "Thought I'd take a few minutes to look things over." He glanced about the living and dining areas betraying no emotion at the sea of white or the disarray of boxes and furniture.

Peter ran through in his mind the list of what needed to be done. "The furnace isn't working," he said. "Sometimes when we tap the thermostat it goes on. Right now I can't get it to work."

Mr. Shanklet stepped to the metal box and slid the heat control up and down. He paused to listen for the furnace starting. There was no sound. "I don't understand that," he said coldly. "The two of you been tinkering with it?"

Brenda stammered, "Peter tried to get it going when we moved in. He was able to start it several times, but lately it hasn't done anything."

Mr. Shanklet's lower lip curled. "Shouldn't touch delicate equipment like that when you don't know what you're doing. It's going to cost more than it would otherwise."

Brenda folded her arms across her chest and bit her lip. "Well, we didn't damage anything," she said confidently. "And we do have to have heat."

Mr. Shanklet paid no attention. He jerked the cover off the thermostat and probed among the wires and levers with his finger. Again he listened, but there was no sound from the cellar. "It was working fine last winter when the Strongs were here. Can't understand what's wrong. But with people tinkering . . . there's no tellin' what might've happened."

Peter swallowed the rebuke and followed Brenda and Mr. Shanklet into the kitchen. "The faucet here." Brenda pointed to the sink. "Water comes out under the handle." She turned it on and stood back so he could get a full view of the stream rippling across the counter.

He stared but said nothing, then turned away.

She refused to follow him. "Mr. Shanklet, can you give us some idea what you're going to do about this? We have to mop up water every time we turn on the faucet. Can it be fixed?"

Mr. Shanklet cast Brenda an irritated look. "It's just a washer. You can get 'em at a discount store. Nothin' serious."

Brenda stepped toward him. "Well, it is serious when this place is such a mess. Water leaks into the cabinets below. I've had bags of flour and sugar ruined . . ."

Mr. Shanklet's brow knit. "Listen, I said a washer will

take care of it. You or your husband can put it in yourselves. Anybody with any sense can do it."

Peter found the back of his neck burning. The lines in Brenda's face deepened. Suddenly Peter had an idea. "Ronalee," he whispered to Brenda while Mr. Shanklet strutted into the living area.

A glint shone in her eyes. "Mr. Shanklet, you must truly have a difficult job."

He turned and stared at her as if not she, but someone else had spoken. "What do you mean by that?" he demanded.

"Well," she groped, "construction work is hard nowadays. And with your being chairman of the church property committee, you've got a lot on your shoulders. At least, I would assume so."

His eyes drew into a squint as if he wasn't quite sure who he was talking to. "You don't think I'm doing my job?"

"No. No, I didn't say that. Not at all. I just sympathize with all you've got weighing you down. I don't want the parsonage to make your life miserable if you're already overburdened."

He took an uncertain step toward her. "Listen, until I came in here, nothing was botherin' me. I just don't like it when people who don't know what they're doin' fool with the furnace. And I don't see why the committee has to fret itself over a ten cent washer any kid could install."

"Well, we live in the parsonage, and the church owns it," she said brightly. "So why don't we work together to make it better?"

Brenda waved her hand over the living area tundra. "Like the painting to be done in here. If the church would buy the paint, Peter and I and the children would put it on. Labor's expensive now-a-days. It would save the church a lot of money."

Mr. Shanklet's eyes grew wide. "Paint? In here?" He stared about like a rodent that had just been run over by a vehicle it never saw coming. "What's wrong with in here? It was just painted last year."

Brenda took a deep breath. "Look at it this way," she said. "This is a magnificent house, an architectural dream — a dwelling worthy of only the finest church in town. But does white paint show off its virtues? Does white carpet demonstrate the rich texture of its design? Do those circles in the ceiling, so artificially made, really demonstrate the fine quality of craftsmanship that went into its construction? That's what concerns me. This decor just isn't good enough for Good Samaritan."

Peter felt Ronalee gazing over Brenda's shoulder, nodding in approval at her technique. He also felt twinges of conscience: God rather puzzled at this revolutionary behavior.

Mr. Shanklet stood in silence, chewing his lower lip. Then his voice came low and threatening. "I don't give a damn what the house looks like. I've got one job in this church." For the first time since he had entered the house, he turned his orbs on Peter. They were glowing with anger. "That's to hold down costs. This house is white because we got fifty gallons of white paint at a closeout. Even Strong didn't take to it, but he was willing to have anything just to cover the cracks in the plaster."

Mr. Shanklet bent toward Peter as if he were about to commit an act of violence. "Let me tell you somethin'. I've done thousands of dollars of work for this church — all for nothin'. They ask me to do it. They tell me I'll be paid for it. But I haven't seen one red cent. The only thanks I get is complaints that somethin' else isn't workin' right." He paused and looked about. "Like this place. You want it to look like an architectural dream? Then you take it up with the Board of Trustees. And when they ask you what it'll cost, look out. They're the tightest bunch of S. O. B.'s you'll find anywhere. It's as if every nickel comes right out of their hides."

Brenda's shoulders sagged in defeat. Peter felt Possibility Posturing foundering on rocks, pieces drifting out to sea.

Mr. Shanklet stopped at the door. "Anything else?" he

asked. His tone of voice defied Peter and Brenda to list one more item.

Peter thought of the plugged drain in the cellar laundry tub. He wanted the fireplace made so it could burn logs. Someone would have to find out if the chimney had a flue. But he shook his head and said nothing.

"We'll work on the furnace when we get time," Mr. Shanklet said. He swung the door open. "In the meantime, stop foolin' with it. You'll just make it worse." With that he slammed the door and was gone.

"Well, nice try," Peter said.

Brenda sagged into the chair next to her cold cup of coffee. "Possibility Posturing," she snorted. She glanced about at the white above and below and all around, at boxes that hadn't been moved since they day they arrived. "I'd like to turn Ronalee loose on him."

Peter laughed. "You don't think she could revolutionize him?"

"Only through intimidation," she replied.

"Like everyone else," Peter said.

"Like everyone else."

Suddenly the phone rang and Brenda went to the kitchen to answer it. She returned with a smile. "It was Marge. A play has just been chosen for the Playhouse. They need ballet dancers. I'm going."

"Good," Peter said. "It'll be good for you, and it'll get you out of this albino house."

17

Peter set out to find the person who had the authority to do away with the brass cross. Bypassing Miss Hensley, he called to Mr. Krohn. Mr. Krohn thought about it for a week and called back. "Charlie Jarvis is the man you should talk to. He's the chairman of the worship committee that doesn't meet anymore."

"Well, let's get together for golf," Charlie said buoyantly in response to Peter's request. "I'll call Krohn and we'll get a fourth. Saturday OK?"

For a moment, Peter couldn't speak. He had lost track of the last time he'd played golf. Where were his clubs? But golf would give him time to make his case. "Yes," he said weakly.

18

Peter dragged up from the cellar the set of golf clubs he had bought on a whim at a garage sale. The handles were covered with mildew, dampness had pitted the shafts, the heads of the irons were coated with fine orange rust. He spent the whole evening with newspapers spread out on the family room floor steel-wooling the rust spots and scrubbing the handles. He made some progress, but the set still looked as if it had spent six months under water. Beneath the mildew, the handles were dull and worn. Pit marks on the shafts stood out darkly against the shine of undamaged metal. The heads on the irons looked a bit better, with the exception of his standby, the nine iron. It was as rusty as an old water pipe; no amount of rubbing could penetrate to pure steel. He thought of leaving it home, but since he didn't have a sand wedge, without his nine iron he would be helpless on close approach shots and in sand traps.

His golf shoes hadn't been used much either. Crunching his way up the walk to the Oakdale Country Club golf house, he was aware of traces of mildew spotting the cracked leather. Behind trailed his rusted clubs in a stained canvas golf bag lashed to his two-wheeled pull cart, also rusty and stained.

The golf house was a single-story white structure with a screen porch; access to the basement pro shop was gained through an outside door. There were no other pull carts in sight. The cellar door next to the pro shop had a sign above it—"Caddies." And over by the first tee gleamed a line of white motorized ride-carts with red and white striped canopies. Peter looked about furtively for a place to stash his two wheeled wreck. There was a privet hedge next to the clubhouse, but it had lost its leaves and would conceal nothing. There was a white and green trash barrel, but the handle of his cart would stick up behind it.

Suddenly Mr. Krohn shouted from the screened porch. "Reverend Campbell. Up here." Peter shielded his equipment with his body, backed it into a scraggly hemlock, and mounted the steps.

Mr. Krohn and the other two members of the foursome stood with glasses of orange juice in hand. Mr. Krohn was clad in black golf shoes, gray trousers, and a gray sweater. A gray golf glove peeked out of a trouser pocket. His banking partner was taller than Peter; he had a shy manner that made it appear he was backing away when Peter shook hands with him.

Charlie Jarvis glowed like a daffodil in a woodlot. Orange trousers, yellow sweater over a red shirt, white golf shoes. About thirty-five, heavy, with a roll of fat beneath his chin, he chuckled as he reached out for Peter's hand. Peter had never seen the face with the black hair and heavy brows before. At least he couldn't recall seeing it on a Sunday morning.

"Nice to meet you, Rev," Charlie said, his smile broadening. "Great day for golf." He turned to Mr. Krohn. "Isn't this a great place for a meeting?"

Mr. Krohn nodded and led them out the door. In front of the pro shop he turned. "What'll it be? Caddies or carts?"

Peter stared at his relic peeking out of the hemlock and gulped. "You won't need that, Reverend Campbell," Mr. Krohn said. "We'll take the easy way. Take the clubs off and come on over here." Peter obediently removed his clubs and wheeled the cart out of sight behind the golf house.

When he returned, Mr. Krohn and his banker friend were loading their clubs on a cart. A strapping black youth had shouldered Charlie's huge leather bag and was hoisting

Peter's canvas antique to his broad shoulders. Mr. Krohn and his banker friend motored ahead while Peter and Charlie trotted along behind. Two other foursomes were standing at the first tee awaiting their time to tee off. Peter did not need a gallery to watch him take his first swing in years. He strutted about trying to create an air of confidence, but when he popped the cloth cover off his driver and drew the club out of the bag, he knew he was fooling no one. The varnish on the head was cracked and peeling; deep pits flecked the wood. Then it suddenly dawned on him. He hadn't brought any balls.

The zipper on the ball pocket of his bag was rusted shut. He bent down on one knee and put all his strength into his thumb and forefinger in order to wrest the zipper down three inches. Barely enough for him to squeeze out a ball. The first one displayed a broad smile, or frown, depending which way he held it. The next ball was obviously a stray he had found. Grass green, its cover brittle, it looked as if it had spent a year or so on the bottom of a pond. The third one had no deep cuts, and it was white, but its egg shape suggested it was ready for retirement. He let the bag drop to the ground and turned around to head for the pro shop.

Mr. Krohn said, "Need balls? Here." He arced a couple toward Peter. They plopped on the grass and ran to his feet, where he picked them up. They were brand new, gleaming paint, spherical—no happy or unhappy expressions staring at him.

Peter was up first. "A privilege reserved for the clergy," Mr. Krohn said. Peter had never heard of that before, but since he felt he was marching to his doom, he didn't care in what order he did it. He mounted a ball on a tee—also thrown to him by Mr. Krohn—and stood back for a practice swing. He was sure he heard bones creaking. The muscles in his shoulders pulled as if he were on a rack. He chided himself for letting himself get so out of shape.

He stepped up to the ball and addressed it with the club head. Shiny ball, withered head. He accidentally tapped the ball and it bounded forward. In the deathly silence that followed, he wondered if Mr. Krohn were a stickler for rules and would count the miscue as a shot. With a chuckle to try to relieve the tension, he remounted the ball. Mr. Krohn cleared his throat.

Peter was almost blind as he brought the club head down. The fairway sloped downhill, so if he could just get the ball moving he would at least get out of range of the gallery. As it was, the ball was teed too high. It rocketed straight up, struck a tree branch hanging over the tee, shot forward onto the fairway, and came to rest about seventy-five yards down range. It was a terrible exhibition of golf prowess, but at least he was off the first tee. Seventeen more to go.

As the match progressed, Peter was so caught up in surviving that he almost forgot the reason he was there. While Mr. Krohn's friend played like a pro, Mr. Krohn and Charlie did not. Mr. Krohn hit a very straight ball. But its flight was like a teeter-totter. Quickly up, quickly down — never more than a hundred yards along the fairway. Having virtually no backswing, his effort consisted of a controlled twitch at the point of contact between the club and ball. True, the ball never strayed from the fairway, but Peter was always amazed at how many strokes Mr. Krohn took to get from the tee to the green.

Charlie was a free swinger. He addressed the ball with a homicidal glare. The club waggled over his head on the backswing like a weapon of malice. As the club head descended, a loud wheeze forced all the air out of Charlie's lungs. The ball whined toward trees or ponds or houses next to the fairway, and in the ensuing silence all that could be heard was Charlie's lungs refilling with air.

Peter thought about raising the question of the cross, but he saw Charlie only on greens and tees — where the golf law banning whispering hung in the air like a funeral pall. Apart from those meetings, the only evidence of Charlie's presence was the crack of a ball against heavy timber or a plume of water in a pond. Peter felt like he was playing alone, except when he approached greens and had to draw out his trusty nine iron. He tried standing on the head to hide its hideous orange color, but after a few holes he figured his corroded treasure had been fully acknowledged by the others.

19

They were sitting with cokes on the golf house porch. Peter was aware that the time for broaching the question for which he had been willing to endure a day of humiliation was running out.

"Cross?" Mr. Krohn asked with a wrinkled brow. "I can't remember a cross. You're not talking about the wooden one. A brass cross?" He looked at Charlie. "I don't think I've ever seen it."

Peter explained how it had been set on the communion table almost every Sunday since he arrived. Charlie shook his head without betraying whether he ever attended church. Mr. Krohn squinted in recollection. "All I can think of is Gottschalk's ball shining up there on top of the hill. I can see that all through the service. Did you know the light shines from different places on the ball as the sun moves? It's quite something what the old boy put up there."

Peter cited the mornings the cross had been out. Finally they agreed that the cross maybe appeared "once in a while." He pointed out how redundant it was with the wooden one. "Besides, it's not the kind of cross a church should have. It isn't a cross of suffering, of sacrifice. It's an ornament that contradicts the gospel's assessment of the price Jesus paid. It denies the mandate that every disciple should take up his cross."

Mr. Krohn's friend listened politely, but without comment. Mr. Krohn kept bobbing his head as if he couldn't figure out how he had missed seeing the brass cross. Charlie Jarvis stared from heavy, drooping eyes as if Peter had no idea what he was talking about. Peter felt his words being carried off the porch by the breeze and having no effect whatsoever.

"I don't see the problem," Charlie said. "I mean the furnishings in the sanctuary don't make any difference to anyone. What counts is what's preached from the pulpit."

Peter recalled the congregation at worship: vacant eyes fixed on Gottschalk's ball, vacant eyes fixed on the maze of organ pipes, vacant eyes fixed on the brass cross. His stomach tightened as it did when he was preaching. "It does make a difference. Communication isn't just words. It's also symbols. While I preach sacrifice, the brass cross preaches life without death, renewal without cost — it proclaims a heresy."

Henry Krohn downed his coke in silence. His gray eyes were so devoid of comprehension Peter wondered if he had developed a sudden hearing loss. Charlie Jarvis pressed his paunch against the edge of the table and shook his head. "I think you're way off the track. Crosses don't mean anything to people. Putting one up or taking one down won't change anything. If there's people who *want* that brass cross there, taking it down will just make them mad. They're liable to quit the church."

Mr. Krohn's head jerked up. "We can't have that. We need all the members we can get."

Charlie leaned back and smiled. His voice came smooth and mellow. "If you ask me, I think we need a whole new approach at Good Samaritan."

Peter sighed and stared at his half empty bottle of coke. His shoulders felt heavy.

Charlie's eyes glowed as if a vision were unfolding before his eyes. "We've got to look at the churches that are bringing in new members. And who are they?" Charlie's glassy eyes searched Mr. Krohn and his friend. "The people with TV and a lot of promotion. Take Jimmy Fennel. He built that place out there on the highway from a tent in a muddy field some twenty years ago. Everybody thought he was a fly-by-night. But he stuck it out. People listened and got saved. He started to grow. Now to my mind, *there's* a successful church." Charlie turned to Peter. "Have you seen it? Have you been there?"

Peter had been past it. The church looked like an airplane hangar. It could be recognized as a church only by the enormous neon sign across the front that said, "World's Largest Worship Auditorium." The boast had not quickened Peter's expectation of the coming of the kingdom of God. He had no desire even to enter the building. He had been in airplane hangars before.

"Packs the place," Charlie went on. "He's got a hundred buses. People come in from all around. Hundreds of radio and TV stations carry his service across the country and around the world. Now that's a successful church for you."

Peter's stomach churned. Mr. Krohn asked Charlie, "How does he do it? Why is he growing while we're barely holding our own?"

Charlie's eyes took on a pontifical air. "I'll tell you why. He's got a simple message and good music." Charlie paused to let the impact of his words settle on his listeners. "That's all it takes."

"Simple message?" Mr. Krohn asked. "What's that?"

"He preaches about ten minutes, maybe fifteen. But everything he says is down to earth. It reaches people where they are. He talks about not feeling good, about being frustrated with your job and with other people. He shows people how God can pick them up and make them successful. Then he has guests speak who've listened to his message and had their lives changed. Why he had on this guy who bought a turkey restaurant . . ."

"Turkey restaurant?" Mr. Krohn asked. "What the hell is that?"

"Turkey every way you can imagine it. Baked, fried, ground up like hamburger, sausage — everything turkey. It's a great food. Tastes good and it's got lots of nutrition. Anyway, he had this turkey restaurant, and then started another, and another, until now he's got a chain of twenty-five. And they're all going great guns. You know why?" Charlie surveyed the puzzled faces before him. "This guy prayed there would be a great hunger for turkey. Can you imagine that? And people started coming in droves. It's stories like that that turn people on. That's religion at work—right where people live."

And eat, Peter thought. He enjoyed turkey at Thanksgiving. Christmas even. But apparently the turkey prayer had missed him. Turkey sausage? Turkey hamburgers? Why on earth were they talking about turkey anyway? He was dragging his rusted clubs around a golf course to get rid of a brass cross.

"You mentioned music," Mr. Krohn said. "What's Fennel got that we don't?"

"It swings," Charlie said. "It's the kind of music people are used to, the kind they listen to on the radio. All Straphe gives us is Bach and a bunch of people I've never heard of. Bach lived hundreds of years ago—I doubt if his records even sell now. It's outdated." Charlie leaned over the table. "You know what? I'll bet half the people in our congregation don't even know how to pronounce his name. They probably call him 'bake' or 'baitch' or something like that."

Mr. Krohn squinted as if in pain. "I can't stand the music I hear on the radio. It's like a bunch of howling savages. If you think that would help Good Samaritan, you're mistaken. The people we've got wouldn't stand for it. And Straphe would leave for sure."

Charlie held up his hand. "I'm not saying it should be just like Fennel's . . ."

"My goodness," Mr. Krohn continued. "If Fennel's the preacher I turned on one Sunday, it was awful. He had his grandmother up there singing. She had this falsetto voice that kept cracking. You'd think the man would be embarrassed to do that to his grandmother."

"Well, there might be a few excesses," Charlie went on. "But we have excesses the other way. We're dead. There's no life, no enthusiasm."

Peter's muscles tightened. Charlie was right. There was no life. But the problem was the brass cross and its heretical religion.

"Well, Reverend Campbell, what do you think?" Mr. Krohn was looking at him. The foursome at the next table sipped their beers pretending they weren't listening in.

Aunt Katherine had once taken Peter to hear an evangelist who had put up a big tent in a field at the edge of town. All Peter could remember was that his ears hurt. Trombones and trumpets blaring terrible notes and a girl covered with make-up blasting out how much she loved Jesus. Peter envisioned her and Jesus walking down some secluded lane exchanging smoochy glances. He couldn't imagine the girl kissing anyone without leaving lipstick caked on their cheeks.

Afterward, he and Aunt Katherine were walking home in the dark when she sighed and said, "I should've known. When I saw that black car and someone said it was his, I should've known we were in for the old pitch. There we were in that stifling tent sitting on those back-breaking chairs, and he rides around in that big car like King Tut. They're all alike." She paused and for a moment the only sound stirring the heavy summer air was the click of their shoes. "No, not all of them. I'm sure there are some who are sincere and try to live like Jesus." She paused thoughtfully; her voice mellowed. "Even one like him." She nodded back toward the tent. "I can't say God doesn't use him to do some good. God has ways we don't understand. But I'll tell you one thing." In the glow of a streetlamp her eyes shone with determination. "He won't get a nickel from me. Let people who like to have their ears blown out support him. And if they won't, then let him sink. It'd be good for him if he had to sell that limousine."

Peter felt no desire to stand as Fennel's judge, but Fennel's ways were certainly not his. "I don't think it's the answer for us," he said. "Not for the people we've got and the ones we can reach."

Charlie's cheeks quivered. "But look at his success. The place is packed every Sunday."

"Success isn't everything," Peter replied. "At least that kind of success."

"But we do need to do something," Mr. Krohn put it. "We can't keep going the way we are. Costs are going up. Our people aren't keeping pace."

Charlie's eyes narrowed. "I think you're making a serious mistake if you don't try to learn from Fennel. Hell, we're marketing something out there. You've got to read the crowd and give them what they want." He turned to Peter. "You may have great ideas, but if you're not connecting, if there isn't that little twitch in the heart while you're talking, people go away unsatisfied. And they go away with the bucks that could put Good Samaritan in the black."

Peter recalled the meeting with the committee that called him. The chairman puffing away on his cigar harking back to Jesus' first followers. "I was called to this church to help people become disciples," he blurted.

Charlie downed the last swig of his coke. His head was shaking. "Disciples. Disciples. They're just turned-on church members. I don't know what else the committee could have meant. What we need is something to make Good Samaritan alive. To make it so people *want* to go there. Sure, disciples. But modern disciples. People who are aiming for success and need God to get there."

Peter didn't know whether the hostility tightening his chest was directed against the committee or against Charlie. Had the committee lied to him? Or was Charlie just another exception?

Mr. Krohn's friend, tired of the conversation, stood up. Two other foursomes had gone through, and the air drifting through the porch was developing a chill.

The second nine holes went the same as the first. Mr. Krohn's friend hit the ball long and straight, Mr. Krohn twitched the ball down the middle of the fairway, and Charlie hacked through rough and woods and sand traps. Peter wielded his antiques as best he could, occasionally with a crisp shot that landed right where he wanted it. But usually the ball screamed right or left for no reason at all.

On the 13th hole, he came on Charlie poking around with his nine iron in swampy black water beneath a grove of weeping willows. Joining the search for the lost ball, Peter asked Charlie, "Can the brass cross be removed? If for no other reason than that I'm the pastor and I want it gone?"

"It'd do more harm than good," Charlie said. "People would get upset. Besides, I don't know who puts it out. The committee hasn't met for years. Everything pretty much runs on its own."

Peter choked down the anger burning the back of his neck. He wanted the cross gone. The cross's removal would make the congregation face what it seemed determined to avoid—that the Christian faith was a costly life. Before he could reply, he found Charlie's ball. It was lying under a brown lily pad.

Charlie lifted it out with a grin. "Winter rules," he said. That enabled him to avoid a one shot penalty, although Peter had clearly seen 'Summer Rules' on a blackboard at the golf house. Charlie dropped the ball over his shoulder for a new placement. It ricocheted off a tree root and splashed back into the water. A smirk covered his face. "I'm entitled to another try."

Peter said, "Why don't you just pick it up and put it on the fairway? Nobody will care."

Charlie glanced about sheepishly, turned, dropped the ball where Peter suggested, and slapped it into a sand trap guarding the green.

20

They had putted out the eighteenth green and were walking to the parking lot when Peter went up to Charlie. Behind Peter trailed his rusty clubs on the two-wheeled wreck he had retrieved from the dumpster: someone thinking it was trash and had thrown it away. Golfers heading for their cars stared at his relic, but he ignored them. It was a relief just to have the game over.

He had to try one more time on the brass cross. But then he thought the better of it. Charlie simply could not understand his concern. He recalled the other aggravation. "Those National Guard fighter planes that fly over during the service," he said. They came every Sunday. He lost his place in the sermon. His mind wandered. He had to restart his sermon twice. Once after the first three planes. Then after the fourth, which was far behind the others. "Can we do something to get them to stop? They're terribly irritating."

Charlie's jaw fell slack as if Peter had just uttered a swear word. "Not on your life," he gasped. "That's our national security up there. They use Good Samaritan as a marker on the run to target practice. We're making a contribution to the defense of our country. Why everyone in the congregation would fight you on that."

Peter was about to respond, but he could see in Charlie's glazed eyes a patriotic zeal that matched his religious mania.

Charlie paused, then his voice came low, as if he were confiding a secret. "I should warn you. There are people in the congregation who are really off the wall. Liberals. Maybe worse. They think the church is supposed to get into politics and change society. They'll be on you. But watch out. They're the kiss of death. Got more people mad and have cost us more members than anything else." He caught Peter's eye. "Just thought you ought to be forewarned."

Peter did not respond. Charlie breathed heavily at his

elbow as Peter loaded his antique clubs into the trunk of his car. "Try Fennel," Charlie said in a lighter tone. "Talk to him. Listen to his TV program. You'll find good tips for getting Good Samaritan rolling."

Peter banged down the trunk lid with extra vigor and looked at Charlie's glassy eyes. "I'll think about it," he said. He got into his car and drove away. The back of his neck still burned.

21

It started snowing the night before Peter was to have an early morning meeting with the woman Miss Hensley labeled as "a liberal." When Peter asked Miss Hensley the woman's name, Miss Hensley's lips curled as if she had found a dead rat in her desk. "Pat Andrews!" she hissed. "Why that woman has cost this church dozens of members. Dozens! The more Dr. Strong tried to reason with her, the worse things got. The woman's fire. Anyone who gets near her can't help but get burned."

Fire wasn't on Peter's mind when he stepped out the front door of the parsonage into the snowy darkness. His foot slid forward. He tried to regain his balance, but overcompensated and fell face down in a drift. He pulled himself up, brushed the snow off his face, retrieved his hat and briefcase, and trudged to his car. Covered with snow from being left out of Jeff's metal sculpture studio, it looked like a huge egg.

Under the scrutiny of the trembling curtain in the next house, he brushed it off and got the motor started. A quick jolt toward the street ended with the back of the car slithering toward the unneighborly neighbor's house and the scream of spinning tires. He hauled the snow shovel out of the garage and attacked the drifts blocking his way. His eyes burned from the little sleep he had gotten after the post-midnight adjournment of the education committee. The shovel felt like it was pulling his arms out of their sockets, his back ached from the strain on muscles unused except for sitting in church chairs. He told himself he would have to do something to remedy his miserable physical condition.

It occurred to him that Ms. Andrews might be having the same trouble he was, and perhaps they should cancel, but she had not called. Besides, after Miss Hensley's fanfare of contempt, he had a burning urge to meet Good Samaritan's alleged liberal. Anyone Miss Hensley so thoroughly disliked might possibly be the kind of person who would help him get rid of the brass cross.

Lights blinked on in neighboring houses. Between salvos of shoveling and old pieces of carpet shoved under the wheels, Peter thought he had a track that would get him out of the driveway. One great burst of the engine shot him rearward until the car landed like a bobcat in the middle of the street. Before him lay untracked snow, but fortunately the street sloped downhill. He attacked at full throttle. The rear end fishtailed, threatening to tear out shrubs at the curb, but he made it to the main road. He ran the stop sign, heaved a sigh of relief at finding the road plowed, and turned toward the city.

The neon lights of the Palace Cafeteria, famous for its low prices and substandard food, glowed along Main Street. He had never eaten there, but it was one of the few downtown places open before seven. Pat had surmised breakfast would be the most difficult meal for a chef to ruin.

She had underestimated. Half a dozen patrons slumped at worn formica tables injecting white mugs of coffee into their mouths as if it were an elixir that would give them the courage to face a new day. What conversation there was consisted of snippets about the snow and how surprised everyone was it came and how the weatherman never seemed to know what was going to happen.

Peter dropped a wet plastic tray on the tubular rack and slid it toward a hairnetted girl slouching behind the counter. The pulp of the orange juice had risen to the top of the shot glasses and dried. Small boxes of cold cereal featuring a broad spectrum of vitamins did not appeal. Neither did a bucket of gray oatmeal that looked like fast-drying concrete. He ordered two fried eggs over light with bacon and whole wheat toast. The girl mumbled in assent through lipstick-less lips. Her tired eyes rested on a stack of cold toast piled on a platter. "No, not that," he said politely. "Would you mind making fresh?"

The girl's jaw dropped, she glanced about as if Big Brother might be watching through the kitchen window, and put two slices of bread into the toaster.

The coffee wasn't bad; it helped cut the hamburger-grease taste of the eggs as Peter sat alone on a yellow plastic chair waiting for Pat.

"Oh, there you are!" The shout came from the doorway. Peter recognized the woman whipping off her coat from worship services. She clomped over to him in black rubber goulashes. "Sorry I'm late," she said, "but I couldn't get up the hill. Had to wait for the plow." Her baggy black sweater somewhat disguised her braless declaration of feminine independence. She swaggered past the table and over to the cafeteria line like a movie cowboy approaching the bar of a frontier saloon. Peter had seen from the membership directory she was single. She appeared about thirty. When she thumped back to the table, she had a slab of oatmeal perched in a white bowl.

She pulled in her chair and threw her long black hair back over her shoulders. She adjusted the chair, mashed down the oatmeal, and drowned it in milk. Next came a generous spoonful of sugar. She slid the orange juice in close so she could submerge the pulp into the liquid with her spoon. That done, and the juice quickly swigged, she started on her coffee. "Gee, I hope we've got time to talk," she said. "This snow's really fouled things up. I suppose I can get to the office late 'cause everybody else'll be held up too."

Peter glanced at his watch. There was a meeting scheduled at the church at nine o'clock; there was no need to hurry.

"I wanted to give you time," Pat said, her green eyes searching him, her mouth arced in the suggestion of a smile. "It must be tough to come to a new church where you have to learn new faces, and things are run differently from what you're used to."

Peter gave his assent to this oft-recurring litany. Frequently it was the prelude to a new demand. But his muscles were too tired to tense. He felt a giddy confidence that Pat was one person he could count on for support.

"I don't want to be pushing you," Pat added. "Let me say it right out. It was fantastic to hear the committee was calling someone from a city church." She mashed her oatmeal around in the milk. "I was afraid they'd go for some jerk from the suburbs working his way up the ladder. Good Samaritan is a sucker for that kind of thing."

Peter hadn't thought about that. As far as he was concerned, there was no ladder. He was either called or he wasn't.

Pat paused and put down her spoon. A strange energy glowed behind her flitting eyes. "I think I should be right up front," she said. "I don't want to sound like I'm sore about Good Samaritan. It's got a lot of fine people. Loaded people, for the most part. And that's the problem. It could stand this town on its end if it wanted to. But it doesn't. Except for a few token projects like scout troops, Good Samaritan doesn't do a damn thing for anybody. Even the groups it allows to use the buildings have to pay rent. All because utility bills hang over us like the Sword of Damocles. The Trustees. They're the power group, in case you haven't found that out. All they do is tell everybody how tight everything is and kill off programs the community badly needs."

Pat hunched over the table like an animal ready to spring. "Drugs are everywhere, but the Mayor refuses to admit it. The Board of Education plays with the desegregation order so only blacks get bused. Business leaders do nothing to hire the handicapped. Zoning is a crap game — developers get whatever they want if they pass enough money under the table. The new expressway is putting poor people out on the street, but the State just pays them a pittance and forgets about them. We need group homes for the mentally retarded, but every time there's a hearing to open one up, hundreds of citizens flock to City Hall to protest. Oh yeah, they're all *for* the mentally retarded. You ought to hear the dripping sympathy. But when they get on their property values, that's the end of compassion.

"Not that the whole town's corrupt. But it's the hands-off attitude of the leaders that gets my goat. They talk a good line, but when you look at what's happening, there's nothing there. And of course nobody wants the churches involved. It's pitiful, but those are the facts."

Peter took a long sip of coffee. He recalled the smiling, confident faces of the committee: "We have a real commitment to the city." Their voices tinkled like a cheap wind chime.

"What about Dr. Strong? What did he do?" Peter asked.

"Nothing much. He went to a ministers' conference and came back talking about desegregation. But when the trustees threatened that if he was serious he'd be out looking for another church, he backed down." Pat sighed in disgust. "What a weakling."

"Well, he was approaching retirement," Peter put in mildly, recalling the glad-handing white-haired man he had seen at meetings.

Pat glared. "If he'd tried, he could've turned Good Samaritan around. The money boys got on him, and that was it. This church has always followed greenbacks. They're its holy spirit." Pat lifted her coffee cup with a shaking hand. "There I go again. Whenever I talk about Good Samaritan I always get upset. Strong's behind us now. We need to think about where we go from here." She eyed Peter. "How do you say we get Good Samaritan involved in the problems of this community?"

Peter thought of the people he had come to know in the church; no ideas came to mind.

Pat plunged into her gunny sack purse. "I've got something," she said. She held up a piece of paper on which was written a resolution. Beneath a single-spaced block of print were lines for signatures and addresses. "This is a petition to the Environmental Protection Agency against Gottschalk Glass." Pat watched Peter carefully for his reaction. Feeling as if he were on trial, he kept his face and eyes expressionless. "They're dumping drums of chemicals in the ravine by Reynoldstown. That's the poor black community west of Oakdale. Reynoldstown has no clout. What Gottschalk Glass is doing is illegal — clearly illegal. But nobody's making a move to stop it or force Gottschalk Glass to clean it up." She shoved the paper under Peter's nose. "Justice, pastor. You sign it and get the Council and the Board of Trustees to sign it. Then I'll believe there's hope for Good Samaritan."

Peter stared down at the petition and twenty-four fresh signatures. "If what you say is true, I'll sign it," he said.

Pat glared. "That's not enough. Anyone can sign. Your job is to make Good Samaritan act responsibly."

Peter felt a sinking within. He had no credibility with either board. To dump a petition on them and demand they sign would further diminish his authority.

"You won't do it," Pat said in a taunt. "Do you know why? Two of Gottschalk's executives are on the Trustees. There's a manager on the Council. Gottschalk Glass could pillage the earth, but Good Samaritan wouldn't lift a finger." The muscles in her face tightened. "That's got to change. People must be forced to face the injustice of their acts. Strong said the church could be educated into social responsibility. Hogwash. People only change when they're confronted."

Pat's eyes rested on Peter. "As far as I'm concerned, you're not the pastor of this church until you show you've got the guts to lead it into justice. Anybody can get up there on a Sunday morning and spout words. I'm talking about changing this corrupt society. For me, that's what Jesus

Christ is all about."

Peter's eyes burned so hot he had to blink. He hated the dull ache of helplessness. What he needed from Pat was support, but the glare in her eyes only redoubled her demand: get the petition passed by the boards, or you've got a relentless foe.

Pat lit a cigarette. "Maybe I'm pushing you pretty hard for the first time we've talked." She paused. "I should shut up and let you tell me how you see the church coming around."

Peter groped back to the committee, to the painting where he saw Jesus pressing on toward Jerusalem, to Aunt Katherine, to his old church. "I was brought here to make the members of Good Samaritan into disciples of Jesus Christ," he said matter-of-factly. The words sounded dry, lifeless — had he spoken them, or had someone else?

Pat's eyes grew large as if holding back a surfeit of energy. Peter could not tell what was boiling within her until she shoved her chair back, bent over double, and howled with laughter. Sleepy heads at other tables turned in irritation. Pat shook uncontrollably. Tears ran down her face. "I can't believe it," she squealed. Another fit of laughter bent her double.

"You mean those trustees? That Council? Those fat cats in the dark blue suits? Disciples of Jesus Christ?" Again she bent double and convulsed.

Peter envisioned others: Miss Hensley glaring hostilely at Mr. Drissle; Henry Krohn, gray Henry Krohn in gray trousers, gray suitcoat, gray hat — talking about moving the church off dead center. Whatever dead center was. Charlie Jarvis trussed in lollypop colored golf clothes hacking his ball through timber saying, "Try Fennel. Try Fennel." John Rhodes aching his way around the church, panting for sympathy. Disciples, he thought to himself — those robed men and women he had imagined with their walking sticks when he was meeting with the committee. If Jesus had faced the members of Good Samaritan at the start of his trek down from the Mount of Olives, he would have hung up the triumphal entry right there and gone back to Galilee. Can faith do what the imagination can't see?

Pat hauled a handkerchief out of her purse and dried her eyes. What lined her face now wasn't hardness, nor contempt for Peter's powerlessness. It was pity: as if he were meat fed into a grinder, or just a damn fool.

She looked at the clock on the wall and stood. "Oh, I'm sorry. I've got to run. Thanks for giving me your time. I mean it." She clomped to the door, put on her coat, and was gone.

It wasn't until Peter took out his pen to sign the petition that he realized Pat had taken it with her. Did his signature count for so little?

22

By the time Peter pulled into the church parking lot, the sun had come out. He gunned the engine to blast through the drifts and slid into the immortal 'Dr. Strong' parking space.

In the office, Miss Hensley cast him a cold look. "Mr. Straphe called. He's waiting to get his driveway plowed out. Then he'll be in."

Peter halted. "How long will that take?"

Miss Hensley turned lyrical. "He doesn't know. Sometimes the jeep doesn't come until the end of the day." Her eyes watched Peter as if to pick up every nuance of his reaction.

Peter made no effort to conceal his anger. "Well, that's great."

"He says we should go ahead without him. He'll bring in suggestions when he comes for choir rehearsal." Miss Hensley's body stiffened. "I warned you staff meetings wouldn't work. Nobody wants them."

Ignoring her remark, Peter threw open his office door,

strode to the phone on his desk, and dialed Mr. Straphe's number.

The voice was Mrs. Straphe's—frightened, overly courteous. "Mr. Straphe, please," Peter said firmly.

"Just a moment," came Mrs. Straphe's timorous reply. "Oh yes, he's in a lesson . . ."

"Then you'll have to interrupt him," Peter shot back. "I want to talk to him now."

There was an awkward pause. "Well, he's told me not to . . ."

"I'll take responsibility."

A moment later, heavy breathing came on the line. "Campbell, what's the idea?" The words shot into Peter's ear like darts, but he did not flinch.

"The staff meeting scheduled for nine this morning. We're all here waiting for you to arrive."

"I told Miss Hensley we aren't plowed out. Besides, the county schools are closed. I'm giving lessons early. This is very inconvenient . . ."

"You're making it very inconvenient for the rest of us," Peter fired back. "Just cancel the lessons. I'll be there to pick you up. You can *walk* to the street, can't you?" Peter found pleasure in letting fly with a bit of sarcasm.

The line fell silent. "Campbell, there are some things you need to understand. I've made commitments to these students . . ."

"And you made a commitment to me that you'd be here at nine o'clock. Perhaps you've overcommitted yourself."

Mr. Straphe sputtered with rage. "But this driveway . . ."

"You could have called any one of us for a ride. I used something called a snow shovel, Mr. Straphe. Unless your driveway's a heck of a lot longer than mine, it might just work for you."

Silence again, then the sound of a hand covering the mouthpiece. Peter had no idea who Mr. Straphe might be talking to. His wife was probably cowering in the corner and the student—if there was one—looking for some escape route from Mr. Straphe's towering rage.

The hand was gone. "I'm going to talk to the Council about this. My contract reads..."

"I know how your contract reads. I've got a copy here on my desk. You don't fulfil half of it, so you don't have a leg to stand on."

There was a long pause, then: "I'll find my way down. But I'm telling you, Campbell, this won't happen again. I've got an obligation to my students. I'm not full-time at that church."

The phone clicked. Peter gazed at it with satisfaction and sank into his chair. It seemed to fit him better.

Suddenly he realized a well-fed penguin was standing at the window looking in. It was one of the women who frequently rummaged through the wreckage of the rose garden. She waved, then bent down to a single stick of rose bush she had uncovered with the shovel gripped in her gloved hands. Peter smiled to himself and shook his head. Such devotion, such persistence. If only it weren't all directed toward dead vegetation.

23

Mr. Straphe's voice rose in the outer office, the door burst open. He lurched in with fire in his eyes. His forehead, which ran from his wooly eyebrows to the top of his head, where it ended in a wall of stiff black hair radiating straight out from the skull, burned bright red. His spindle legs carried him with a series of jerks; his arms gesticulated to speech he had yet to begin to utter. "This is an outrage!"

Peter stared at the darting eyes. "We can talk about it later. We're already behind schedule, thanks to you."

Mr. Straphe paced like a rabid dog. "Strong never had meetings. This is ridiculous." He leaned over Peter's desk as if about to spring. "Do you realize how much money I'm losing? You may think musicians are rich. Well, they're not.

There's *nothing* in my contract about staff meetings."

Peter leaned forward until his face was only inches from Mr. Straphe's. "But conferring with the pastor is. And the pastor is free to determine how that conferring will take place. It was you who made the commitment for this morning."

"But the snow . . ."

" . . . started falling yesterday, and a message could've been left at my home last night or this morning." Peter stared into Mr. Straphe's puffed orbs until they diverted their attention elsewhere.

With a wheeze, Mr. Straphe tore off his coat and dumped it onto a chair. John Rhodes, bearing three chairs from the outer office, dragged himself through the door, followed by Miss Hensley. Her grudging pace spoke for itself. Behind her came Mrs. Peck with an eager smile.

Peter hauled his own chair around in front of the desk so they could form an informal circle. He had learned in seminary it was good psychology not to put a desk between himself and people he wished to win to his views. Mr. Straphe kept his gaze fixed on the garden windows as if he were looking for a way out. Mrs. Peck stood until Miss Hensley had set her chair as far as possible from Mr. Straphe. Then she put her chair in to fill the gap. John Rhodes planted himself against the door, tilting the chair back like a policeman guarding the hospital room of a Mafia member.

Peter stared at the disarray. "I thought we'd form a circle," he said sternly. No one budged. Mr. Straphe pushed back his sleeves and took a long look at his watch. The cold hostility hanging in the room made the blanket of snow hiding the cadaverous roses seem like a tropical beach.

"Originally, I wanted us to plan for Lent and Easter," Peter said.

Miss Hensley's black gaze fixed on the pad of blank paper perched on her lap; Mr. Straphe glanced at the floor, the outside wall, Peter's bookshelves, the clear ceiling—

everywhere but at him. Mr. Rhodes crossed his eyes as he performed minor surgery on a thumb nail. Only Mrs. Peck paid attention, her sweet smile resting on Peter with a hint of pity.

"But now that we're here," Peter continued, "I think we should talk about something else." He might as well have been addressing a storeroom of mannequins.

"Since this is a *Christian* church"—he quickly quelled a surge of doubt that swept through him—"we're not just a staff, but a family—a Christian family. This should say something about our relationships with each other."

Miss Hensley raised her knife gaze from the pad of paper. "Is something wrong?"

"I'd like to know why you so much dislike the idea of having staff meetings," Peter replied.

Mr. Straphe's eyes fixed on Peter's necktie. "Strong never had one in thirty-five years. The church ran without a hitch. Why we need them now is beyond me. What a ridiculous waste of time. I checked my contract. I'm going to take this to the Council." The strands of hair radiating from the back of his head looked like the tail of a peacock in full strut—an angry, black peacock.

Miss Hensley continued to stare at her blank pad. Mr. Rhodes did not look up from whatever he was doing to his thumb. Mrs. Peck held her smile on Peter. Her voice came so quietly he could hardly hear it. "Well, we could at least . . ."

Mr. Straphe's foot came down with a crash. He turned to Mrs. Peck with a homicidal leer.

Mrs. Peck shrank back in her chair. "I . . . I mean it wouldn't hurt . . . if we tried it . . . just once."

Peter was about to encourage her when the phone rang. He glanced at it with irritation. Miss Hensley rose like a robot and headed for it. "Only if it's an emergency," Peter said. Miss Hensley listened for a moment, then said, "Yes, he's right here." She shoved the phone in Peter's face. "Emergency," she hissed.

A banshee howl knifed into Peter's ear. It turned into a

frail woman's voice pleading: "Is this the Rev'rent? Is the Rev'rent there?" Peter acknowledged. "Oh, thank God," the voice said. "I need to talk to someone real bad. It's ter'ble, Rev'rent, jus' ter'ble. You can't believe what I'm goin' through." A howl dissolved into wrenching sobs.

"I know you're a busy man, Rev'rent. Bein' new to that church an' all that. But I need help. I can't take any more."

"Can you tell me what's wrong?" Peter asked, unable to flush from his voice the anger he felt at his rebel staff. "Where are you? I'll come over."

"Oh, no!" the voice shrieked. "No, no, don't do that." There was a pause. "That would make it worse. Then he'd get me for sure."

"Get you? Who would get you? Where are you?" He envisioned an elderly lady alone with an intruder in the house.

"That man down the hall. He's eighty-five, Rev'rent, and he chases women. I know that's hard for a man like you to believe, but that's God's truth. Eighty-five, an' he's still doin' things like that. He's threatened to come into my room . . ." The voice broke off into another howl. "I can't take it, Rev'rent. That look he gives me. I'm scared out of my mind."

"Where are you?" Peter asked again. John Rhodes had given up on his thumb and was glancing about impatiently. Mr. Straphe glared with contempt. Was that a smirk on Miss Hensley's face? He had a hunch Miss Hensley knew who this woman was. She was the kind who had a dozen emergencies a day — all in her mind. How could he get rid of her without appearing calloused?

"I can't tell you where I am," the woman replied. "I don't want you comin' here. If he even knew I was talkin' to you like this, he'd do somethin' ter'ble. He's jealous, that's what it is. He don't let me out of his sight. He's in the bathroom now, but when he comes out, I'll have to hang up. I'm so frightened. He's eighty-five, and he still don't have the sense to leave poor, innocent women alone. I've told 'im, told 'im he ought to work off his energy down in the poolroom or go out to the garden. They should look at his head down there in X-ray and find out what's wrong with him. A man shouldn't be like that—not at eighty-five. Don't you think so, Rev'rent? You're a wise man. You know what God thinks about these things."

Peter's hand tightened on the phone. He had a fierce impulse to hang up. There was no other way out. The woman's voice suddenly came more quickly. "Oh, there's the toilet flushing. Here he comes. I've got to get off." The phone clicked.

Peter stared at the receiver, then turned to the smirking grins of all but Mrs. Peck. He fixed on Miss Hensley. "That was an emergency?"

She cocked her head with a self-righteous air. "Dr. Strong always talked to her. The poor woman's desperate. A *Christian* doesn't turn his back on someone in need."

Peter ignored the sarcasm. "Who is she? Where is she?"

Miss Hensley shook her head. "We've never known her name or where she calls from. Some nursing home, probably. But there are several around."

Peter took a deep breath to ease the stricture in his chest. "Well, I'm making one change here and now. When that woman interrupts something, she's not an emergency. If she needs help, she can leave her number, and I'll get back to her. Is that clear?"

Miss Hensley's gaze drifted back to the blank pad. She said nothing; Peter could not perceive even the slightest nodding to indicate she would heed his demand.

John Rhodes banged down the front legs of his chair and leaned forward. "I've got something we need to work on. Tell me who I'm supposed to take orders from." He nodded toward Mr. Straphe. "Straphe here leaves me notes saying where I'm supposed to set chairs and move pianos. He's got thirty people in that choir, but do you think they move anything? No sir."

Mr. Straphe's eyes bulged with anger, but before he could say anything, Mr. Rhodes continued.

"And then the office out there." He motioned toward the opaque glass partition. "Every time I come through, I'm told—do this, do that. I hired on at this church to work for one boss: the chairman of the Board of Trustees. But everybody else thinks they have the right to tell me what to do." He scowled at Miss Hensley. "I'm gettin' good and fed up. Let's work on that one." He sat up straight, rolled up the sleeves of his flannel shirt as if preparing for a fight, and waited for Peter's response.

"We do need to work on that," Peter said. "We need to work on it *together*."

"That's nonsense," Miss Hensley put in. Her frame arched forward, her eyes leveled an evil gaze at Mr. Rhodes. "I only pass on to him what the trustees give me. Mr. Krohn can't be here all the time. And Mr. Rhodes doesn't have the brains to see what needs to be done. There was a job list for him sometime back, but do you think he follows it?" Her mouth quivered with contempt.

Mr. Straphe looked at his watch. "Every half hour is another lesson. So far, this has been a complete waste of time. Fifteen minutes and I'm off." His cheeks puffed in defiance.

Peter's mind spun. Spying a folder on his desk, he picked it up. "The Wednesday night studies in Lent," he said. "I want to use them for . . . "

"Forget it," Mr. Straphe said emphatically. "The church brought in hot-shot speakers for the Wednesday nights last year and nobody came. Blew a fortune for nothing. Just the same handful of people who would come to anything."

Miss Hensley nodded in agreement. "We sent out a huge mailing. It wasn't worth the postage."

Peter offered other ideas for Holy Week, but they all bounced off sullen faces and glaring eyes. Mr. Straphe would conduct no extra music. John Rhodes threatened that if the church held additional services it could jolly well go out and hire another custodian because he was overworked—and he wasn't no slave.

Suddenly Mr. Straphe jerked to his feet. "This is a total waste. Here." He thrust a sheet of paper in Peter's face. "Here's the music for the Sundays leading up to Easter. The anthems are longer than usual, so it'd help if you'd cut down the length of your sermons. People tune out anyway. And the Sunday before Palm Sunday we'll have a cantata. The whole service is set to music, so you can take the day off."

Peter clenched the sheet of paper and restrained his anger to avoid crushing it into a ball. Before he could reply, Mr. Straphe had grabbed his coat, shot past Mr. Rhodes, and was gone.

Mr. Rhodes picked up his chair with slow, arthritic movements. "I can't get nothin' done sittin' here, and they don't pay me for overtime."

Miss Hensley stood stiffly. "Is that it?" The pad in her hand was blank. She nodded to Mrs. Peck to follow her out.

Sighing inwardly, Peter watched them leave. He could think of nothing more to say. He hated to admit it, but he was glad to see them go. It would be a long time before he tried to have another staff meeting — at least with this staff.

Outside his window, two penguins were stuffing straw around stubby rose bush remains. Through the sanctuary above the garden, Gottschalk's ball glistened in the winter sun. And from the communion table, the brass cross silently mocked. "It has to go," Peter muttered aloud. "Even if that's the only thing I do here."

24

That afternoon Peter was working on his sermon when he looked up to see a dark shape looming against the opaque door of his office. Miss Hensley shrieked from beyond as if she were being assaulted. "You can't go in there! You're not allowed!"

Adrenalin pumped Peter into action. When he opened his door, he had to jump back to avoid being trampled by a grizzled man with orange hair, his bent body clad in a shapeless wool coat and baggy corduroy trousers.

In the outer office, Miss Hensley writhed. "I told him," she shouted. "He's not allowed to bother you." Her face was white, her breath came in sharp gasps. "I'll call the police." Her trembling hand reached for the phone.

Peter sized up the man—reeking breath, yellow teeth, piercing gaze. "Now just wait a minute," he said to her.

Miss Hensley clutched the phone. "Dr. Strong said never to let them in. Tramps. That's all they are. They get off freight trains on the other side of the hill and come here for a handout. They used to come in droves, but Dr. Strong stopped all that. It was like we were some kind of rescue mission. You can't do anything with them. All they want is money to buy liquor." Her lips curled in disgust. "You can *smell* it on his breath." She waved the phone about like a weapon.

"Now Rev'ernt," the man began in a subdued voice. Peter stood in the doorway between the man and Miss Hensley. "I don't know what that woman's talkin' 'bout, but you don't seem like the kind o' preacher who'd turn a man away in his hour o' need."

"Dr. Strong . . ." Miss Hensley repeated.

"I'll talk to him," Peter said. He shut the door, aware that Miss Hensley was still standing with the phone in hand.

The man sat down. "Name's Henchard. Jim Henchard. You may've heard of me."

Peter thought for a moment. He had not.

"Good friend o' Billy Graham's. Oral Roberts, too. Great men. Used o' God. I know 'em all. Farwell too. Smart man. They preach to millions." His eyes narrowed, his head nodded as if he were leaning over to pray. "Giants of the faith. I know some you prob'ly never heard of." His stare suggested condescension that Peter had not been inducted into the higher levels of the kingdom.

"Look here." Henchard pulled a thick paper out of his jacket pocket and held it up. In the center was his picture, one of those instant photos from a booth found at bus stations. Glued around it were newspaper and magazine pictures of Graham and other evangelists. "Know 'em all."

Peter looked at his watch. He had several people to visit in the hospitals, and he was trying to get home before Brenda cleared dinner from the table. "What can I do for you?" he asked.

Henchard's pale eyes held him in a penetrating gaze. "No, no," he said. "Not what can you do for me. It's what I can do for you."

Peter could think of nothing he needed. Suddenly the phone on his desk buzzed. "Mr. Krohn on line two," Miss Hensley said.

Peter pressed the outside button.

"Krohn here," came the staccato voice. "Sorry to bother you." Henchard's eyes searched the glass walls, the papers lying on Peter's desk, the rows of books on the shelves, the rose garden abandoned for the present by the penguin gardeners. Krohn spoke quickly. "I want to nip a problem in the bud. You remember the couple next door I told you about?"

Peter recalled. Apart from the twitching curtain, he had yet to meet them.

"The fellow called me. Very upset. Says the cars are left out every night. I don't mean to get involved in your business, but you know—for the peace of the neighborhood. Plus everyone knows the house belongs to the church. We've got a reputation to uphold."

Peter's throat tightened.

Krohn's voice went on: "One more thing. 'Course I don't know what he's talking about. Says somebody's in the garage with a welding machine. The old guy might be hallucinating or something."

"He's not," Peter said sharply.

"No?"

"My son, Jeff. He welds out there."

"Welds? Cars?"

"No. Sculpture. He's very good at it. He won a prize last

year." Peter's chest swelled as he recalled Jeff mounting the high school stage to receive the plaque for Neanderthal. Of course the committee had had to come to the house to see it.

"Sculpture? That's clay, stone."

"Or metal," Peter added.

The phone went silent for a moment. "Well, that's a new one on me. I don't know what we're going to do. The old guy says it keeps him awake at night, you know, the flicker. There's so much junk in the garage he says he's afraid you'll never put the cars in."

"Well, never's a long time."

"Are you set on this, Campbell? I mean we've got to get along with those people. Welding? Did you tell anyone before you came? Isn't it unusual for a kid to be doing something like that?"

"It is a little different," Peter conceded. "But it's a hobby, just like any other. Some people keep bees, others breed rabbits . . ."

"But the whole garage?"

"He'd take the basement if he could. Someone would have to install a blower to clear the fumes. And there would have to be an outside door so he could get finished pieces out."

Krohn paused. "Well, that's the damnedest thing I've ever heard. When the old guy calls again, I'll tell him. But in the meantime, talk to your son. Tell him he's got to find another hobby."

The hair on the back of Peter's neck bristled. "You tell the old guy to mind his own business," he said.

"What's that?" Krohn asked.

"Never mind," Peter replied.

When he had hung up, Henchard was leaning over Peter's desk with his eyes wide. Acrid breath came in waves. "I'm goin' to Washington to talk to the President."

Peter stared without blinking.

"I had a vision 'bout the end o' the world. Time's run out. The Lord told me to warn the President."

Peter pushed back his chair to find clear air. "And what should *he* do?"

Henchard leaned farther forward, almost toppling onto the desk. "Tell the nation. Call it to repent o' its sins. We're a profl'gate people. Stiffnecked. Like Sodom and Gomorrah. Fire's gonna fall from heaven." He hauled himself up until he was standing. His arm made a broad sweeping motion as if a curtain of flame were descending over the rose garden. "There'll be nothin' left. Nothin'. Every man, woman, and child—gone like that." He snapped his coarse fingers. "Churches too," he added with an accusing look at Peter. "They've sold out. Liberal. Mamby-pamby. Don't believe in hell fire, in white throne judgment, in the last day when the book'll be opened and everyone will have to give answer." Henchard lunged toward him. "Ain't that right? Maybe not you. But a lot of 'em."

Compared to what Peter had so far confronted at Good Samaritan, hell and white thrones and books opened were quite remote. Even the end of the world created no tremor. It would put an end to the roses and the glass—and Miss Hensley.

Henchard groped back to the chair and dropped into it as if his sermon had exhausted him. "Just a hundred bucks," he said. "That'll get me to Washington and back."

"Why back?" Peter asked. "If the world is coming to an end, won't one way be enough?"

"You never know the exact time." Henchard's tone was serious. "I'd hate to be stuck in Washington. It's the devil's city. Once I warn the President, I'm free."

Peter had only twelve dollars in his wallet. There was a small petty cash fund in the office, but Miss Hensley guarded it the way mythical dragons breathed fire over hoards of gold. "I don't have a hundred dollars," he said flatly.

Henchard leaned back and crossed his legs. "Stopped 'bout four hundred miles west o' here, Rev'ernt. Catholic church. The priest gave me a hundred. Just reached in the till. Fine Christian gentleman. Like Graham and those others."

Peter shrugged his shoulders. He didn't mind staking Henchard to a meal, maybe a room for the night. But the President could get along without the doomsday message. "I just don't have that much."

Henchard nodded toward the rose sticks probing up through melting snow. "Looks like you've got a fine garden out there, Rev'ernt. Fountain, too. How d'ya get that thing to work in freezin' weather like this?"

Peter gazed out at the swaying plume. "Antifreeze," he replied.

Henchard cocked his head. "Expensive stuff."

"The garden and the fountain were a gift."

"Must've cost a fortune."

Peter looked at his watch and sighed in irritation. "We don't keep cash. I can give you ten."

Henchard's face drew up into a pout. He lurched from the chair. "Don't put yourself out." The words rang with sarcasm.

Peter stood and reached for his wallet.

Henchard spun toward the door and glanced back in contempt. "Sorry I bothered you."

Peter held out the ten. Guilt grew in his chest like an explosion.

The grizzled beggar flung the door open. "Real help for God's servants! This is some church!" He turned and stomped into the outer office. He had taken only three steps when two uniformed policemen came into view and blocked his path. Henchard halted like an animal at bay.

"You're under arrest," one of the policemen said.

Peter rushed out. "What's going on here? This man has done nothing wrong. What's the idea?" Then he saw Miss Hensley standing off to the side with a look of smug satisfaction.

"I called them," she said. There was a note of triumph in her voice. "This man is a trespasser on church property."

Peter's gaze alternated between Miss Hensley and the

policemen. "This is ridiculous. She's made a mistake."

Henchard cowered before the police. Speech had deserted him.

The policeman said, "We were called here to make an arrest. Who's pressing charges?"

Peter opened his mouth to speak, but Miss Hensley cut him off. "I am. If I can't do it as an employee of this church, I'll do it as a private citizen. This man has no business coming in here. If we don't show we won't put up with his type, we'll have freight train loads pouring in on us."

Peter felt such loathing he could hardly speak. "The man's innocent," he said. "He came here for a handout. This is a church. He should feel welcome."

The policeman shifted his weight. "Who's pressing charges?"

"I am!" Miss Hensley shrieked uncontrollably. Her head trembled, her arms jerked about like those of a scarecrow in a gusty wind. "I have that right."

Peter felt like wringing her spindle neck. Krohn worried about the image created by leaving cars out overnight. Did he ever think of the image Napoleonic Miss Hensley created in the office? Putting an innocent man in jail was to side with Pilate and Caiaphas and those who pounded the nails into Jesus. But she did have the right. He turned to Henchard. "I'm sorry."

Henchard's look softened. "It's all right. I don't hold it against you. You got problems of your own, I can see that." He paused. "Prophets expect to go to jail. It's in the Bible. I've been there before."

Sparing Henchard the humiliation of handcuffs, the policemen marched him out. When they were gone, Peter felt the brittle cold of the office. Mrs. Peck, out of Miss Hensley's line of sight, shook her head in despair. If he had uttered his feelings, Peter would have sworn. When the storm had quelled a bit, he said to Miss Hensley, "This is unforgivable."

She refused to look at him.

"How you can do that to a poor man who's down on his

luck, I can't understand," he said. "If you think you can do that and keep working here, you're sorely mistaken."

Miss Hensley said nothing. Peter turned to his office and was passing through the door when her threatening voice came to him. "You make one move against me, and you'll have the shortest pastorate in the history of Good Samaritan. People are already dissatisfied. It wouldn't take much to make them see you'll never work out."

Peter shut the door behind him. Miss Hensley's voice rang in his ears. She could smear him before the congregation. But the thought of being ousted from Good Samaritan didn't have the sting she intended. Not to have penguins outside the window. Not to have to face Miss Hensley each morning. Not to have Mr. Krohn dinging him about the driveway. A strange calm settled on him.

Part Two

1

B*lessed are the peacemakers*. The phrase stood out on the gilt-edged page as if in lights. Peace, Peter thought. The cessation of conflict, of each person seeking his own way. Good Samaritan could use a sermon on that. He hauled out a yellow pad and held his pen poised to write down subpoints.

Outside the windows, dear penguin members of the garden club bent down to scrutinize the dark twigs they had nursed through the winter. One produced a magnifying glass, and the four ladies hulked down on their hands and knees like dogs beside a black stick. Each peered through the glass, then there was a long, heavily gesticulated discussion of the horticultural patient, as if verbiage had the potential to resurrect the dead. When they hauled themselves up, the ladies did not seem to mind the mud caked on the knees of their pants.

Nothing came to Peter's heat-slaked mind. He sat back, pulled out his handkerchief, rubbed his forehead. The handkerchief became soaked, sweat beaded and trickled down into his eyes. Directly overhead, the white mid-May sun grew hotter and hotter. It was as if the curved glass ceiling magnified the heat. He stood up, shed his jacket, loosened his tie, and rolled up his shirtsleeves. A stroll around the office in search of shade revealed there was none. His breaths came in short gasps, there were moments when the office tilted, he almost fell and had to catch himself.

He picked up the phone. "Miss Hensley, it's time to turn on the air conditioning."

"Oh, it's not too bad," came the compassionless reply.

The outer office had an opaque wall to the east that afforded shade. "You're not feeling the full effect yet," Peter said. It also occurred to him that Miss Hensley's fish-like flesh might make her impervious to temperature changes.

"We're not allowed to turn on the air conditioning this early in the season."

"Allowed—by whom?"

"The Trustees. It's so expensive to operate they allow us to use it only when there's a heat wave." Her tone was stern—the usual when she was responding to a request of Peter's. "There are louvers at the bottom of your windows."

She was right. Peter turned the black knobs and felt a faint breeze brush the hairs on the back of his hand. What relief it might bring would be imperceptible.

He turned back to brood over the yellow pad. The pad was still blank a few moments later when he heard the staccato chug of an engine. A small yellow tractor wobbled through Benedict into the garden. (The architect of the church had designed no other entry, so heavy equipment had to wheel right through the building.) Without a pause, the tractor drove its bucket into the sod covering the area into which the rose garden was to be expanded.

Between heat and noise and yellow dust rolling in through the louvers, Peter found himself nursing a headache. He tried to ignore the distractions, but it was difficult to develop the theme of peace with the glass around him trembling and his desk shaking every time the beak-like bucket on the tractor ensnared heavy clay or rocks. He could not help but swing his gaze over to the convulsing machine, its slender operator wearing a baseball cap wrenching it about as if he and the ground were engaged in mortal combat.

Three members of the garden club stood next to the door of Benedict. Festooned in baggy pants and shirts and wearing oriental sun hats, they alternately pointed at the tractor and bent over existing rose plants like doctors searching through bedcovers to see if the patient was still there.

His yellow pad containing only a few scratched notes, Peter did not realize the tractor had been shut off until his ears were searching about for its chug. His notes said he would talk to the congregation about its interest groups and how divisive they were. He would liken them to men rowing a boat without coordination. The efforts of some cancelled out others', with the result that the church went nowhere. He would paint a picture of peace — the sacrificing of pet interests for the sake of Christ. And then he would show them trading in their ecclesiastical obsessions for concern for the world. He saw it in a dim vision — the Council and the Trustees allocating money for the hungry, the homeless. Good Samaritan would finally do something for others, and the people would be glad to see their resources well-used.

2

The sound of a knock pulled Peter from his reverie. Miss Hensley ushered into his office the three ladies Peter had seen in the garden. "These are members of the garden club," she said. "It's very important they talk to you."

Peter nodded slightly, resentful of Miss Hensley's interruption just when his sermon was coming to life. Besides, he was out of uniform: his collar was open, his tie pulled down, his jacket off. Sweat dampened his shirt. He thought of putting the ladies off until later, but their gaze was determined. "I'll get you chairs," he said.

"No," Mrs. Clayton replied sharply. "We're terribly upset." She was over seventy, her face a patchwork of wrinkles in paper thin skin. The pants and heavy shirt two sizes too big made her look like a midget. Sweat dampened the rim of her straw hat. Her cheeks quivered. "Christopher Stone, Charlotte Armstrong, Mrs. Arthur Curtiss . . . all dead."

Peter stiffened. Three people dead? He did not recognize the names: they must be friends of the gardeners. Had the gardeners come to ask him to officiate at a triple funeral service? What a job that would be. "An accident?" he gasped.

"We don't know," Mrs. Clayton said. Her sad eyes searched the carpet. The eyes of her companions, Mrs. Brown and Miss Arbaugh, rimmed with tears.

Mrs. Clayton continued, "There isn't a sign of life."

It flashed in Peter's mind that a crash must've just occurred on the highway in front of the church.

Mrs. Clayton's sad gaze remained fixed on the carpet. "We broke twigs off. They're all bone dry."

Peter suddenly exhaled the air he had been holding in. "Oh, roses," he mumbled. The image of three caskets arrayed in the chancel vanished.

Mrs. Brown said, "As a matter of fact, we can't find one single plant in the whole garden that looks like it's going to leaf."

Peter tried to look concerned. Compared to what he thought had happened, a few comatose roses were nothing at all.

"It's unbelievable," Miss Arbaugh added, her eyes flitting about as if she suspected some diabolical plot. "If Miss Hayes were alive, she'd be totally ill. It isn't just the money. It's the labor . . . the love . . . the hours of care that have gone into the garden. It was to be a show place. It was to make Good Samaritan the rose center of the county." Her voice rang with anguish.

Peter could think of nothing to say. He wasn't a gardener. He knew nothing about roses or any other flowering plant. He had hoped to learn more if he ever got free from some of the responsibilities of running churches. "I'm very sorry," he said with as much sympathy as he could muster.

Mrs. Clayton smiled through her tears as if he were a life-long ally in her battle against the horticultural grim reaper. "We need your help." Miss Arbaugh and Mrs. Brown nodded in agreement. "We get no cooperation from the Trustees. We're willing to do the work, but the garden club doesn't have the money to replace the plants we've lost, as well as buy new ones for the expansion. Miss Hayes expressly said in her will that she wanted the garden to fill the entire center of the church. When she was on her deathbed, we promised her we would carry out her wishes."

Peter tried to recall the garden budget from Mr. Krohn's papers. His mind was blank. "She left a bequest, didn't she?"

"Yes," Mrs. Clayton replied. "And we've been using it. But with prices going up and the Trustees making us pay for all the grading and preparation"—she nodded toward the tractor standing idle on the scarp—"and now that we've got to buy all new plants . . . it isn't enough."

"As a matter of fact," Mrs. Brown said emphatically, "Miss Hayes' money is almost gone. And look where we are." She waved her arm toward the clay tundra.

The muscles around Miss Arbaugh's mouth tightened. "The church must help. The trustees have thousands of dollars in investments. What's the use of having all that money if it isn't used for something worthwhile?"

Sweat trickled down Peter's back. His armpits were soaked. The sun glared down like an interrogator's lamp. He hadn't come to Good Samaritan to grow roses. He came to lead disciples, and he had never seen in the New Testament that disciples needed roses. Why didn't these weathered women grow roses at home to satisfy their horticultural cravings? He resented the determined gazes that assumed because he was the pastor he had to satisfy their desires.

Mrs. Clayton leaned forward abruptly. "We're asking you to get the trustees to grant us the money to expand and finish the garden."

Peter shrugged his shoulders. "I don't have the authority."

"You're the pastor," Mrs. Clayton said. "If *you* can't get things done, then something's wrong. Dr. Strong always got what he wanted."

Peter conceded something was wrong. But it wasn't what Mrs. Clayton thought. He glanced at Miss Hensley, leaning against the door frame with her bony arms crossed, her pale ears scooping in everything. "I have no jurisdiction over the Board of Trustees," he said.

"But you're on it," Mrs. Brown declared loudly.

"*Ex officio*," Peter replied. "Without vote." He stepped back to see if he could find air in which to breathe. Between the women's intent gazes and the sun and the headache still throbbing behind his ears, he felt as if he might faint.

Mrs. Clayton clomped forward to close the gap. "That makes no difference. We're talking to a trustee of this church right now." Mrs. Brown and Miss Arbaugh nodded as if on cue. "We want the Board to authorize the completion of the garden. We've stopped the man with the tractor. He won't start again until the trustees act. All the dirt down to a foot and a half must be dug out and hauled away. Fresh topsoil has to be brought in. That's the only way we're going to get rid of whatever is killing those plants."

A muscular man in khaki pants, a khaki shirt with the sleeves rolled up, and boots caked with yellow clay walked up behind Miss Hensley. "Who's in charge here?" he asked brusquely.

Peter waited for Mrs. Clayton to reply, but she just cast the man an irritated look and turned back to Peter.

Peter was not in charge of the garden, but he was in charge of the church — as much as he wrested authority from Miss Hensley. "I'm the pastor," he said quietly.

"Name's Jackson, Rev'ernd. I need to know what's goin' on here. I was contracted to grade the garden out there. Now my man tells me he's been told to stop. We've got a fixed price on the project. When my machine and man are sittin' idle, I lose money. What's the holdup?"

"*We* told him to stop," Mrs. Clayton said. "The whole garden needs to be redone."

Jackson put his hands on his hips. "The contract is for one day. That tractor's to be on the other side of town tomorrow morning. Nobody said anything about doing the whole garden."

"We're sorry," Mrs. Clayton said. "But we can't plant

roses in soil that kills them. It's got to be replaced, and this church has to pay for it."

"Apparently there's some misunderstanding," Peter said. "Why don't you have your man finish what he came to do? Then when we determine what more we want done, we'll have you come back."

"No!" Mrs. Brown shouted angrily.

Mrs. Clayton's tone was diplomatic. "We're sorry, Mr. Jackson, but there's no use doing any more until we get authorization. We think we can get it now. Can you wait a few minutes?"

Mr. Jackson looked at his watch. "Very few. I can't afford to have equipment standin' idle."

Mrs. Clayton turned to Peter. "Now you call Mr. Krohn and get him to authorize what we need."

Peter did not move. Only the whole Board could approve a large capital expenditure. "We can't do anything until the next meeting."

Mrs. Clayton's face turned crimson. "If the pastor and the chairman of the Board of Trustees can't authorize fixing up a mere garden, then Good Samaritan has gone to the dogs. I want you to call Mr. Krohn. Now."

Peter glanced at the phone. All Mr. Krohn had to do was say no, and that would get the ladies off his back. He dialed Mr. Krohn's office. "I'm sorry, but Mr. Krohn is in a meeting," came his secretary's melodic voice. "Can I have him call you back?"

Peter glanced at the garden club ladies. Their faces were hard with determination. "I'm afraid it's urgent," he said.

"Emergency?" came the query.

Peter hesitated. "Well . . . yes . . ." The phone went on hold. Peter shifted his weight. Mr. Jackson stared again at his watch. The three weathered faces lost none of their determined pucker.

The phone clicked. "Krohn here. What the hell's up?" His voice was gruff, angry.

"It's Peter Campbell. We've got a problem . . ."

"That damn neighbor again? Why don't you put the cars in the garage and be done with this nonsense?"

"No, not that. The rose garden."

"The rose garden! Not that damn thing again. That meeting you called me from is the annual review."

Peter glanced at the three gardeners; their eyes impaled him like daggers. Miss Hensley stared in cold satisfaction. Mr. Jackson was pacing. Peter explained the predicament to Mr. Krohn. At each pause, Mr. Krohn could be heard gasping.

When he finished, Mr. Krohn shouted, "Damn the garden. That Hayes woman hardly ever came to church. She just didn't have any family. Those women roped her into that garden club and put it in her head to leave a bequest. It was too small to begin with. The garden should never have been started."

Mr. Jackson stopped and glared. "I'm charging for down time. It'll cost you for the man and the machine just as if both were working."

"What's that?" Mr. Krohn shouted.

"The contractor," Peter replied.

"What does he want?"

"He wants us to know he's charging for the man and the machine while we argue."

"Tight son of a gun. Who told him to stop?"

"The ladies from the garden club."

Mr. Krohn groaned. "You might know. They always take over, and we end up with nothing but trouble. Expensive trouble." He paused. "What can I do to get us out of this?"

Peter felt relief that Mr. Krohn's was shouldering some responsibility. "The women want the Trustees to authorize redoing what was done last year as well as finishing the rest."

"Now?" Mr. Krohn shouted so loud the determined women nodded in affirmation.

"Can it be done?"

Mr. Krohn sputtered. "Of course it can't. The trustees work during the day. We can't meet every time the dear ladies of the garden club decide they want something done with their damn roses."

Mr. Jackson resumed pacing with his brawny arms folded across his chest. "Fifty bucks an hour for man and machine."

"What's that?" Mr. Krohn asked.

"The contractor again," Peter replied. "Can you come out?"

"Come out? Now?" Mr. Krohn made no attempt to disguise his rage.

The three women had heard him. They vigorously nodded their sunhatted heads.

"The ladies from the garden club insist," Peter said.

Mr. Krohn's gasps came more quickly. Peter pressed the phone hard against his ear to muffle the expletive he could feel coming. Mr. Krohn swiftly consigned the ladies and their dear roses to the eternal underground hothouse. "I've got business," he went on. "This meeting." He paused. "Look, we'll break for lunch in half an hour. Tell the contractor to take his lunch hour now. I'll be out."

Peter hung up the phone and turned to his audience. Grim smiles lined the ladies' faces. Mr. Jackson grudgingly agreed to go to lunch. "But I'm charging for the time the machine has been down already," he said. Miss Hensley's black eyes stared in cold satisfaction. They reminded Peter of the eyes of a spider as they must appear to a venom-drugged insect wrapped in silk at the edge of a web. He was aware that he was carrying out her agenda: satisfy the demands of influential people in the congregation. Mrs. Clayton's husband was on Dr. Strong's list of people for whom he was to play doormat.

The notes for his sermon lying on his desk appeared strangely remote. *Blessed are the peacemakers.* Hopefully, the sermon would blunt the mania for roses. If he made himself clear, if he could get anyone to listen.

3

Miss Hensley had left for lunch when gray-suited Mr. Krohn arrived. Even though Peter had brought other chairs into his office, only Mr. Krohn sat down. Peter went to his desk, glad to be out of the line of fire.

The ladies surrounded Mr. Krohn and started their assault. Miss Arbaugh: "Christopher Stone and the other roses wouldn't have died if the trustees hadn't been so tight." Mrs. Clayton: "We asked the trustees over and over. Even though they sit on thousands of dollars in investments, they did nothing. What better investment is there than a garden that will be the county showplace?" Mrs. Brown: "The ladies of the garden club have given hundreds of hours of work — worth a fortune if the church had hired it done. Now it's all lost."

Sweat poured from Mr. Krohn's forehead as if he had contracted malaria. He dabbed his eyes and face with his handkerchief, but the handkerchief was so damp the flow of perspiration was unstanched. His cheeks quivered. "I don't have the authority to spend the Board's money," he said. "Investments can't be liquidated on short notice. The Council has to be involved in the decision." His puffed eyes glanced about for some route of escape. There was none. Certainly not from the sun glaring down in hot persecution.

Peter felt a sympathetic urge to help, but resisted. He had had enough of the gardeners' ire. He had fewer answers than Mr. Krohn did. If Mr. Krohn just held his ground, the ladies' anger would expend itself and give way to peaceful compromise.

The light on his telephone blinked. He waited for one of the secretaries to pick it up, but then remembered they were out. He could let whoever was calling hang up, but pangs of conscience tightened his chest. It could be an illness, a death; or a pulpit robe salesman. He picked it up.

A high-pitched howl pierced his ear. "Rev'rent Campbell?"

He should hang up. She would never know. He could just tell Krohn and his attackers it was a wrong number. But he was a pastor; he was supposed to help people. "Speaking," he said softly.

"He's at it again. I'm ter'fied. Eighty-six he is now—he had a birthday. And he still don't know 'nough to leave women alone." There was a wrenching sob. "I'm 'fraid, Rev'rent. Some night, he's gonna get me. Sure as I'm here on this phone talkin' to you, he's gonna come into my room when I'm not lookin' out for myself, and that'll be it."

"How can I help?" Peter asked quickly. "Do you want me to come over?" The gardeners were circling Mr. Krohn like buzzards waiting for a wounded animal to drop. Peter carried the phone back into a safe corner.

"Oh no, no," came the frightened reply. "Then he'd know I was callin' you. That'd be worse. He watches me. In the dining room, all the time I'm sittin' there eatin', I can feel his eyes. An' when I'm in my room, he paces the hall—back and forth, back and forth. He thinks I can't see 'im, but I do. And I know what he's after." She sniffled. "There' oughtta be a law. Man like that's dangerous. You know what I think?"

Peter sighed. "What?" he asked.

"He should be locked up. Man like that's gonna hurt somebody some day. I'll bet he already has. Nobody knows 'cause he ain't been found out. But a man like that don't get to eighty-six without hurtin' somebody. No sir."

The ladies directed Mr. Krohn's attention to the garden. Mrs. Clayton stood at the window, her bony hand pointing out key features of the devastation. Mr. Krohn's face burned red. His eyes swam in sweaty heat. It suddenly occurred to Peter that Mr. Krohn's system might be pushed beyond its limit.

"I've got this awful bloatin'." The plaintive cry jerked Peter back to the telephone. "Day an' night. I can't eat. I go to the bathroom—it don't do no good. They give me enemas—

ter'ble things—poison. Still I'm sick. I tell that doctor when he comes around—which ain't much. He looks at me an' tells me I'm all right. He doesn't know, but I do. Do you know what's wrong with me?"

Mrs. Clayton turned to Mr. Krohn and stamped her boot on the floor. Her eyes hurled darts. Voices were loud, strident. "What?" Peter said lamely.

"Cancer," the voice announced in a pontifical tone. "My stomach's full of cancer and I'm going to die, but they won't tell me. Now what do you think of a doctor like that? Here I am full of cancer, and he takes one look at me and tells me I'm fine."

Mr. Krohn looked as if he were on the verge of delirium tremens. He was sunk down in the chair, his shoulders sagged forward. He resembled a snowman melting in the sun. "I have to go," Peter said into the telephone. "I'm sorry . . ."

"They should operate," came the reply. "That's what they should do. But they won't. Do you know why?"

"Miss whoever you are," Peter said quickly. His brain floated in heat. His mind spun from the cacophony around him, the violent looks. Mr. Krohn stared up at the women as if he were a small boy who had just been caned.

"Money," the voice went on. "They know I don't have nothin'. They won't operate when there's nothin' in it for them. Now what do you think of that, Rev'rent? Isn't it somethin' that in this day an' age doctors won't operate on you just 'cause you don't have no money? What's this world comin' to?"

Peter started to hang up, then paused. "I . . ."

"Nobody cares about anybody anymore. It's ever'body for hisself. Dog eat dog. That's it. And it's gettin' worse. The doctors, the nurses, nobody cares. So you die. So what? Don't you think that's ter'ble, Rev'rent? I know you're a man of God. You don't think like that. But other people do . . ."

Mr. Krohn stole a glance at his watch. The gesture raised the ladies' fury. From the tone of their voices, it was clear

Mr. Krohn would not get out of there until he gave them a commitment. He kept saying, "I can't do it. I don't have the authority." Whatever ground might have firmed up for a compromise had already dissolved. Peter had to step in before Mr. Krohn had a stroke. "I'm sorry," he said into the phone, "but . . ."

"You don't have money and they turn their backs!" the voice shrieked. "Like that man down there. Nobody does nothin' 'bout him. They see his look, the way he follows me, his pacin' back and forth in front of my door . . ."

The office door shot open and Miss Hensley thrust her head in. "Mr. Jackson is out here waiting for a reply," she said sharply.

Peter held the phone in front of his face, then lowered it, trailing a stream of plaints, until putting it in its cradle silenced it. He looked at Miss Hensley's crow form. Had she knocked?

She glared at Mr. Krohn and the red-faced gardeners. "Mr. Jackson is impatient. His lunch hour is over, and he must know what he's supposed to do."

"He stays until the whole garden is finished," Mrs. Clayton shouted. "If we send him away, we'll pay for the day and have nothing accomplished. He can't leave the garden torn up like that." She gestured angrily toward the holes dug that morning.

Mr. Krohn's liquid eyes alternated between his watch and the garden ruin. His voice was weak. "All right. Let him do whatever you want."

Mrs. Clayton leaned over Mr. Krohn as if to make sure she heard him. "Then we can start redoing the whole garden?"

Peter stepped forward; blood pulsated through his overheated body. "No," he said more loudly than he intended. The women whirled toward him. "We must work through the trustees in orderly fashion. If you start the garden, you commit the trustees before they've decided."

Mrs. Brown glared. "How can you say what the trustees

will do? You're only *ex officio*. You have no vote. Mr. Krohn here is the chairman. He has the authority to speak for the Board."

Peter turned to Mr. Krohn. "Tell them to wait. We can't run a church by blackmail. They'll commit us to spend money we don't have." Peter's head throbbed from a full-blown headache that ran from his forehead to the base of his neck. His voice drifted back as if it came from someone else.

Mr. Krohn lurched unsteadily to his feet. "I can't stay another minute." He turned to Mrs. Clayton. "Do what you want. I don't know where the money will come from. If that Hayes woman had left more in her will, we wouldn't be having this trouble."

Mrs. Clayton bristled like a wolf closing in on its prey. "Why, how dare you talk about Miss Hayes that way! She was a generous member of this church. Why the idea of you . . ."

Mr. Krohn's sweaty hand grasped the doorknob. "I'm sorry. I meant nothing against her." He directed his weak gaze at Peter. "Campbell, call me later." The door shut, and Peter was left with the ladies. Ignoring him, they rushed to the outer office. He could hear them all talking at once, instructing Mr. Jackson what he was to do.

Even with the door shut, the voices came. If Mr. Jackson was saying anything in reply, it could not be heard.

Peter wiped his face with his wet handkerchief and sat down. Before him lay the notes for his sermon. *Blessed are the peacemakers.*

He picked up the stack of scribbled yellow sheets, tore the stack in half, halved the halves, then halved them again until he had nothing but tiny pieces of yellow confetti which he let flutter down into his wastebasket.

4

Later that afternoon when Peter turned into the driveway, he was greeted by the blue flicker of Jeff's welding torch. The barrel-shaped maze of pipes, rails, steel bands, and plates had grown to the joists and ran from the open doors to the back wall. Trojan was the size of the steam locomotives that had plied the railroad yard near where he had grown up. He fell back in astonishment.

Jeff shut off the torch, slid the welding mask back on his head, and stood in reverie. His grimy, perspiration-streaked face glowed with satisfaction.

When Peter could finally muster words, he asked, "How much bigger will it get? How will you move it?"

Jeff gestured with animation. What Peter was looking at was the body. The neck and head were yet to come. Jeff pointed to oil-soaked timbers he had found at a junk yard with which he was going to block in the ceiling joists after he cut a hole for the head. Leaning against a corner of the garage were rusting wheels from an old streetcar. The flanges would be ground off and the wheels mounted on the base so Trojan could be pulled, just as the ancient horse was through the gates of Troy.

Jeff's brow wrinkled. "Mr. Shanklet was here. He says I've got to finish Trojan by winter."

"And what did you tell him?"

"I said I didn't know when I'd be done. There are too many uncertainties."

"And?"

"Mr. Shanklet said he'd go to the Board of Trustees." The furrows in Jeff's brow deepened. "I could be making your job in the church harder."

Peter laughed. "It couldn't be much harder than it is now. The church promised we could use the house as we wished. We told them you had this hobby." He gazed up at

Trojan's full height. "Although I never dreamed we were in for something like this."

Jeff's gaze lowered to the stained concrete floor. "Then do I have to set a date?"

"No," Peter replied. "Use it as long as you want." Again his eyes swept over the cylinder of iron and steel. "But watch the weight of it. We don't own a tractor."

Jeff smiled. Down came the mask with its cobalt window, the torch popped into ignition; with a blue hiss of power, he applied himself to a rail on the flank still glowing red hot.

5

Inside the parsonage, Jackie was staring glassy-eyed out the window.

"What's wrong?" Peter asked.

Jackie's face puffed red. "The gym teacher won't speak to me. The Principal claims I lied when I said the gym teacher promised us a track team." Jackie turned toward him. "She did promise. A whole bunch of us heard her. He's also mad because we wrote a letter to the school board."

She looked pensively at Peter. "Am I making things worse for you? There are church members on that board."

"You could be," Peter replied. How much worse, he had no idea. "But I like it that you want the track team to help kids make something of themselves," he said with resolution. "Don't worry about me."

The usual vibrant pink returned to her cheeks. He put his arm around her shoulders. "Any fight is hard," he said. "Harder on you than anyone else."

She looked up at him. "I don't want to quit."

"Good," Peter said. "You're doing something very worthwhile."

6

On Peter's office desk lay a thick volume encased in a black cover. It looked like a theological treatise, but on the front it read: 'Report and Recommendations by the Trustee Committee to Study the Rose Garden.' It was the proposal the trustees were to take action on that evening. He picked up the tome and examined the table of contents: the original plan, Miss Hayes' bequest, a biography of Miss Hayes, various plans that had been proposed, unusual roses, and then, at the end, a motion to the Board of Trustees. Peter thumbed to it. It proposed fifteen thousand dollars for the garden's expansion and completion.

Considering the dire financial straits the church was in, the amount was excessive. But, Peter reminded himself, what he held in his hand was merely a proposal. Through debate, the trustees would hammer out a compromise. Besides, he had to concede, he knew nothing about roses.

He turned to look out at the garden. An overnight thunderstorm had turned it into a sea of gullied mud drying under the morning sun. No water plumed from the white fountain—the pump had mysteriously failed. The useless sculpture surrounded by brown clay looked like an architectural scab. What the ladies so enthusiastically described as a landmark had to be the most grotesque attraction in the state.

It would be best if the whole area were grassed in and forgotten. That could be done for a fraction of fifteen grand, and it would free the church from gardening so it could get on with discipleship. Picking up the report and thumbing through the rest of it, Peter noticed no grass alternative had been proposed. Perhaps it was too simple, or the garden club was blackmailing their spouse trustees. If the meeting came to a stalemate, Peter could propose grass as a compromise—with perhaps a few hardy perennials and evergreens, if the garden club ladies were persistent.

The intercom buzzed. "There's someone here to see you. Shall I send her in?" Miss Hensley's voice vibrated with its usual frigidity.

Peter waited for an explanation of who the someone was and why she had come, but he could hear nothing but Miss Hensley's sharp breathing. She had a strange custom of identifying visitors or not identifying them as she chose. No motive had yet emerged except a diabolical delight in surprise.

Miss Hensley held the door open, standing well back to allow the visitor to enter. She was a young girl, perhaps in her twenties, although it was hard to tell because her blond hair styled into an immense cloud of curls made her face look small and babyish. Most obvious was her silk blouse, far too small, far too tight for her generous appointments. Miss Hensley's black eyes fixed on him to get the full effect of the girl's entrance. When Peter had drunk his full, Miss Hensley announced with a hint of derogation, "Mary Jones." Then the door swiftly shut.

Peter motioned Mary to the plastic chair, settled into his own, and loosened his tie. The heat was so intense he no longer felt a twinge of guilt that he did not keep his tie and suitcoat on. "Well, what can I do for you?" he asked.

Mary leaned forward, locked her hands around one knee, and gazed down at the carpet. Her cheeks puffed red with anguish. "I don't know where to begin." Tears welled up in hazel eyes glancing about as if some clue as to where to start might slide into her field of vision. "So many things've gone wrong. Life is so messed up." She looked up sheepishly. "I'm not sure I should even be here. I don't come to church much. I haven't given any money for a long time."

Peter felt sympathy for the despair in Mary's voice. To give her his full attention, he shoved the Trustee's garden tome to the side and rested his arms on the top of his desk. "Those aren't requirements for getting help if you need it."

The crimson in Mary's face intensified as if she were mustering courage. "It's Red. That's the guy I live with . . . *was* livin' with . . ." Sobs escaped her heavily lipsticked lips; the mascara around her eyes ran until she dabbed it with a tissue drawn from a canvas purse. "I just don't see how things are goin' to get any better."

Her skirt was above her knees, her blouse looked as if one button, maybe two, would pop off with such force they would fly across the room. Peter found it difficult to concentrate. "Maybe we need to see what's wrong before we can decide that." He used his best counseling tone.

"About a year ago I moved in with this guy. That's Red. I'd only known him a month or so, but we hit it off." She stared down at the floor again. "My folks didn't approve. I don't know why. It's what everyone was doin'. So they told me I couldn't come home if we broke up. They moved out of town anyway, which was a help 'cause they couldn't bug me anymore."

"But you didn't get married?"

"No. Red didn't want to. He told me if we got along okay, then we'd have a church weddin'. I told him that'd be nice, and I never thought no more of it. I really thought he loved me. He treated me good an' took me places. He made me feel like I was somebody." She leaned back and stared with a vacant look at the ruined garden.

"That may not sound like much. But I never felt like I amounted to much when I was a kid. There were six of us, all girls, and my folks couldn't cope. They'd shout all the time, my father got drunk, it was a rat race. We all wanted to get away."

"Things were pretty bad," Peter remarked sympathetically. He had learned that the best counseling technique was just to echo what a client said. It also saved him trying to think up wise responses.

Mary's sad eyes fixed on him. "Yeah. Well, anyway, I thought Red was a clean-livin' guy. Oh, he had a beer once in a while, and he'd go out on his motorcycle. But most of the guys I knew did that—and a lot worse. You know what I mean. I don't see nothin' wrong with a beer and a ride, just as long as he didn't get carried away."

Peter did not know much about beer or motorcycles, but he did not have to pursue either because the buzzer on his phone rang. He stared hostilely at the intruding instrument. He had told Miss Hensley repeatedly not to interrupt him while he was counseling. He wrenched the receiver to his ear. "Miss Hensley, I asked you . . ."

"I told her you were busy, but she said it's an emergency. Mrs. Clayton, line two."

"Emergency?" Peter exclaimed. "What is?"

"I don't know. She was very insistent. I don't like to pry." Peter chuckled to himself. "Maybe somebody got sick or died," Miss Hensley said gravely.

Stifling a groan, Peter pushed the button.

"Oh, Dr. Campbell." Mrs. Clayton's voice ululated like the call of a jungle bird. "I've had such an awful night. I didn't get a wink of sleep. My husband was beside himself trying to calm me down. I can't believe what the Trustees are doing. Have you seen the proposal?"

Peter glanced at the black treatise. "It's here on my desk. I was reading it this morning."

"Isn't that a disgrace? There's that church with all that money. Those buildings were donated by Mr. Gottschalk, and so was the ground. We haven't a dime of mortgage on the property. All those funds in securities and savings accounts. And the trustees are telling us all they can give us is fifteen thousand dollars and we'll have to raise the rest. Dr. Campbell, do you know how far fifteen thousand dollars goes in a rose garden?"

"Well, I'm not too well versed in roses . . ."

"I'll tell you. It goes nowhere. Hauling all that dirt out and bringing in new soil and manure will be very expensive. Do you know the price of manure these days?"

Peter paused. He was way over his head. It was a waste product. "It shouldn't be too much," he said. Fortunately

Mrs. Clayton could not see the smirk on his face. Manure was not something the faculty at the seminary had ever discussed—not formally, at least.

"A hundred dollars a load," came the pontifical reply. "And a load doesn't go far. I tried to get a lower price just to calm my nerves, but that's the best I could do. Demand is up, and you know the market—supply and demand. Topsoil's as bad. Then getting it in is expensive—it has to be unloaded outside and taken through Benedict—you'd think Mr. Gottschalk might've thought about our having to haul materials into the garden once in a while; it's ridiculous to have to run a tractor through the building." As she drew a breath, Peter could hear wind whistling through her dentures. "Well, anyway, I've been sitting here. Actually, I sat up all night trying to figure how much we'll need for a minimum garden—as large as Miss Hayes wanted it, but with some economies. I can't come up with anything less than thirty-five thousand dollars. That's twenty thousand more than the trustees are willing to pay. And do you know, Dr. Campbell, that thirty-five thousand dollars is based on standard roses—ones that have been around for years? If we went to the new hybrids—they're so much prettier—the price would go up another five or ten thousand dollars."

Peter's mind drifted. He glanced at Mary. She was wringing her hands and staring at the floor. Obviously Mrs. Clayton considered his counseling expendable. The melancholy look in Mary's eyes tugged at him.

"Well, Dr. Campbell, you've just got to do something. You're the pastor of Good Samaritan, and a fifteen thousand dollar rose garden will be an embarrassment. It'll be smaller than the one we started last summer. We'll have to skimp so much on roses it'll look like we bought them all at a discount store. That's probably where we *will* have to buy them. Can't you see what a disappointment it will be?"

Peter could not see. But he could tell from the tone of Mrs. Clayton's voice she was not asking for a reply. "I'm just *ex officio* on the Board of Trustees," he said. "I wasn't present when the committee worked out the proposal."

"But you're the *pastor*. I don't care if you're ex official — whatever that means. You're our leader. If you stand behind a garden we can all be proud of, then the trustees will do what you say. Dr. Strong always got his way." There was a heavy pause. "'Course now that he's gone . . . maybe we can't expect . . . well, we've got to have help. This proposal just won't do. I've been a member of that church for over sixty years. It's where Horton and I were married. Our children were baptized there. It's all we've known. But now, in our hour of need, if the church no longer cares . . ."

It suddenly occurred to Peter he was being threatened. "I don't think that's the case," he said quickly, hoping he understood what he was responding to. "There are other programs needing money . . ."

"But they're supported. The Sunday School always has enough. We do well with our foreign missions. Look how much the women raise at their strawberry festival. No, there's no need as great as the garden. And once it's in and paid for, there will only be maintenance. We'll get perpetuals that bloom year after year. We're only asking this once. And it's for Miss Hayes. You didn't know her, did you?"

"No," he replied. She had died over two years ago. But he felt he was getting to know her. She was a green woman with a huge red rose for a head.

"She was a dear. And to think that in her dying breath she thought of Good Samaritan and wanted to leave something people would remember, something that would bring cheer season after season. Don't you think that was thoughtful?"

Peter wasn't at all sure. The garden certainly added little cheer to his own life. "Well, it's a generous gift," he conceded. "It's just too bad it didn't cover . . ."

"That wasn't Miss Hayes' fault." The tone was sharp. "She had no idea her money wasn't well invested. And who would've guessed that something would kill every plant we put in? That's why we've got to have manure. That's what my horticulturist says. 'Not enough manure.' So if we don't get what we need, we might as well quit." Her voice faltered. "I tell you, and I say this with tears in my eyes and sixty years of my life spent in that church, if that garden can't be completed, then I would be ashamed to remain a member any longer. Any group of people who call themselves Christian and would let down a dear poor soul like Miss Hayes, well, I just couldn't in good conscience be party to that. It would be too bad. It would be terrible for Horton. But that's how I feel. Some people may think it's not right. But I know my duty, and I know the duty of Good Samaritan. We've got a name and a reputation to uphold, and disregarding and desecrating the dead . . ."

Peter felt his brain bulging from all the words Mrs. Clayton pumped into it. "I don't think it would be desecrating . . ."

"Desecrating," came the sharp reply. "I choose the word carefully. I stayed up all night trying to think which word was best, and that's it. I'm sorry to be saying these things to you, Dr. Campbell, but that's the way I feel. I know you're on that board. It may not be official, but you are the pastor. We need thirty-five thousand dollars for that garden and not a penny less. I would like a commitment from you that you'll stand behind what's needed and fight that insulting proposal from the committee."

The expletive that came to Peter's mind for the garden he could not utter to Mrs. Clayton. "I can't take a position like that," he said diplomatically. He felt like a politician being interviewed on TV—pumping words while avoiding solid promises. "I'll be fair," he added.

"I had hoped for a lot more than that," Mrs. Clayton said with an abrasive edge. "Well, like I said, Dr. Strong isn't here anymore. We'll just have to fight the battle ourselves. But we will win. You can be sure of that, Dr. Campbell." The phone clicked, and Peter stared at the dead receiver. Only then did he realize his hands were trembling. Anger burned the back of his neck. Mrs. Clayton had given no thought to Mary Jones.

7

Mary was sitting quietly in the chair, her eyes heavy with sadness. Peter felt an urge to take her side against all her foes. "Sorry to keep you waiting."

Mary sighed. "I guess you got your problems too."

He searched his mind to recall where she was in her story. "Red," he said. Then he remembered—beer, the motorcycle.

"I thought he was a regular guy," Mary continued. "He was supposed to have a job, too. Gas station mechanic. Well, I always left for my job before him, and when I got home, most of the time he was already back at the apartment. I didn't think nothin' of it, 'cause Red always said his boss didn't have much for him to do." Her body shuddered, she crossed her arms as if she were cold. "Well, when I came home, I'd notice the ash tray full of cigarette butts, like he'd been smokin' all day.

"He'd shrug it off and say he was uptight and had chain smoked for a while. Then I got to noticing there was lipstick on some of those cigarettes. I asked him 'bout that, and he said his old girlfriend stopped by to talk over her problems. I knew he had an old girlfriend, so I let it go at that. You see, all this time, I thought Red was a neat guy."

The sun blazing down on Peter's forehead made it hard for him to concentrate. Suddenly it popped into his mind what tons of manure on the rose garden might do to the sanctuary on a hot, rainy Sunday morning. He envisioned members of the congregation clad in their fine summer wear casting each other strange looks.

"Then he told me his boss wanted him to work nights— no one would bother him while he took engines apart. I pleaded with him 'cause I don't like to be alone at night, but . . ."

The phone buzzer jolted Mary to a halt. Her jaw hung

slack. Peter stared at the intruding instrument with irritation. He ignored it, but it buzzed again. He thrust the receiver against his ear. "I'm counseling . . ."

"It's Mr. Jarvis," Miss Hensley said in a steely tone. "He *insists* on talking to you. He says it won't take long."

Peter opened his mouth to scold Miss Hensley for her lack of respect, but with a click she was gone. Angrily, he pushed the outside button.

"Hello, Campbell?" came the ebullient voice.

Peter made no pretense at cordiality. "Speaking."

"It's Charlie Jarvis. You remember me?"

How could he forget the golf game where he got nowhere trying to persuade Charlie to remove the brass cross? Charlie had a fixation on Fennel, the neon evangelist.

"I just got wind of this business coming before the Trustees tonight," Charlie said. "Needless to say, I'm upset. Fifteen thou' for a bunch of roses is heresy, it's apostate. We're already putting a fortune into upkeep. The utilities are running sky high. Out of respect for the Gospel, this proposal must be voted down."

"That's an option," Peter said coldly. "I'm sure we'll debate the proposal thoroughly, and the outcome will be a fair compromise."

"A compromise isn't what I'm looking for," Charlie said. "I'm for *no* money for the garden. We've got our priorities all fouled up. There's a world out there crying to be saved. We could put the money into radio and TV. There's so much need it's a crime to spend on ourselves. It's unchristian. That's what it is." His voice grew louder, more emphatic.

"Part of being a Christian is drawing the line on materialism. It's devious. The devil's always tempting people to spend money on things they don't need. Now if we'd get like Fennel over there, we'd be on the right track. They've got a huge budget, and it all goes to mission—TV, radio, trips around the country and abroad. That's what all the churches ought to be doing. And do you know what?" The only what Peter could think of was getting Charlie off the line so he could continue with Mary. "Fennel's on a fixed salary. People think he's a spendthrift because of the house in Bermuda and the jet and his wife's designer clothes, but when you're out there meeting the world, you've got to look first class. Christians would never make it if they wandered around looking poor." There was a pause as if Charlie were searching for the track of his argument.

"I'm dead serious about this, Campbell. I know I'm putting you on the spot, but there are times when ministers have to take a stand. This is one of those times. If this proposal is approved by the Trustees, as far as I'm concerned, Good Samaritan is finished. We'll have sold out to the world—lock, stock, and barrel. There'll be no way back but prayer and repentance, and I don't see much of that in the wind. The life of our church is on the line."

Peter could feel what was coming next. Sales pitches always had to work up to a climax.

"I know I'm asking a lot of you. You only sit in with the trustees—no vote and all that. But those men respect you. They did Dr. Strong. You take a stand—no money for the garden—and they'll back you up. There's no question of God's will in the matter. People don't give money for roses. They give it for God. I'm counting on you to set the Trustees right. I'm praying for you."

While deciding whether he should thank Charlie for the prayer, Charlie hung up. Words stuck in Peter's throat: had the abrupt ending given Charlie the impression Peter would do his bidding?

8

Mary's eyes were fixed on him. "Boy, they don't leave you alone, do they? Maybe I should come back some other time."

Peter leaned back to ease the tension in his neck. "Go right ahead. This doesn't usually happen. There's a meeting tonight, and some people are a bit concerned." He wiped the perspiration off his face and grimaced up at the persecuting sun.

Mary stared at the carpet. "Then one night I got this call. It was three in the morning. Red had been gone for hours. He sounded worried. He was swearin', shoutin'—like he'd lost his head. 'Lock the door,' he says. 'I'm at a pay phone at the police station. They picked up the gang.' Well, that was the first I'd heard about the gang. It was motorcycles, and I had no idea what they were doin' at three in the morning. 'Who's comin'?' I ask him. 'The fuzz,' he says. 'If they find out where I live, they'll bust the place. Don't let 'em in.' I ask him, 'Why not? There's nothin' here.' He swears somethin' terrible. I never heard him like that before. It was like he'd lost his mind. Then he hung up." Mary squirmed in the chair as if she were reliving that night.

"I didn't know what to do. I was scared stiff. I had a girlfriend, but I didn't think she'd want me callin' her at three in the morning. There was nothin' she could do anyway.

"I tried to go to sleep, but my nerves. I was shakin'. I didn't know nobody in the other apartments. I kept seein' those police comin'. I knew I should welcome police, but Red was always kind of funny 'bout 'em. Whenever he'd see a police car, he'd look the other way and speed past. Like he was afraid or somethin', but I always thought it was just him."

Mary leaned forward, her face drawn. The redness had given way to a bloodless pallor. "Then somebody was knockin' at the door. I . . ."

The buzzer cut her off. Mary glowered at the phone. Peter felt like bundling it up and hurling it through the window. Miss Hensley was doing this purposely. He threw the receiver into his ear. "What now?"

Miss Hensley's response was cold, even. "Mr. Straphe is threatening to quit. I thought you might want to talk to him." Sarcasm cut like a knife. If it were up to Peter, the absence of Mr. Straphe from his life would be a blessing. No more mad charades at the organ. No more having to get past his guard dog wife to talk to him. No more having the worship service come off like a potluck where no one knew what anyone else was doing. But if Mr. Straphe did quit, the Council would want to know what Peter had done to prevent it. Duty over rancor. He pushed the button.

"Make it fast."

"I will," Mr. Straphe said angrily. "Fifteen thousand for a damn rose garden? Is that what the Trustees are voting on tonight?"

"It is." Peter heard defiance in his voice. There was a sadistic enjoyment in countering the dictatorial choir director.

"I can't believe it. Traitors! The whole bunch of them — traitors!"

Peter felt aloof, as if he were a feudal lord looking down at a dissatisfied peasant. "Can you come to the point?"

"When the new organ was built, certain sections were left out because the fund drive fell short. The trustees promised that when extra funds were available, the organ would be finished. If those trustees spend one nickel on that garden without purchasing the rest of the organ, well, as far as I'm concerned, they're a bunch of liars — and I'll say it publicly. Then maybe the people in this community will see Good Samaritan for what it is." Vengeance rang so loudly in Mr. Straphe's voice Peter wondered if people sounded like this before they committed homicide.

Straphe's tone changed to condescension. "You may not know it, Campbell, but I've put my life's blood into that church. When I came ten years ago, that choir didn't know a whole note from a toilet seat. They sounded like a bunch of Saturday night drunks. I'm not exaggerating. Well, I worked with them. Slaved with them. It was slow, but they came along. Now they're the best choir in town. They've put Good Samaritan on the map. When people think of fine music, they think of us. But if those trustees are going to rob me of what they promised, then I'll have no more of it. If they want to spit on me, I don't have to take it. There are dozens of choirs around that need good directors, directors who know quality music. I don't need Good Samaritan." Mr. Straphe's voice rose to a shout that pained Peter's ear. "I tell you, Campbell, if one nickel goes to that garden, then I'm out. You can tell the trustees that. Then we'll know how much my services are appreciated around there."

"There'll probably be a compro . . ." The phone had already slammed down at the other end. Peter was talking to no one but the phone company's impersonal buzz.

9

Mary squirmed in the chair. "Do people always get so mad?"

Peter flicked the perspiration from his eyebrows. His shirt clung to his back as if he'd been swimming with his clothes on. Not a breath of air could be felt coming through the louvers. He had a yearning for a large straw hat to shade his head, his body. "No," he replied absently.

Mary half rose from her chair. "Maybe I should come back some other time."

Peter tried to recollect where they were. He forced a smile onto his face. "No. Go ahead. That should be the last interruption."

Mary sank back onto the chair. "Well, there was this knockin' on the door. I was in bed in my pajamas . . ." Her voice trailed off as a shadow loomed at the office door.

Miss Hensley poked her bird head in. "It's Pat Andrews. She insists."

Peter's anger gave way to disbelief. How could Miss Hensley be so calloused? What was behind her straight teeth, pale flesh, black eyes? Was what he saw in the bob of her head sadistic triumph? Behind her, Pat paced with a deeply furrowed frown. Peter had no choice but to ask Mary to excuse him.

Without a word, Pat led him out into the entry. She took a series of puffs on her cigarette; smoke rose to the glass ceiling where it billowed out in a mushroom cloud. She had yet to set eyes on him. She was clad in red slacks, tan sandals, a loose cotton shirt.

Finally she turned on him with a stern expression. "I'm liable to lose my job for coming out here, but if the trustees voted on this proposal without my doing something, I couldn't live with myself." Anger gave her voice an ominous sound.

"I know I shouldn't interrupt you," she added with a hint of apology. She shifted from one leg to the other. "Let me get it straight. The trustees are voting on fifteen thousand for the rose garden. Is that right?" She held her voice in careful restraint.

Peter nodded. "It's just a proposal. It will be debated, altered — surely the trustees . . ."

Pat planted her hands on her hips. "This is the last straw. I've watched this church retreat from the city. I voted against accepting this monstrosity from Gottschalk. I was afraid that when we got away from town we'd forget all about the people there. And that's exactly what's happened.

"I've bided my time. I told myself there's no use getting angry and just alienating people. I talked to Dr. Strong. He said it would take time 'til people saw they had an obligation to the city." She paused to draw on her cigarette. The tip burned bright red. "Well, I've waited. I thought if the church couldn't send people, it could at least send money. We can get kids from the university to do the work. But now, if this proposal goes through. If we appropriate funds we don't have for a damn rose garden – well, then I've had it. This church is doing precious little for anyone now, and if the trustees approve this recommendation, then as far as I'm concerned, it's finished."

Peter groped for words. "They haven't voted yet." He had been in Good Samaritan long enough to know she was right. Nobody did anything for the city. If she quit, the church would lose a voice it needed. "Nobody knows what the outcome will be." He detected a pleading tone in his voice.

"I know that," Pat said sharply. "I don't want to fly off the handle." She paused. "But I know this church too well — how it's been drifting. Unless someone takes a strong stand, the Board will vote the money. If for no other reason than just to get the issue over with." She pressed her cigarette out against the sole of her sandal and threw it into the umbrella rack. "I want to know. What's your position?" Her eyes searched Peter's face.

Peter glanced at the parking lot and the line of trees bordering the highway. Part of him didn't care what happened. He was supposed to be counseling Mary Jones. He had not come to Good Samaritan as her referee. Yet he was the pastor, he could not run away. Compromise — that was the only hope. But what it would be escaped him. The women would have to get some kind of garden, Straphe his organ, Jarvis his evangelism, Pat her programs for the city. It wasn't fifteen thousand they needed, but a hundred thousand. And how many other projects lurked in the minds of parishioners too timid to voice them? "It's a bad time to make any decision," he said.

Pat's eyes held him like meat skewers. "I'm asking you — do you favor fifteen thousand for the garden or not? It's a simple question."

Peter felt like a politician in front of TV cameras. No, he did not favor the proposal. But he did not have Pat's freedom to just walk away from Good Samaritan because he disagreed with it. "I'll work for a just compromise," he said. "That's the best I can do."

Pat's mouth curled in disgust. She pulled her eyes from him as if he posed some threat of contamination. "There are times when compromise is a cop-out. This proposal involves fundamental issues of right and wrong. You can't please everybody. You know that."

Peter did, but the real question was whether it was possible to please anybody. Between Pat's livid gaze and the heat pouring through the glass from above, he felt he was being spit-grilled. His only instinct was to get away, to forget there was a garden. "I'm for a just compromise," he repeated. "I know that isn't satisfactory to you, but there's been no debate. There may be angles we don't know."

Pat's head shook in disgust. "I had hoped to hear something different. You sound like Strong. Always trying to please everyone. Great in the pulpit. But in practice . . . well, you don't deliver." She turned to the windows and gazed out. Her face radiated hot frustration. "Sometimes I think all ministers are mice," she mumbled.

She stepped toward the outer doors and stopped. "Is the meeting open?"

Peter had given the question no thought. He saw no problem. "I'm sure it is," he said resolutely.

Pat smiled. "Well, that's a stand. Maybe you're not totally hopeless." She pushed open the door and rushed out.

For a moment, Peter thought she had meant her remark as a compliment. Then he allowed himself to hear the sarcasm. He didn't like it.

10

Mary stood staring out at the garden scarp. "I really should go," she said apologetically. "You've got more problems than I do."

Peter motioned her back toward the chair. "I'm going to see you through," he said.

She caught his seriousness and sat down. "Well, it was the police," she went. "I got up, put my robe on, and by the time I got out to the sitting room, they were shouting. 'Open up, or we'll break down the door. We've got a search warrant.' There were six of them. They ran past and started tearin' into everything: kitchen cabinets, the oven, drawers. They cut open the cushions on the sofa, dumped the dirt out of the plants I'd bought. I screamed at them. They were ruining everything.

"'Who are *you*?' one of them asks. He was mean lookin', with a scar on his forehead. I wanted to say, 'his wife,' but that would've been lyin', so I said, 'I'm his girlfriend.' 'Where's the stuff?' he asks me. 'What stuff?' I reply." She looked earnestly at Peter. "I really didn't know anything about drugs. Like I said, Red was a nice guy. He treated me right."

Between the drone string of Mary's voice, the brilliant orb overhead, and the stifling air, Peter found himself launched disembodied on a sea of heat. Mary's story drifted as if from another room. Her young face and earnest innocence shimmered before him like a surrealistic painting.

"Am I boring you?" She was staring at him as if she had just awakened him from sleep.

Peter blinked his eyes. "Oh no," he said. "It's the sun, the heat. It gets terribly warm in here."

Mary wiped beads of perspiration from her cheeks with her finger and nodded. "Where was I?"

Peter had no idea.

"Oh, then this cop comes outta the bedroom with plastic bags. 'Here it is,' he says. I'd never seen the stuff in my life. 'Coke. There's more of it.' I went in. They were haulin' it outta the mattress. You know a bed's got two mattresses, and, well, the one underneath is hollow. Red had been puttin' the stuff in there. I never knew nothin' about it." Her eyes grew large as if she still could not believe what she had seen.

"Then they tell me I've got to go with them to the police station. There I am in my pajamas and robe. Can you imagine that? 'I need to get dressed,' I tells 'em. 'Okay, sister,' one of 'em says. 'Two minutes.' I looked terrible. I hadn't slept. All I could find was jeans and a sweater and sneakers. I tried to do somethin' with my hair, but they dragged me out." Her voice dropped to a sad dirge.

"It was ter'ble. They asked me all kinds of personal

questions. Told me I was holdin' out, tryin' to protect Red. I was scared. I called my girlfriend, but she couldn't come. She said she didn't feel well." Mary looked hard at Peter. "I think she was lyin'. When she heard it was drugs, she just didn't want to get involved.

"Well, after a while they let me go. I guess they believed I didn't know nothin' 'bout what was goin' on. But Red was still there somewhere an' . . ."

The buzz of the phone stopped her dead. Peter lifted the receiver. "Mr. Krohn," Miss Hensley said icily.

"Can't he wait?" Peter retorted. There was no response. He pushed the button.

"Campbell!" The voice was angry.

Peter moaned.

"Krohn here. Secretary says you're busy, but this can't wait. I don't know how your morning's gone, but mine's been hell. Phone's rung a dozen times. Everybody wants to tell us what to do with the proposal for that damn garden. I'm supposed to be making a living down here, but I can't get a damn thing done with all these calls." The surge of energy halted, the voice dropped. "Campbell, who let this thing out?" The strain of accusation was undisguised.

"Not me," Peter said, trying to focus his attention in the hot haze. "I just got the proposal, I've been tied up ever since."

"Papers are to be sent to trustees only. They're to keep their mouths shut. This damn thing's all over the church. People want to come to the meeting and make demands. Others threaten to resign. They'll cut their giving. I can't believe all this furor over a stupid garden. That Hayes woman is a thorn in the side. She should never have left the money in the first place. Those women won't see anything else. We're desecrating her . . ."

". . . grave," Peter added.

"Oh, you too," Mr. Krohn exclaimed.

"Yes," Peter replied. "My morning has been like yours."

"That's what I wanted to know. Who let this thing out?"

Peter had no idea. "Only the committee and the office have had it," he said.

"Well, I suppose we won't find out. People will clam up now that it's become such a hot potato." Mr. Krohn paused. "I wanted to ask you. The people who called me claim they've got you on their side. Is that right?"

"No," Peter replied.

"That's what they say. Those garden club women think you're going to speak for them. You want the garden because of what it will do for Good Samaritan."

Peter felt an impulse to expatiate on his feelings about the garden. His compromise of grass—he could see it now as his eyes ranged over the yellow tundra. It was the best idea. "It's a lie. I've told everyone I would work for the best compromise. That's all."

"You're only *ex officio*."

Peter caught the appellation of powerlessness. "I know."

"No vote."

"Discussion only. I've read the by-laws."

"Then there's that Andrews woman," Mr. Krohn said. "One of those bra-burners if you know what I mean. Says there's going to be a demonstration. People from the city will picket outside the door. She was incensed when I told her the meeting was closed. Has been for a hundred sixty years. We're not changing the rules just for a bunch of domineering females who want to take over the church."

The hair bristled on the back of Peter's neck. He hated closed meetings, the false illusion of power, the comfort of approving the irresponsible. "Can't we reconsider that?" he asked.

"Reconsider what?"

"The closed meeting policy. If people are allowed to observe the trustees work out a just compromise, then tempers will die down and we can get on with more important things."

All Peter could hear was Krohn's angry breathing. "No. The trustees have the full responsibility of running the church. We're not sharing it with anybody else. I know the Board." There was a pause. "You keep using the word 'compromise.'" To Peter, it was the only solution. "I hope you haven't given people the idea we're going to satisfy all of them. The Board has certain prerogatives. We've always guarded our right to decide what we think best..."

"Isn't that what compromise is?" Peter asked.

"No," Mr. Krohn said emphatically. "That's not what I mean."

Peter tried to articulate a response, but Mr. Krohn had an urgent call and excused himself. Peter was left with the dead phone and words he wanted to speak.

11

Mary was standing with one hand on the doorknob. "This place reminds me of the police station," she said. "I've got a feelin' something ter'ble is goin' to happen."

Peter nodded toward the chair. "It's quite all right. You must feel badly about Red."

Mary paused, then sat down. "Oh, I got over that." Her face softened.

"Don't you want help? Isn't he in jail?"

"He was sent up for ten years. But you know, when I thought about how he'd lied to me and how he was runnin' around with other girls and how he'd been stashin' all that stuff in the apartment—well, it made me mad. He had no right to do that to me. Don't you think so?"

Peter leaned forward. "You have every reason to be angry with him."

"Well, that's what I thought." Mary pursed her lips in satisfaction.

"But don't you need...?"

"For Red?" She looked at Peter as if he were dense. "He's gettin' what he deserves. I never want to see him again."

Then why the story? Peter wondered. Perhaps with the

heat and the interruptions he had missed something. "I don't understand. What can I do for you?"

Mary clasped her hands on one knee and shrugged her shoulders. "Well, there's this other guy. He's not like Red. He's tall and has blond hair. He's real nice, if you know what I mean. He tells me I'm the greatest girl he's ever met."

Peter repressed a stifling sense of déjà vu. "And you're living together?" he asked.

Mary stared without blinking. "Well, it is cheaper. Instead of two apartments, we only have to pay for one. But I don't know if it's goin' to work out. I like him a whole lot, and he says he likes me." She paused, her lips trembled. "But, well, it's like this. I just found out he's already married. This girl showed up at the door when Brad was gone an' she had two kids an', well, Brad hadn't said nothin' 'bout that, an', well, I just don't know what to do."

Mary looked at Peter as if the answers to the mysteries of her life were written somewhere inside his head. He felt an impulse to scold her because of her lack of discretion, but that faded into an urge to embrace her as if she were a small child. "Mary, have you ever thought of trying morality?"

She cast him a puzzled look. "More what?"

"Mor-al-i-ty," Peter sounded out phonetically.

"What's that?" she replied.

Lectures Peter had heard in seminary ran through his mind, but they were beyond Mary's grasp. His too, in part. "Well," he began, "it's a way of thinking that says you don't live or sleep with someone of the opposite sex until you know that person and you've made commitments to care for each other and stay with each other no matter what happens."

A sparkle shone in Mary's eyes. "You know, I like the sound of that. To care for someone. To stay with someone. That would be really nice." She stood up. "Maybe that's what's been missing in my life."

"But you don't live with them *until* you've made the commitment," Peter repeated.

Mary nodded. "I understand. That's what I need. You've been a help. Thank you." With a light step, she turned, opened the door, and was gone.

Peter sagged back in his chair, pressing his wet shirt against his flesh. Images of the past hour floated on a misty sea of heat. There was Mary's face in the center, with no idea whether he had any notion what she was talking about.

12

The black cover of the Trustee garden report was hot to the touch. Peter slowly scanned the pages, but there was nothing to even suggest that the committee had considered grassing over the garden.

Suddenly, his eye caught movement outside the window. Five women from the garden club were gesturing, measuring with a long yellow tape, driving in stakes. Peter stood up in hot terror that they would notice him and barge in to lobby for their proposal.

He remembered he needed to get his hymnbook from the sanctuary. In the glass tube leading to Benedict, John Rhodes lapped at his side. "If you want my opinion, the garden should go. It's a pain in the you know where. It brings those women down here"—he gestured toward them beyond the glass wall of the tube—"and they keep tellin' me what to do. I can't take it. My wife says my nerves've never been so bad."

Ignoring John, Peter plowed ahead. He swept into Benedict, but the door crashed behind him before he could stop it. Leotarded women sat about with their legs crossed in the lotus position. Mr. Drissle was perched on top of a table with his head bent slightly forward, his eyes staring straight ahead. Peter weaved on tiptoe through the Buddha bodies.

"Is that that damn custodian again?" The glass walls amplified Mr. Drissle's voice and gave it a Wizard of Oz echo. "Oh, Campbell," Oz went on. "You've got a schedule. Why are you in here disturbing us?"

Out of the corner of his eye as he kept striding, Peter could see Mr. Drissle's wiry body uncoiling. "Campbell, do you feel how hot it is in here?" The temperature felt the same as Peter's office. The only difference was the pungence of human sweat hanging in the air. "The custodian and Miss Hensley say the air conditioner can't be turned on until there's a heat wave. As far as I'm concerned, what's in here right now is a heat wave like I've never seen before. We pay a fee for this course. I demand the air conditioner be turned on. We can't meditate in a furnace. Unless . . ."

Peter strode toward the doors on the other side.

". . . you're trying to kick us out of here . . ." Peter thought he heard Mr. Drissle's Peter Pan slippers following him, so he lengthened his step. He attacked the doors as if to tear them from their hinges and went on up toward the sanctuary.

His hymnbook was on his chancel chair. Turning to go back down to the office, his eye caught the communion table. The traitorous intruder was back. For six weeks it had been missing, but there it was—taunting, mocking.

All the anger of that morning rose like a hot shaft of pain. He fought with all his might to resist picking up the brass cross and smashing it on the stone floor. Of course it wasn't the source of all his problems, but it represented all that was wrong—religion without sacrifice, religion as sanctified ego-tripping. Even the hanging wooden cross gave offense. There should be no cross in Good Samaritan. People who did not believe in sacrifice did not deserve crosses.

The destructive surge ebbed, leaving Peter limp. He thought of the meeting that night. Even though the brass cross would not be dealt with, the meeting could still be a beginning—a new direction. Miracles did happen. By some totally unexpected stroke, the trustees could vote to give the fifteen thousand away to help others. A beginning. That was all that was needed. Then, one day, *they* would remove the brass cross of their own volition.

13

Relaxing on the family room sofa with his tie loosened, Peter picked up the evening paper: PRESIDENT SEEKS HIGHER DEFENSE BUDGET; PEACE TALKS IN MIDDLE EAST STALL; GRAVE OF MASSACRE VICTIMS FOUND; DROUGHT WORSENS; NURSING HOME RESIDENT RAPED. Nothing about the crisis of the rose garden at Good Samaritan.

14

When Peter arrived at the church, he was greeted inside the narthex by milling blacks, whites, beards, long hair, jeans, conversations—some in Spanish—sharp, earnest. Faces confident of backing a just cause bobbed about in a haze of cigarette smoke. Peter felt comfortable among them in his worn cotton pants and brown sweater, his attempt to free up the Board from its blue suits with the jackets always buttoned.

Pat Andrews stood at the door leading into the tube to Assisi. Cigarette in mouth, she gestured for everyone to step back and let Peter through. "Everything will get worked out," she shouted. With jaw set and eyes hard, she blocked Peter's way. "They told us we can't be admitted."

Peter halted.

"You promised," Pat said loudly enough for those nearby to hear. "We're waiting. I don't know how much longer I can hold them back." She nodded toward brows knotting with frustration.

"I'll talk to the trustees," he said.

Pat jerked the cigarette from her mouth. "Good luck. They say they've got a hundred sixty years of tradition on the line."

The semi-circular meeting room in Assisi looked out on

the church lawn. Around the oval conference table sat the trustees in their buttoned blue suits. Their heads bobbed with indignation as they voiced displeasure at the disheveled horde in the narthex. Mr. Krohn presided from the end of the table in his gray suit—his uniform, as Peter had come to know it. Power threatened hung heavily in air still warm from the day's sun. At Peter's entrance, heads turned, lips moved in greeting. Reflected in the curved glass outside wall, Peter saw himself diminished, misshapen.

He went to his seat near the foot of the table but declined to sit down. Mr. Krohn glanced at his watch. The meeting never started before 7:30, so there was always some fidgeting as the trustees avoided any topic of conversation which might take them past the last few seconds of the countdown. To draw their attention, Peter loudly cleared his throat. Heads swiveled toward him. Gray hair and no hair far outnumbered black and brown. This was the most venerable board of the church. Men scrounged their way here through years of service on the Council, or they gained instant membership by civic recognition—the amassing of small fortunes through business or professional prowess. It was as if Jesus had discarded his ragtag fishermen for a boardroom full of bankers, lawyers, and corporate managers.

"I'd like us to reconsider the rules," Peter began. "We should be grateful that people in the community feel strongly enough about Good Samaritan to devote a night to hearing us debate. Christians are people of light. We shouldn't be intimidated by letting the world know what we do and why. It's an opportunity to show our real concern for people—the kind of concern Jesus demonstrated. If our decisions are just, we should not shy away from public scrutiny."

Their faces were masks of officiousness—a polite way of saying the minds behind them were turned off. Eyes were fixed, jaws set, cheeks rigid, arms resting authoritatively on the table.

Mr. Krohn called for a vote. "Since it's not 7:30 yet, our action is not official," he said. Peter's recommendation lost unanimously.

He started to sink to his chair, then paused. "But gentlemen, what do we have to lose?" He glanced at the faces on both sides of the walnut table. "If we don't let them in, they'll get angry. Something could happen that would embarrass the church. If we let them in and show that we're willing to hear all sides and then make our decision—how does that hurt us?"

The trustees sat like statues as if the question were rhetorical. Mr. Krohn glanced at his watch. "The hour has come." Lines of strain in his face softened. He looked at Peter. "I'd like to ask the Pastor to open our meeting with prayer." Heads bowed, but Peter, looking down at the table, didn't feel like praying. There was nothing on his mind he wanted to say except to ask God to help this Board loosen up and deal with people openly. After a disconcertingly long pause, he blurted, "Father, may your will be done." Then he excused himself to inform Pat of the Board's decision.

The blood drained from Pat's lips; her teeth ground as if she were biting the end off her cigarette. Bearded faces behind her murmured angrily. Being on the butt of arbitrary power was not going over well. "I've done the best I can," Peter said apologetically. "I told you, I have no vote. I just sit in. You'll have to take my word for it that they'll come up with a just decision. They know about the city and its needs. It's just that there are other needs too." Surely the Board would come to a compromise, perhaps the grass alternative—or, better yet, just give the money away. If people wanted roses, let them donate whatever it would take to finish the garden. Most of them had the money to do it.

Pat shook her head. "I've been in this church a lot longer than you have. *You* may think the decision will be just. *I'm* telling you it won't. They'll approve the committee proposal, and that will be it."

The mood of the crowd turned hostile. Word of the Board's refusal rippled back; voices grew louder. Strident shouts rose near the outside door. Peter had a fleeting premonition they would rush forward and turn violent. He hadn't been in a situation like this since the riots in the inner city. "You've got to trust me," he said to Pat. He cringed at the pleading tone in his voice. "I have full rights of debate. I'll do everything I can to get a compromise that will be best for everyone."

"It won't happen," Pat said sharply. "It never has. Now that we've pressed the issue, it surely won't. You're going to learn some things about Good Samaritan you haven't seen before."

Peter bristled at the suggestion he was naive. Yes, he was new to the church. But he had met with the trustees before. Although as best as he could recall, all they'd dealt with was utility bills, and debate had gone past midnight.

Pat shouted to her followers to stand back from the doors so Peter could return to the meeting. They jostled each other in bad temper. Peter wondered if they were really under Pat's control, but he could not stay to find out. If he didn't get back to the meeting, the proposal would be passed without his participation.

The chairman of the committee on the garden stood reading the report in a dry monotone. Expressions on the trustees' faces were the same as when Peter had appealed for a change in the policy. With darkness now fallen, the glass outside wall had turned to a black mirror reflecting the entire Board—shrunken, misshapen.

Suddenly, a dull chorus of voices could be heard. It rose not from members of the Board, but from the black void beyond the windows. Angry shouts, taunts hurled like darts from the dark. The glass trembled; fists pounded on it, a line of black, white, and brown fists thudded across the length of the room. Bodies invisible, fists shot from darkness, rapped the glass, disappeared, then struck again. The tempo increased, the wall rumbled like thunder, resonated like a giant gong. Loose panes rattled, the room shook like the innards of a bass drum.

Drowned out by the noise, the committee chairman

halted his drone. The trustees turned to Mr. Krohn. His eyes flitted about as if he were besieged by rapid pulse and rocketing blood pressure. How to deal with unruly demonstrators was not covered in the by-laws. He had no precedent to tell him what should be done when a hundred people stood at the windows using them as a percussion instrument.

Peter's anger dissolved into thin pity at the helplessness before him. Trustees stared about as if there were no such thing as people pounding on plate glass windows. Or, if there were, they were found in some subterranean part of the culture into which the trustees never ventured. Peter stood. "I'll try to get them to stop," he shouted. Mr. Krohn cupped his hand behind his ear. Peter repeated his pledge. Mr. Krohn nodded.

The narthex was empty. Outside, the sky glowed from the distant lights of Oakdale. Fresh dew dampened Peter's shoes as he strode up the hill toward shapes silhouetted against the lighted glass of the Board room. Pat Andrews stood behind them, her eyes fixed with a look of satisfaction, her arms folded across her chest as if she could stand there all night.

Peter puffed from the climb up the hill. "They've got to stop," he shouted above the rumble. "The trustees can't hear."

Pat stared blankly, drew a pack of cigarettes out of her jean shirt, and lit up. A cloud of smoke grew about her in the still air. "Good," she said. "Maybe we'll finally get our point across."

"But if they don't resolve the issue tonight" — Peter could not contemplate the church hanging in limbo for days on end, irate members calling him to vent their anger. "You've got to trust the process," he pleaded. "They know what you stand for. They've got to be impressed that people are giving up a night to come here."

Pat flicked ash off her cigarette. "When they make their decision, we'll see if you're right."

Peter's heart had slowed from the climb, but it was increasing again. "Don't you see? They can't make a decision with all that racket. You can't hear the person next to you in there."

Pat drew close to him. Her voice dropped. "Look at them," she said. "You and those trustees think you're dealing with a bunch of punks." That wasn't quite what Peter saw. The energy they put into their pounding amazed him. There was nothing that would have sent him to take their place.

"You're witnessing a very rare confrontation. Inside that room are the people who control Oakdale. They determine who the schools hire and what they teach. They decide who gets charity funds and who doesn't. Their money backs political candidates who can change a neighborhood in a matter of weeks. Through their clout in Washington, they influence when and where we go to war and what people in the world starve or eat.

"The people on this side of the windows are the controlled," Pat continued. "Blacks, hispanics, poor whites. Students who realize the world they must find a place in is controlled by those who have money. Some of these people work for the men in the room. They know more about them in some ways than they know about themselves."

Pat's explanation seemed too simple. The men in the room would never acknowledge they had power over anyone. They only did their jobs. They had their own frustrations. He heard them talk about how the government regulated business and nobody could make money any more because so much of it went to Washington.

Pat's cigarette glowed brightly as she took a long draw. "What you see here is the frustration of a hundred people who are tired of being pushed around. They want to be part of the decisions that affect them. And tonight, the Board of Trustees has denied it to them. Just as those men deny it to them in every other way. They don't want to hear what people really need. They like to determine what the needs are and then provide their own solutions."

Peter felt a sense of déjà vu. What Pat was saying he had heard from radical ministers in the Synod. In the sixties, spokespersons for ad hoc groups had demanded time on the agenda. It was all power and control and denial of self-determination for the masses. Their rhetoric was laced with Marxist slogans. Peter knew there needed to be changes, but this was not the way.

The crowd took up an obscene chant, repeating it over and over. The shouting grew louder, the pace of the pounding faster. Peter felt power escalating, power that had to find some outlet. "You've got to stop them," he shouted. "They're getting out of hand."

A smug smile crossed Pat's face. "They *are* out of hand. I couldn't stop them if I wanted to. It's anger. Frustration. But that's all. They won't break anything or hurt anybody. They just want the trustees to know there are people and issues they don't know anything about."

Peter's muscles tensed. "You're going to let them go on?"

Pat smiled in condescension. "You sound like a trustee yourself. When they've gotten all their anger out, they'll go their way. They won't have gotten anywhere, and the trustees will probably screw us on the garden, but we'll have made our statement. That's one thing the powerless in this country have gotten used to. Make your statement. It doesn't change anything, but at least you know someone had to recognize you exist."

Peter shook his head. The demonstrators formed a circular human chain rotating against the glass. Those passing the windows pounded their way from one side to the other. Those on the outside clapped their hands and kept cadence with the obscenity. Hostility hung in the air, but there was also a hint of carnival. In the glow from the meeting room, Peter could see smiles on the faces of the demonstrators — as if they found pleasure in what they were doing. Perhaps Pat was right. At least he saw nothing to indicate they intended anything further than disruption.

15

Back in Assisi, Mr. Krohn was hurrying along the corridor outside the meeting room. His short body strutted like that of a victorious Napoleon. "Now we'll get them," he snarled. "Riff-raff, radicals." He looked hard at Peter. "I'm sure there are Communists among them. Always disrupting. Always making trouble wherever they can. Why don't they all go to Russia and stay there? Why do they always want the benefits of a Capitalist system they despise?"

What had Mr. Krohn done? Peter wondered. He followed the little man back into the room. The glass roared like a thousand timpani. The trustees stood staring at the passing hammering fists with blank expressions. When they saw Mr. Krohn had returned, they nodded in satisfaction.

"What have you done?" Peter shouted at him. Mr. Krohn stared in incomprehension. Peter shouted louder. From reading Mr. Krohn's lips, Peter got the answer: "Just wait and see."

Mr. Krohn stepped brusquely to the windows and rose up on tiptoe to look over the heads of the demonstrators. Peter's line of vision was already that high from where he stood. What Mr. Krohn was looking at was a long procession of red flashing lights racing from town along Valley Road.

The blood in Peter's veins froze. He looked again, blinking his eyes. He went to Mr. Krohn and grasped his arm. "This isn't the way!" he shouted. "This is no good. You'll incite them to violence. Leave them alone. They'll get tired and go home. We should postpone the meeting and go home ourselves. That's better than having a battle between the police and them." Peter gestured toward the window. Mr. Krohn threw him a blank look. Obviously he had not heard a word he said.

Peter turned to the rest of the trustees and raised his voice until his throat burned. "This is disastrous. Good

Samaritan will become a riot zone. We're overreacting. You should know more about the people who are demonstrating. Then you wouldn't be so paranoid." But the trustees couldn't hear either. They looked at him as if he were a poor mime, the theme of whose act went over their heads.

He turned back to the window. Into the parking lot turned the parade of red lights — fifteen cars. They must have called out the county police as a backup. At the end of the procession came a white truck. When it passed under a parking lot light, he could see in big red letters on its side: TV 7 ACTIONEWS.

The hammering suddenly stopped. A bright white light appeared in the sky over the city. It moved north, and then headed directly toward Good Samaritan. Peter thought it was an airliner with its landing lights on. But when it drew nearer, its erratic motions revealed it to be a helicopter. Its bright light probed the lawn and stopped above the demonstrators. They stood in reeling confusion, their gazes alternating between the police getting out of their cars under the blaze of TV arc lights and the helicopter thucka-thucking overhead.

"By God, this'll show 'em!" Mr. Krohn shouted. "Now they'll know who's boss. Wait 'til they spend the night in jail. Then they'll think twice about coming here and telling us how to run our church." The other trustees nodded. Lined up at the window with their padded shoulders, they looked like a cadre of undertakers awaiting the lowering of a casket.

None of them noticed Peter drawing back toward the door. A wave of nausea swept across his stomach. *Blessed are the peacemakers*. The trustees relished battle — war. Did they really want to see heads bashed, blood run? Revulsion took charge of him.

To save time, he headed for the emergency fire door. Disregarding the bold red letters: 'For Emergency Use Only,' he threw it open. The alarm buzzer went off behind him, but he kept right on. The light blazing from the helicopter blinded him. He shielded his eyes and glanced at where the demonstrators had been. There was nothing but grass. They were farther up the hill — dark shapes stopping occasionally to wave their arms. They were shouting, but whatever they said was drowned out by the helicopter's whine and the flap of its rotor. He had seen TV 7's chopper before, hovering over traffic jams and house fires. It was Oakdale's snooper in the sky. Its pulsating thucker battered his ears, sent his brain spinning. It would only make the situation worse. He waved at it to go away and then stopped. There was probably a camera up there recording his every move.

He turned toward the bottom of the hill. Under glaring TV lights glinted a wall of plexiglass — riot shields behind which crouched policemen tightly clenching nightsticks. He had seen it all before on TV. The wall moved slowly up the hill. Suddenly he realized he was the only one left in the no-man's line between the police and demonstrators. Assisi was dark. The trustees had turned out the lights so they could get a better view. Not one of them had followed him out to lend a hand.

Blessed are the peacemakers. The plexiglass line drew closer. The helicopter swooped over it and stopped directly over his head. Two cameramen came stumbling up the hill trailing electric cables. They crouched down and focused their cameras on the police line. The wash of the helicopter ruffled his hair, buffeted him like surf. He felt as if he were an actor on the cardboard set of a B movie.

The line slowed and began to encircle him. "I'm the pastor," he shouted. "You've come far enough. Let's talk this thing out." Through the shields he could see nothing but grim faces framed by riot helmets. Blank eyes looked right through him. These were not men, but machines, robots programmed to put down riots.

He shouted again, waved his arms. No expressions appeared on the faces. His words were blasted away by the thucker and whine of the Eye in the Sky. The crouching cameramen had their lenses trained on him.

He felt no urge to run. This was just an act, a dramatic gesture to drive the demonstrators off.

Suddenly two helmeted officers broke from behind the shields and grabbed his wrists. Peter looked at them in surprise. Their rough grip burned the flesh above his hands. Their faces were masks of determination. "I'm the pastor!" he shouted at the top of his voice. "This is my church. You have no right to do this."

Saying nothing, his captors thrust his hands behind his back and clapped cold handcuffs on his wrists. Again he shouted his plea, but they spun him toward the line of shields and pushed him through. He almost fell. Grabbing his arms, they half dragged him down the hill toward the flashing lights. "We got one," a policeman shouted at what appeared to be a superior officer standing at the open door of a police car, microphone in hand.

"Good," came the reply.

"I'm the pastor!" Peter shouted. The officer paid no attention. His eyes were on the hill where the helicopter hovered over the advancing line. He spoke into the microphone.

Peter glanced toward the narthex. Surely the trustees had seen the mistake and would come out to explain to the police their error. But the narthex was empty and dark.

He gazed up the hill. The demonstrators had broken into dark knots. One circled past Gottschalk's ball, another was passing out of sight over the top of the hill, the third had moved off to the left and was dispersing in a grove of trees. The police line had reached the sanctuary, a wave of insects creeping toward the ridgeline silhouetted against the star-studded sky. No one stood in its way.

The two policemen brusquely pushed Peter into the back seat of a patrol car and locked the doors from the outside. A heavy mesh screen separated him from the officers. With the din of the helicopter diminished, he said, "I'm the pastor. I'm the pastor of Good Samaritan. Go ask the trustees." The policemen paid no attention. They screeched out of the parking lot onto Valley Road and headed toward the city with the siren screaming. Cars pulled to the right like frightened rodents; Peter and his captors swept past as if a life were at stake.

Finally the officer in the passenger seat turned to him. "Yeah, and I'm the President of the United States," he said sarcastically. "Why don't you save your story for the booking officer?"

With that, Peter slumped back in the seat. This was a nightmare. He shook his head to wake himself up. But the scream of the siren and the people staring at him from Oakdale's sidewalks looked too real for a dream.

16

The booking sergeant sat behind a desk in a heavy mesh cage with a recording clerk beside him. He made no response to Peter's protestations, just kept asking questions in a monotone voice as he filled out a form. Peter warned them they would get a black eye for arresting the pastor of a major church, but he might as well have been talking to statues in a museum.

They charged him with disobeying a police order. He knotted his fists and argued that he had heard no order to disperse because the helicopter made it impossible to hear. Besides, as pastor of the church he had a right to be anywhere on the property. The booking officer asked him to sign the paper and press his fingers on an ink pad and then on a paper. Peter looked at the stone face and deemed he had no choice or there would be another charge. Then he was marched through a steel door with an oversize lock into the cell area.

The jail was old. The brown tile on the floor had been worn down to the black backing. Bare light bulbs with green reflectors illuminated a corridor lined with cells. Urine yellow paint covered the ceiling and walls. Vertical bars that kept inmates from upsetting decent society were rusty.

Unlocking a cell with two double bunk beds, the warden

apologized that all the single cells were taken. Peter did not reply. He could not allow himself to believe he was being placed in a cell. Even the heavy door clanging behind him and the sharp metallic click of the lock were emanations from a fantasy. He was the Reverend Peter Campbell, pastor of prestigious Good Samaritan Church.

There was another occupant in the cell. An elderly man with orange hair was slouched like a two hundred pound bag of flour in the back corner of a lower bunk. His hands were clasped across his bulging stomach the way funeral directors arranged clients for viewing. His head was thrown back, and out of his half-open mouth rumbled a deep guttural snore. The noise of Peter's entry had disturbed him not at all.

Peter sat down on the other bunk and held his face in his hands. His mind would not stop whirring. This could not be happening. He had not been arrested and thrown into jail.

But as his mind slowed, it dawned on him that everything had happened just as he had experienced it. I *am* the pastor of Good Samaritan. But I'm in jail because the police say I disobeyed an order to disperse. That isn't it. He rubbed his face. I'm in jail because I came out of Assisi to try to keep the peace. They put people in jail for that?

He glanced over at his snoring cellmate. There was something familiar about the face, the tufted hair, the stout torso. But with the eyes closed and the head back so that Peter was staring up the other man's forested nose, it was hard to tell what he looked like.

Peter removed his shoes and lay on the bed. It reminded him of beds he had known as a boy at summer camp. The suspended mattress hung down like a hammock. He put one arm behind his head and stared up at the parallel line design on the mattress fabric above. His mind continued to slow, muscles released their grip. His eyelids grew heavy with weariness. He yawned, stretched, and in a few moments had drifted off.

17

When Peter awakened he looked at his watch. Three hours had passed. His cellmate was in the same position as before; from his mouth came the same liquid rumble. Peter pulled himself up with a jerk. Why hadn't someone come to see him? The trustees knew he was arrested. The whole debacle was probably shown on the eleven o'clock news. Why was he being allowed to stay there in humiliation? *When I was in prison, you visited me.* It occurred to him that he was part of a line of the unjustly imprisoned: Jeremiah, John the Baptist, the apostles Paul and Peter. Jesus himself was held over night by the kangaroo Sanhedrin court. Rare company. It brought some relief.

His cellmate stirred, licked his thick lips, opened his eyes. When he saw that Peter was looking at him, his head jerked up, and he pulled himself to a sitting position. Peter had seen him before. But where? He searched his mind, but nothing came. With the baggy corduroy trousers and shapeless wool coat, it was surely not at Good Samaritan on a Sunday morning.

Then when Peter caught the glare in the man's gaze and heard his name, it came. "Henchard," the man said. "Jim Henchard." He looked Peter up and down from the loafers on his feet to his cotton slacks, crew-neck sweater, and curly hair. "What's a man like you doin' in here?" His eyes blinked. "Who are you, anyway?"

Peter swung his feet over, placed them on the floor, and met Henchard's gaze with a bold stare. "I'm the Reverend Peter Campbell, pastor of the Church of the Good Samaritan." He felt no qualm, no shame in saying it. To the contrary, his chest swelled in recognition of the place he held under unwarranted persecution.

Henchard's eyes blinked as if he were staving off an attack of disorientation. "A rev'ernt? Can you beat that? A rev'ernt here in this hell-hole?" He shook his head. Then a glint shone in his eyes. His rough hands searched through the pockets of his jacket and finally drew out a thick, folded sheet. He smoothed it on the bed. "You're not goin' to believe this," he said.

As Peter looked over the sheet, he was sure Henchard did not recall that he had been to Good Samaritan and already given Peter his spiel. Henchard pointed to his own picture in the middle of the sheet and cited with an arrogant smile his friendship with those pictured around him: Billy Graham, Oral Roberts. There was smiling Rex Humbard. Peter said nothing.

The punch line came as if Peter were sitting in the opulent office of a huge Protestant cathedral or were the father of a sprawling Catholic enterprise. Henchard looked at him beseechingly. "I need money," he said. "God told me I've got to go to the President and warn him the end of the world is comin'."

Lies, Peter said to himself. He chided himself for being so guilt-ridden and gullible when Henchard had come into his office at the church. Henchard was like a lot of the people around him. Things weren't what they said they were. The trustees who had not come to visit him. He could serve *ex officio* on their board, but when he was arrested he ceased to exist. And the committee that had called him to lead Good Samaritan to discipleship. They had lied. There was no other way to put it. They had doffed church talk and tried to sound interested in discipleship so they could rope Peter into their glass temple. All they wanted was someone tall in their pulpit. Discipleship—they hadn't the faintest notion what the word meant.

Without a hint of accusation, Peter said, "Mr. Henchard, I've heard everything you've just said, and I don't believe a word of it. You're not an evangelist. You don't know those other evangelists. You're not going to Washington to warn the President. And the money you collect for your mission just goes to booze."

Henchard's jaw dropped; his eyes pinched up like those of a buzzard inspecting poisoned carrion. "I don't know what you're talkin' 'bout. Why I never before heard a Rev'ernt talkin' like this. You mean you don't *believe* what I'm saying. Don't you know the apostle Paul says the people of God *believe* all things?"

"Yes, I do," Peter replied. "But the Bible also says, 'Beware of wolves going around in sheep's clothing.'"

Mr. Henchard slouched back on the bed. "Well, I never," he mumbled. "Never in all my days have I heard a preacher talkin' like this. Lord, what is happenin'?"

"I'm not sure," Peter said loudly. "Except that a lot of things aren't what they appear to be." What they actually were, he could not be certain. But one thing he did know: it was time he took a fresh look at Good Samaritan.

18

Peter sat at his desk in the burning sun with his tie off and sleeves rolled up. He was now reconciled to the daily broiling. The secret was to get to the office early in the morning, work fast, then get out before dizzy spells began.

Outside the window, the garden tundra dried in the hot sun. The color and texture of adobe, looking as if a Mexican house had dissolved around the fountain and was flowing farther down the hill with each rainstorm, the ruin was now a bargaining chip the ladies of the garden club were using to demonstrate their anger at the Board of Trustees for taking no action at its meeting.

From the outer office came the shrill voice of Wesley Stone, the Synod bishop. Peter wondered why Wes hadn't been by since he had been called to Good Samaritan. A long interval, considering Peter had gotten to know him while requesting denominational funds appropriated for inner city projects. The funds were always delayed, so he had to go in person to see what was the holdup. And without exception

Wes met him with lips bowed in compassion: "The hungry and poor of the city are our first concern." He patted Peter on the back. "You're doing a great job. The entire Synod is beholden to you for keeping the church on the cutting edge of social reform."

Only now those words resounded with the same tinsel ring as Jim Henchard's protestations of his bedfellow relationships with electronic evangelists. Peter had never allowed himself to see that in Wes before. Now he realized the money was delayed and he had to crawl for it because Wes wanted to use it for other purposes—projects politically advantageous to his bid for archbishop. He had been making his run during those years. Behind the cellophane compassion in his eyes lurked a glare of ecclesiastical ambition, the pious thrust for power—cloaked with ingratiation. "Why, if the church asks me to serve, I would interpret it as the call of God." How many men, Peter wondered, had ever declined high office because they were willing to admit to their own incompetence?

The thought of high office reminded Peter of the three hours he had had to sit in jail. Sure, he was one with Jeremiah and the others. That had alleviated some guilt, but it hadn't made the ordeal pleasant.

"Peter, I can't believe it," Brenda had said when he was let out of the cell. She was standing in the booking office in her red sweatsuit. "I saw it on the 11 o'clock news. Why didn't you call?"

He hadn't thought of it. It was a dream. The trustees saw what happened, and he was sure they would explain the mistake.

"Well, I paid the bail fee," she said. "Let's get you home."

He had gone, but he still felt like a prisoner. No one on the Council stopped in, as if what had happened to him was a non-event, a bad dream the church had already forgotten.

On the Sunday afterward, when the National Guard Weekend Warriors screamed overhead he stopped his sermon dead. Why should he have to shout over such a racket?

After all, the planes were there by Good Samaritan's choice. His request to the Council that it petition the Air National Guard to alter its Sunday morning operation had been soundly defeated. "America needs a strong military defense." "The pilots are patriotic young men who need practice, and if Good Samaritan can be at their service, that's a small price to pay for national security." The weekly dissection of the sermon seemed to bother no one. As Peter waited for the fourth plane to fly over, he thought perhaps the congregation might prefer twenty minutes of jet whine in place of a sermon, since Communist aggression seemed more on its mind than Christian discipleship.

19

The phone buzzed. "Bishop Stone," came Miss Hensley's cold voice.

Wes bounced into the office and extended a hand strangely limp considering he had narrowly lost the campaign for archbishop. Drooping eyes showed his sixty-three years which made him too old to run again. The bald dome of his head, reddened by the summer sun, set off boldly the white fringe of hair that ran in a circle from temple to temple like a fallen halo. His small hand was stiff, his movements as he sat down in the plastic chair, staccato. Apparently being a bishop required him to exude energy, although Peter envisioned him at home at the end of a day unwinding like a toy soldier and slumping behind the TV like most regular people. Maybe sub-regular, because he couldn't envision Wes popping the tab off a beer or kicking his shoes off, or even slipping out of the black clerical suit and reverse collar that Peter had never seen him without. He and the suit were one, just as he and his position blended into a single smooth integration of language and movements and saccharine smile that someone somewhere must have declared was the look permanently sculpted on God's face. The *imago Dei*.

From a gold chain around Wes's neck hung a brass cross. Its vertical member about the length of a cigar, it had the same smooth sheen as the furtive imposter that appeared on Good Samaritan's communion table.

Peter had admitted into his office a symbol of desecration. Miss Hensley could broil the building's inhabitants, John Rhodes could bellyache about how the church persecuted him, but the brass cross glinting against dull black fabric had to go. He felt like jerking it from the bishop's chicken neck and throwing it in the trash. But pastors of status churches didn't do things like that to their bishops, so he just brought his chair around in front of the desk so he and Wes could look out on the dissolving adobe house. "Well, what brings you to Good Samaritan?" Peter asked.

Wes's imago smile broadened. Peter could see nothing to smile about, certainly not the garden or what had happened to him the past week. "I hadn't planned to drop in so soon," Wes replied. There was a hint of pique in his voice, as if by showing up ahead of schedule he were lowering himself. "I usually wait 'til a man's been in a new position for about a year and then stop by to see how he's doing." Wes tugged at his nose as if he were being bitten by a gnat. His eyes slid without expression across the dry clay of the rose garden. "But I've been getting so many calls from your parishioners I thought I should come a bit earlier."

"Calls?" Peter asked. No one had said anything to him about calling the bishop.

"Phone calls." As if there could be some other kind. The back of Peter's neck burned at the thought that while he endured the week of silence, parishioners were bending Wes's ear. "This the rose garden?" Wes asked with a wave toward the tundra.

Peter confirmed that it was.

Wes sighed loudly. "Does look like it needs work. That's what the calls were about. Sounds as if you've had some bad luck with the soil."

Peter nodded reluctantly. He didn't give a damn about

the roses. What about the Board of Trustees, the police, his being thrown in jail?

Wes's eyes played over the garden as if it were populated with starving children. "All those roses the women planted dying. It's a terrible shame."

Peter suppressed the rage tightening his throat. "They've had the soil tested," he said coldly. "Nobody can figure out what's wrong. The women want to dig down two feet and bring in new."

"That's what I was told." Wes squinted up at the blazing orb heating the room. "That must've been some trustee meeting."

Peter waited for him to continue, but Wes seemed caught up in the interplay of the sun on curved panes. Peter twisted about in his chair and pulled one leg up across the other. He was never comfortable with Wes's meandering way of getting at whatever he wanted to talk about. When Peter had wanted money, he had to sit through hours of hard luck stories about churches and ministers. It was Wes's way of exerting his authority. At times, Peter was tempted to apologize that the inner city got any funds at all. The thought of it further stiffened his muscles. "What are you here to talk about?" he asked. He made no attempt to disguise the irritation in his voice.

Wes's head bowed as if he were sinking into prayer. "Nothing much, I hope," he said.

"That's not very specific."

Wes cast him a vacant look. "It's just that the people who called were very concerned about the way the incident at the trustee meeting was handled. And having everyone see it on the TV news that night. It's given the church a bad image." He paused, waiting for Peter to reply.

"Yes, it was stupid of the trustees to call the police," Peter said. "If they'd waited, the demonstrators would have gone their way, and we could have continued the meeting." His flesh crawled as he remembered the look of triumph on Mr. Krohn's gray face. Triumph over what?

Wes's smile turned into a grin of condescension. "I'm afraid you misunderstand. It wasn't the police the people who called me were upset about. It was you. What were you doing waving at the helicopter, challenging the police line — they think you were protecting the demonstrators."

Peter pulled himself up straight. Blood pounded in his ears. "I'll *tell* you what I was doing. It's what those callers could have found out if they'd had the decency to come in here instead of prattling behind my back." His hands jumped on the arms of the chair; the sun's heat fueled the fire growing in his chest. "I was trying to keep peace. If the demonstrators and the police had clashed, there would've been bloodshed. You've seen it yourself on TV. All I was trying to do was keep police from knocking heads and prevent people a bit overenthusiastic about their ideals from doing something they would regret." He paused, holding his rage in check. "I didn't invite the police. I didn't invite the TV people. I just went out to do what I thought a pastor should do."

Wes's expression did not change. "But the demonstrators were trespassing on church property. They were breaking the law."

Peter glared at him. "I don't like to think that people walking on church property are trespassing. It may well fit the Pharisees, but I don't see any territorial imperative in Jesus."

Wes's chin rose until he was looking down at Peter. "You *sound* as if you sided with the demonstrators."

"Am I on trial here? Who are my accusers? Isn't this a strange way for people in this congregation to deal with a problem?"

Wes's pallid hand waved him off. "Now, Peter, let's not get overexcited. I am your bishop. I have a right to know what happened."

The anger burning in Peter's throat leapt free. "Well, I'll tell you what happened. It's not demonstrators I'm concerned about. What do you think of a Board of Trustees that watches its pastor get arrested and doesn't lift a finger? I sat down there in that stinking jail for three hours with an alcoholic who thinks he's Elijah, and no one from the church came to see about my well-being. Since then, there's been a conspiracy of silence you could cut with a knife. Where's the Christian concern in this church? The compassion? I'm beginning to think all they want is to fight for their own causes. There certainly was no attempt at the trustees' meeting to keep the peace."

Wes fingered his brass cross as if it afforded protection against angry ministers. "You've got it all wrong. They think you sided with the demonstrators. Some even think you authorized their being there. You did keep going out to talk to them during the meeting."

"To prevent violence," Peter almost shouted. "No one else made a move to do anything."

Wes's nose rose several degrees. "Except call the police. Which is precisely what they should have done because what the demonstrators were doing was illegal."

Peter took a deep breath. "Was it immoral too?"

Wes hesitated, then said, "Whatever is illegal is immoral."

Peter rolled his head back and smiled. "I wish your seminary professors could hear you now. You could rewrite the Bible."

Wes's face turned a shade redder. "We're getting off the point. You talk about peace. Well, I'm trying to hold a church together that's bent on tearing itself apart. And the pastor is in the front line of those doing it."

The sun's heat poured down like hot lead. Peter checked his watch. He was past due for getting out of the office. He wanted Wes and his toy cross gone. "I don't think we're getting anywhere roasting here and arguing. What do you want me to do?"

Wes's eyes took on a sardonic glint. "The most important thing has already been done."

"What's that?"

Wes's eyes shone like those of a child who has just beaten his friends at a game. "The trustees met and resolved the problem of the garden."

"Met?" Peter exclaimed. "When? Where?" His head whirled in protest.

"Two nights ago at the Delaware Club."

Peter's chest hurt as if he had been kicked. For a moment, he could not speak. "How could they? I didn't receive any notice. I'm *ex officio*."

Wes's eyes glowed with power. "They voted thirty thousand."

Peter gulped a mouthful of suffocating air. "Thirty thousand? When the request was only for fifteen? And they met without giving me notice?"

"They invited me to take your place. Legally, that can be done you know."

Peter's neck stiffened. He leaned forward. "Only if I'm incapacitated. Or if I extend the invitation."

"Well, details. They're nothing to worry about. I told the Board I was sure you'd approve of what they did."

Peter's hands clenched the arms of the chair. "I can't believe it," he gasped. "An illegal meeting . . . thirty thousand . . ."

"We saved you a lot of trouble," Wes said. "There's some question about your competence to handle this congregation. I know Dr. Strong was here a long time and that can make problems for a new man."

Peter fired back. "Who says I lack competence?"

Wes rubbed his hands together and pressed them palm to palm as if he were again resorting to prayer. "Well, let's put it this way. Every congregation has certain people who are leaders. Some are on the boards. Some aren't. A pastor has to deal with those people — if he's truly competent, that is. They're the ones who've invested themselves in the church. They look out for its well-being. It's just that there's a feeling abroad you haven't been doing that. These people feel neglected. There's word that you haven't visited them.

They expected you to join the Delaware Club, but you seem to have no intention of doing so. To put it simply, in their eyes you lack style."

Peter knew who most of them were. The well-heeled who had put money into the church over the years. Some up-and-comers who expected instant recognition in every organization they joined. "You mean I won't lick their boots," he said.

"Peter, let's not lose control." Wes's tone waxed paternal. "I'm sure you realize leading a congregation like this is a very complicated business. The people I'm talking about are used to having their own way. And why shouldn't they?" Wes's head nodded as if such knowledge were self-evident. "They've worked their way up the ladder. They've earned respect in the community. They're the fabric of which this great nation is made." Wes dropped his hands and faced Peter squarely. "They're also the biggest contributors to this church. Look at what Gottschalk has done. And Miss Hayes."

Peter let his eyes stray over the gully ruin of the garden, his brain numbed at the hours he had put into the fracas over finishing it. As for Gottschalk—he peered up at the blazing white sun and swore silently to himself. An elderly parishioner dying of cancer had told him about Gottschalk's generous gift: "Gottschalk Glass made the four round buildings for a private botanical garden that went bankrupt before they were delivered. Gottschalk had no place to put them, so he dumped them on Good Samaritan as a tax write-off." Peter hauled out his handkerchief and swabbed the sweat trickling down his face.

"I don't see that kind of ministry as Christian," he said. "Jesus went to the poor. The letter of James says we shouldn't ignore the needy and honor the man with the gold ring."

Wes's hands flicked in irritation. "Don't give me a Bible lesson. I've been in the ministry a lot longer than you have." His voice rose. "Neither Jesus nor James ever had to lead a wealthy twentieth century congregation. If they had, they would've altered their approach. All this first century idealism isn't worth a damn when it comes to the day-to-day running of a church. You've got to be practical. That's all these people understand. Your job as pastor is to deal with them where they are. They don't know about poor people in Palestine or some man with a gold ring. They know about a full sanctuary and a well-run organization and a balanced budget and programs that draw people and put the church on the map. All they need from you is a little help to get through the week — affirmation that God is well-pleased with their hard work. That's all. These ideals some ministers get in their heads just mess things up. People get mad. There are fights. Churches are damaged for years. We've had too many already. That's why I've come to you. I don't want to see you hurt. And Good Samaritan is too fine a congregation to be torn up by indiscretions." Wes's voice floated in the burning air.

"You came out of concern?" Peter asked.

"Why certainly. I am the bishop of this Synod. The well-being of its ministers and churches is my responsibility."

The words rattled like Henchard's spiel about his friendship with the evangelists. Wes was doing the same thing he had done when Peter wanted funds for the inner city. Words, nothing but words. An awkward silence was broken only by the clack of typewriters in the outer office. "Ticks me off those trustees met behind my back," Peter said softly. He turned to Wes. "It was illegal. You know that. They're required to notify all the members."

"They notified me," Wes replied calmly. "They were afraid if they notified you there would be a demonstration at the Club. Surely you understand their anxiety."

"They think I marshalled the opponents of the proposal?" Peter asked.

Wes pursed his lips. "They didn't say that. It's just that there's a leak somewhere. They wanted to make sure everything was kept in confidence."

Peter felt the stabbing implication of guilt. "And I suppose the fact that no demonstrators came shows I'm the source of the leak?"

Wes's eyebrows jumped with irritation. "It doesn't prove a thing. They needed to make a decision. Now it's done. For the peace and unity of the church it was the only course."

"Even if it was illegal?"

Wes's cheeks puffed; tiny red lines traced intricate patterns across the whites of his eyes. "Dammit, Peter. Don't you see I had to do something to prevent a real disaster?" His head quivered in frustration. "I'm beginning to wonder why I even came to talk to you. You're so stubborn. You always have been. All you could see in the inner city was the need for money." He glared at Peter. "And I gave you thousands."

"It wasn't yours to give," Peter said. He was about to demonstrate the link between Wes's political ambitions and the disbursement of funds, but he found such an accusation distasteful. "What did you really come here for?" he asked.

The redness in Wes's face diminished, a pietistic grin appeared. "Your trustees need help announcing their decision to the congregation."

Peter made no response.

"They need *your* help, Peter. They don't know what will happen when word gets out."

Peter laughed out loud. "So the trustees have gotten themselves into a helluva mess, and now I'm brought in to bail them out?"

"They did the best they could. They wanted to make the decision peacefully." Wes paused, his face sagging with a look of pious beseeching. "Look, this whole situation is very trying. Good Samaritan is the plum of the Synod. It's the biggest church, it has the strongest influence. As you know, the pastor of this congregation speaks for the denomination in this part of the Synod."

Peter felt an impulse to suggest such a statement was inane, but resisted.

Wes pressed his hands together as if again entering into prayer. "When this congregation has trouble, it sends waves through every church in the Synod."

Peter wished he could swat down such droning and step on it like an insect. "Money? Is that what you're talking about?"

Wes's droop of compassion vanished. "What?" he asked.

Peter felt the conversation tilting in his favor. "The contribution to the Synod budget. Good Samaritan's is the biggest. Isn't that what you're driving at?"

Wes's eyes drifted off to the garden as if in the midst of the adobe he were witnessing a rerun of the Transfiguration. "That never crossed my mind."

Peter stood up, crossed to the windows, checked the louvers to make sure they were open. His head felt like it was floating on the perspiration soaking his shirt collar. His muscles were as flaccid as jello left out of the refrigerator. He sat on a corner of his desk and looked down at Wes. "What is it you want me to do?"

Wes looked up. The pleading tone was back. "The trustees are very worried about how their decision will go over."

Peter saw weatherless faces singing a hymn, eyes glazed during a sermon. "Well, I can tell them. When they announce it, some people will feel this church is going to the dogs. Others will grin with satisfaction because their side won. And the rest—most of them that is—will sit there like they're at a wake where the body hasn't arrived."

"You're cynical," Wes said.

"Not cynical. Realistic."

Wes drew out a pair of wireless spectacles, carefully placed them on his nose, and stared at Peter. "I'm not sure I know what you're up to."

Peter waved his arms. "Don't get excited. Part of it is that I'm giddy from the heat in here."

Wes glanced about as if his improved vision confirmed the presence of excessive warmth. "By gadfry, it is hot. I thought it was me. Why don't you turn on the air conditioner? With all this glass on a sunny day like this . . ."

"Trustee regulations. Your wealthy church is saving

energy. The air conditioner goes on only when we've had a fatality."

"Fatality?"

"Heat prostration."

Wes squinted as if his ears had suddenly gone bad. "Like this every day? I never knew."

Peter nodded. "We love it. It makes us a hardy bunch of sacrificing disciples."

Wes's eyes wobbled as if they were coming loose in their sockets. "The trustees want you to keep the decision under wraps until this Sunday. Then you're to announce it in the worship service. Before you do, you're to tell how they arrived at it, how it was their responsibility to make it, and how the congregation must abide by what they've done."

"And the reason they voted thirty thousand instead of fifteen?"

"They would have lost members otherwise. They did what was best for the church."

"You mean for a few horticulture-minded members with bulging bank accounts."

"I can't believe you're not taking this seriously. The trustees are afraid it could split the congregation. They're up the creek."

Peter stared out at the garden scarp and said nothing. As far as he was concerned, the trustees could stay up the creek. That's what they had done with him. Only worse. They'd let him rot in jail.

Wes blinked as if the sun soaking into his black uniform had brought him to the threshold of sunstroke. Peter thought of suggesting Wes seek shelter, but it had been Wes's decision to come and sit in the sun to beguile Peter into his twisted plan.

"Look, maybe the meeting wasn't done the way it should've been," Wes said. "I don't know all the angles. There are times when matters are very touchy."

Peter pulled out his handkerchief and swabbed the sweat dripping from his chin. "I have an idea. You come Sunday and announce the decision. I'll even relinquish the pulpit of your most prized church so you can deliver one of your eloquent sermons." Peter envisioned the rhetorical bowing and scraping—the congregation was wonderful, the church great, the commitment to Christ heartwarming. It was like sitting under a spigot of hot syrup. Wes and the congregation could even adulate each other's brass crosses.

Wes's head shook jerkily. "I can't," he said. "I'm already committed."

Peter threw his head back in abandon. "Break the commitment. This is an emergency. A time for altering the rules—just like you did with the trustee meeting."

Wes rose from the chair, his knees wobbling. Whatever response he had planned to use if Peter refused seemed to have been baked out of his mind. His eyes swam in overheated fluid. "I've got to leave," he gasped. "Peter, I'll say it once more. I'm damned tired of arguing with you. Do what your trustees want, or you're going to be in a helluva lot more trouble than just sitting in jail. I can't imagine what's come over you. I trust that when you've thought this over you'll act responsibly." With his arms extended scarecrow-like to keep him balanced, he turned toward the door, lurched through it, and was gone.

Peter leaned back against the desk. He could not recall ever having stood up to Wes so stubbornly. A hint of the concern Wes felt for the trustees still hung in the air. There was none in him, none at all.

20

Peter was looking out the living area window when Mr. Shanklet turned in to the driveway. Immediately Peter went out to head him off, but Mr. Shanklet had walked past Mr. Tazano's wrecker and was in the garage.

Mr. Tazano, black-haired, stocky, wearing black pants and a white T-shirt, was holding the stepladder while Jeff cut through garage joists with a power saw. Mr. Tazano's junkyard was the source of most of the iron that had gone into Trojan, and he was glad to come whenever Jeff needed help. He also supplied the oily lumber with which Jeff was shoring up rafters weakened by cutting. The garage reeked of sawburned wood, oil, and welding torch burn which Peter surmised was permanently embedded in the walls and roof.

"What's going on?" Mr. Shanklet shouted with the veins in his neck bulging. They also stood out on his forehead where his crew cut laid bare a generous portion of scalp.

Unable to hear above the scream of the saw, Jeff ignored Mr. Shanklet. Mr. Tazano's eyes darted uncertainly, he ventured no answer.

Mr. Shanklet jerked forward, grasped the ladder and gave it a slight shake. Jeff looked down, took in Mr. Shanklet with Peter standing behind him, and shut down the saw.

"What's the idea?" Mr. Shanklet sputtered.

Jeff pointed to the hole he was cutting above Trojan's front end. "This is where the head goes. The garage is so small I've got to make more room." He was matter-of-fact, as if Mr. Shanklet ought to know what had to be done without asking.

"You're destroying property that docsn't belong to you," Mr. Shanklet said. His eyes took in Trojan filling the garage from front to back. "This thing's a monstrosity. It's too big, too heavy. You should never have been allowed to start it."

Peter stepped into Mr. Shanklet's line of vision. "I told the committee that called us. If you weren't warned, it's their fault."

"This floor." Mr. Shanklet scrutinized the concrete. "It'll never take weight like this. This is a garage. For cars. So they won't be left out overnight and get the neighbors riled up." His arms writhed. He pointed to the house with the window where the curtain twitched but the people never appeared. "Those people are threatening to take the church to court."

"That's the church's problem," Peter said. "The church forced us to take this house."

Again Mr. Shanklet ignored him. "I want this mess out of here in a week," he shouted. "I don't know where you'll put it. I don't care. One week. That's it." His face burned red, veins throbbed.

"Well, it won't be done in a week," Jeff said quietly.

Mr. Shanklet was heading back to his car. "One week. I'm reporting this to the trustees. Maybe we'll take you to court."

With a jerk, he got into his car, slammed the door, and sped off.

Jeff turned to Peter and sighed. "Boy, am I getting tired of him."

"Don't let it worry you," Peter said. "They can't do anything to us."

"But your job?"

"Don't worry about that either. Trojan's the least of my problems."

Jeff climbed down the ladder. "There is one thing." He bent over and studied the floor where Trojan's legs rested on it. "There are some hairline cracks I don't think were here before. The concrete's real thin, like they got a cheap job."

"They probably did," Peter conceded.

"So if it needs fixing after I'm done?"

"We'll take care of it. You're doing fine." Peter looked up through the hole in the joists. "How high is the head going to go?"

Jeff hesitated. "Well, the head on the real Trojan was real high."

"How high?"

"To the peak of the roof," Jeff replied, averting his gaze. "Dad, it's got to be authentic. It's a lot smaller than the original. But at least it's got to look like the original."

Peter sighed. "I suppose so," he said. He looked at the ports in the flanks, strands of metal shaped so Trojan had a tail. Such fine detail. So artistically rendered. He felt expansive. "It's great work, Jeff. And I'm not saying that just because you're my son."

Jeff smiled. "Thanks, Dad." He climbed the ladder, lifted the saw into position, and turned it on. The blade screamed, sawdust sifted down, Mr. Tazano held the ladder firmly.

21

Jackie's recruits vacated the family room, and the house resumed its usual quietness. Jackie came up with wrinkles in her broad forehead. "Dad, I'm worried."

"About what?" Peter asked.

"We decided to tell Diane's father to go ahead and sue the School Board. He offered to do it for nothing."

"Well, what's wrong with that? Nothing else has worked."

"Dad, there are church members on that board. Two of them. Things are liable to get worse for you."

If what Jackie said was a threat, Peter did not feel it. While he was still uneasy when the house was full of her burn-out recruits, if she rescued one of them, her cause was of value. "I'm not worried," he said.

She eyed him closely. "You're really coming around."

"What does that mean?"

"Don't you remember at first how threatened you were by those kids?"

"I'm still threatened," he said.

"Oh," she replied, and then shook her head as if illogical fathers were the new vogue.

22

Brenda came up to Peter. He had just arrived home. "Are you ready for a shock?" There was an impish glint in her eyes.

Peter smiled. "I think I'm beyond that. What's up?"

"This play I'm dancing in. It's very theological."

He cast her a puzzled glance. "Theological? Since when is there shock in that?"

Her eyes danced with energy, the dimples in her cheeks deepened. "I'm Eve," she blurted.

"Eve?"

She nodded.

"Before or after the invention of clothes?"

"Before."

"So that's the shock. An apocalyptic confrontation with human skin."

Brenda smiled. "We're doing it discreetly. But you have to remember this is Oakdale. What *we* think is discreet might not pass muster with everyone else."

"No question about that," Peter said. Certainly the public Oakdale would have something to say. Privately most of them probably relished human flesh. "I'm not worried. If that's the shock you're wondering about."

"Well, I didn't think you needed more problems, but this play is very important to me." She paused. "Not just because I'm getting back to ballet. It's got something very important to say. I believe in it."

Peter kissed her. "If you believe in it, then I believe in it," he said.

23

The congregation sat restlessly in the baking sun. Men wiped bald heads and sweating brows. Women sat stiffly beneath broad-rimmed hats that shaded smooth faces. Small children wiggled and folded bulletins into airplanes and asked their parents when the service was going to end. Teenagers stretched, sighed, and looked about to see if they could catch anyone sleeping.

The brass cross was back. Denying blood, denying suffering, denying any discomfort for the sake of Christ, Good Samaritan's idol taunted from its perch on the communion table. Peter could live with it only because he was certain one day it would be gone.

The sermon on self-denial finished, Mr. Straphe led the choir in an anthem that depicted Jesus at the beck and call of whatever egocentric whims popped into the vacant minds of believers. Mr. Straphe was clearly on the side of the shining idol.

Announcing that Mr. Krohn had an important message from the Board of Trustees, Peter kept his voice free of emotion. The gray Board chairman rose from his pew with a jerk as if he had been stabbed by a hatpin. His face was twisted into the same scowl it had worn when Peter had told him firmly he would not do the Board's dirty work of reporting its action to the congregation.

The small figure pushed his way to the aisle and started forward. At the standing microphone in the chancel, he turned to face the congregation. His hands groped into his trouser pockets, out, into his jacket pockets, out. He fumbled with the front button of his jacket, fingered his shirt collar as if it were choking him.

The trembling in his voice was amplified by the PA system and the echo off encircling glass. He started as if he were reading a history book: the dear ladies had planted roses and then they died. They planted more roses, and they died. Experts found the soil contaminated, so it was replaced. More roses were planted; they died. Plantings multiplied, the slaughter doubled, tripled, quadrupled. A report on thousands of infants dying every day in remote reaches of the Third World could not have elicited the same sorrowful tone as the mounting heap of comatose roses.

Enter the Board of Trustees — Lone Rangers mounted on horses of compassion handing out sacrificial bullets of garden resuscitation proposals. Poor Miss Hayes' bequest had been exhausted by the plant-consuming plagues. A digression into the saintly virtues of that gullible soul who hardly darkened the door of the church. In her dying breath she had thought of nothing but Good Samaritan, the most beautiful place in the State for a rose garden. Peter recognized the words and phrases as verbatim Mrs. Clayton. Her hawk eyes in the third pew never wavered from Mr. Krohn's diminished frame. From the sadness welling up in his voice, Mr. Krohn sounded as if he would have to stop and stanch the surfeit of emotion stuffing his nose.

And how the trustees had suffered in order to make the decision. While seeking God's will, they were set upon by long-haired savages who pushed their way into the church and hurled threats. These ragtag malcontents were part of a conspiracy to disrupt Good Samaritan and plant seeds of Communist sedition. Outside the window of the meeting, they hurled obscenities and threatened to damage the property. But the trustees held their ground and called the police.

Not a mention of Peter's attempt to avoid bloodshed. Nothing about unjust arrest and being thrown into the town jail for three hours. Just Lone Rangers and trespassers and Miss Hayes and dying breath. She'd said a lot in her dying breath, Peter surmised.

Then to the catacombs of the Delaware Club. The Lone Rangers fulfilling their bounden duty to Miss Hayes, to the garden club, to the entire congregation and its upstanding image in the community. Bishop Stone's name bounced off the surrounding glass like variations on a theme. He had counseled the Board, suggested the meeting place; he was there to help make the decision. Everything was on the up and up. Not a mention of the illegality that Peter had not been notified, that they could be censured by the Synod Judicial Commission were he to charge them with violating the Standing Rules.

Mr. Krohn's hands clenched and unclenched. His voice wound tighter and tighter, rose in pitch. Peter had a premonition that if the speech went much further, Mr. Krohn might surpass the limits of his gray body and pass out.

Mr. Krohn halted as if all his energy had been expended on the preamble. Only the decision remained to be uttered. He stood perfectly rigid as if what he was to say had stuck like a chicken bone in his throat and he needed the Heimlich procedure to get it dislodged. His voice high and strained, he said, "The Board of Trustees decided . . ."

One, two, three, in the sky above the center dome flashed the Weekend Warriors. Shadows, glints of silver; panes rattled, the structure swayed, the congregation looked up as if its judgment were drawing nigh. Mr. Straphe's eyes rolled heavenward in his circular face framed by peacock hair standing straight out.

Mr. Krohn's hands slid in and out of his pockets. He too looked up, but the sky had given up its charges. Their thunder diminished to a complaining rumble, a summer storm foundering on the peaks of distant mountains.

He lowered his head and resumed as if his speech had been rewound on a tape recorder. The trustees had met at the Delaware Club with the blessing of Bishop Stone, who was present, and the Board had decided to appropriate for the garden . . .

Plane number four. Peter had been expecting it. It usually came late, but he could never predict how late. When he stopped his sermons and waited, it seemed like hours. Invariably, if he resumed after only three, the fourth shredded what was left of his discourse. He could not restrain the smile creeping onto his face.

Mr. Krohn hauled out his handkerchief, wiped his face and brow. With the handkerchief somewhat shielding his lips, he blurted, "The Board voted thirty grand for the garden." The handkerchief came down with such a jerk it looked as if an alert for incoming artillery had just been sounded and Mr. Krohn was about to run for cover. But he didn't. He just stood ramrod stiff as if he had no idea what to do next.

Pat Andrews shot to her feet. She was a third of the way from the back in the center section. "I can't believe it," she hissed. Mr. Krohn flinched. Her outburst drew squints from other quarters of the sanctuary. A few worshippers stood with angry looks. Shaking their heads, they pushed their way to the aisles, paused to scowl at Mr. Krohn, stomped to the doors and vanished.

The rest sat. Some whispered in angry tones. Others, including bug-eyed Mrs. Clayton, embraced Mr. Krohn with benevolent smiles. Most looked as Peter had predicted—a wake without a body. Maybe they knew nothing about roses or Miss Hayes or thirty grand. Or maybe when they came to church they left behind their receiving apparatus so nothing said could penetrate to their centers of control.

When the back of Mr. Krohn's neck lost its quartz pallor and blood resumed flowing, he dismounted the chancel and jerkily returned to his seat.

At the door, Peter warmly grasped sweaty hands and wished their bearers a cheery good morning. Questions about his opinion of the garden decision flew at him, but he deflected them all. "Ask Mr. Krohn." "Ask Bishop Stone." "Ask members of the Board," he told his inquirers.

It was clear the trustees had misjudged the size of the opposition. It went far beyond Pat Andrews and her demonstrators. Charlie Jarvis almost wrenched Peter's arm from its socket. "It's a travesty. It's a desecration." Charlie's salesman vocabulary was too meager to get his anger off his chest. All he could do was wheeze in Peter's face and vow, "The Board hasn't heard the last of me."

One voice Peter did not deflect. It came from a woman he only occasionally saw at worship. Thin, in her late thirties, always alone, blond hair pulled back, clad in a loose stylish dress with a cowl neck. He was hardly aware she was talking to him.

"I think you should know something about Miss Hensley. She's got a circle of gossips she leaks things to. She's always done it. I don't think Dr. Strong knew. If he did, he did nothing about it. It could nail you. That's what I'm concerned about."

Then she was gone, an apparition sweeping through the glass tube toward Assisi. But the words remained.

24

The morning sun struck a corner of Peter's desk, leaving the rest of the office in cool shadow. The louvers beneath the windows were open, but with no breeze flowing across the garden ruin, no air came in. Miss Hensley sat perched forward in the plastic chair as if it were coated with a corrosive. The cords in her neck strained with tension, her cheeks were as rigid as slabs of ice, her eyes burned with the overflow of a brain with a superhuman penchant for control.

Peter let her sit in silence. What evidence he had was circumstantial. There was a time he would not have acted on such a basis. But since his involuntary stay in the local jail, a strange abandon had come over him.

Miss Hensley sighed and adjusted her position in the chair. Peter leveled his gaze at her. "Miss Hensley." He intended the chill in his voice. "It appears that information privy only to you and to me has been getting out of the office to the congregation."

The bony frame pressed into the chair and grew stiffer, the eyes filled with black contempt. The pallid lips quivered but said nothing.

"People not on the Council have called me in advance of meetings to tell me how the Council should vote. Prior to the meeting of the trustees on the garden" — he nodded toward the furrows of clay outside the window where Mr. Jackson, the contractor, was looking about — "dozens of people knew what the proposal would be. None of them are members of the Board."

Peter paused and waited for some sign of dis-ease, a slight squirming of the pallid body that would indicate a tremor in the soul. There was none. Just eyes pinched in contempt as if Peter were some vermin that had stolen its way into the church.

He leaned forward. "Do you know anything about these,

these leaks?"

"Nothing," Miss Hensley said in a tone that could have been made by a machine.

"As I said," Peter continued, "only you and I had access to that information . . ."

"And the people who wrote it and those who helped them, and anyone they might have talked to." She spit words like a machine gun. "We aren't the only ones who know what's coming before the boards. And in case you haven't noticed it yet, people in this church like to talk."

She was right, of course. Others did have access. But Peter had no evidence any of them had broken their trust; no one had come up to him and whispered that anyone other than Miss Hensley was leaking information to the congregation.

The bony frame roused itself. "If you're accusing me of leaking" — she said the term with a shudder as if it described a crime so heinous she was incapable of contemplating it — "information, you're sorely mistaken. I've worked for this church for over twenty years, and in all that time, no one has ever accused me of doing anything underhanded." Words hissed through her teeth like the darting tongue of a viper.

Peter paused to take stock. He wished he could fall back on hard facts, but he would never bring himself to play the role of detective. That was not his calling. He could mention that a woman had told him she knew information was leaking out of the office, but he would not call the woman to have her repeat her statement before Miss Hensley. And if Miss Hensley truly was an old hand at spreading rumors, then people would fear her ability to start rumors about them. In the conspiracy of silence that gripped Good Samaritan, words could be the most deadly of weapons.

Softening his expression, he said, "Well, I was just concerned. I think you understand. It looked as if information was getting out through the office."

The flesh around Miss Hensley's eyes pinched in with innocence. "I can't believe I would be accused. Are people spreading lies?"

Now she was the inquisitor, and he the defendant. He shrugged his shoulders as if the question were trivial. "Oh, there might have been a word or two. Nothing serious."

Miss Hensley arched with indignation. Was there a glint of fear in those black eyes? "Who? Who said I was spreading things?"

"Just rumors," Peter said. "Nothing anyone would bring into the open."

Her cheeks trembled as if she suffered from a nervous tic Peter had not previously noticed. "Why, I've been smeared."

Peter waved his arms loosely. "No, no. It's nothing to get upset about. Just a rumor." He paused. "But information has gotten out. The boards are holding me responsible for making sure it doesn't happen again."

Miss Hensley stood with a jerk. "Well, then you'd better make your accusation against members of the boards. The nerve." Her fists clenched. "After the way I've slaved for this church. If that's the thanks I get." Self-pity rang in her voice. Her arms writhed as if she were combating an invisible foe.

Peter leaned back to observe the show, as if he were part of a theatre audience awaiting the climax of a dramatic conflict. The complaining tone of voice, the eyes flashing with anger could be the start of a scenario leading to a tearful resignation. He was ready to draw out his pen so she could sign a document before she changed her mind.

Her eyes flamed. "I'll get even with them." She turned stiffly to the door and stopped. "Ingrates. After all I've slaved." Her voice crackled with revenge.

Peter did not reply. He was amazed that the boards were the target of her anger and not him. Or was she hiding rage at him beneath that fire of righteous indignation? The door closed behind her with a bang.

Reflected sunlight glared up all across his desk. Perspiration beaded on his forehead and trickled down into his eyes. Even though it was only mid-morning, his shirt was soaked.

When Miss Hensley buzzed to indicate he had a phone

call, he could hear no hint of pique that he had accused her earlier that morning. Perhaps she had already ventilated her anger by piping out to her grapevine complaints that she was being persecuted. Her phone light had been on non-stop since he had talked to her. Yes, she could smear him—he saw that now more than he had before. Yet he felt no regret for what he had done. Any church that would let him sit in jail would also leave him imprisoned behind a secretary who held over him the threat of rumor. It wasn't right.

The ground rumbled from the direction of the garden. Partitions had been removed from Benedict, a yellow tractor with a digging bucket on the front and a dozer blade on the back had trundled onto the ruin. A thin man wearing a baseball cap guided the machine; behind trailed Mr. Jackson, Mrs. Clayton and several more garden club members festooned in old shirts, baggy pants, and an assortment of wide-brimmed sun hats. Their gesticulations swept over the whole garden, including John Rhodes—his body slouched in weariness as he approached them from the sanctuary.

25

The intercom buzzed. Miss Hensley's frigid tone announced that Miss Andrews had arrived for her appointment.

Pat entered the office dressed in loose slacks and a shapeless Indian pullover that looked as if it were made of burlap. Ignoring Peter, she rushed to the window and gazed out. "So they're starting today!" she hissed. "Scared to death we'll get the trustees' action reversed. Chickens!" The epithet bounced off the glass like a bullet.

The rasp of the tractor's engine increased as its bucket came up with a crumbling heap of yellow clay. It trundled out of sight through Benedict to dump its load into a waiting truck. Then it returned. At that rate, removing two feet of soil would take more than a week.

Pat sat down. "I'll make it short and sweet," she said. "I've come to the conclusion I no longer have a place in this church."

Peter recoiled. While he did not agree with all Pat's views or with the way she expressed them, she was still an important member. She wanted change. She wanted the church to be aware of people who were hurting. She helped keep its members from sucking in all the light of Christ the way a black hole drew in illumination. "I hope your decision isn't final."

"It is. Look at the record. We fought the trustees and lost. We appealed. They refuse to listen to us. We went to Bishop Stone about the illegality of the meeting. He just smiles and talks nonsense. There's nothing left for us to do but appeal to the denomination. For that, we've got to get a lawyer. When I get to the place where I've got to sue my own church in order to get the right things done, then I'd rather quit. What we'd gain isn't worth the price."

"You're not the only one who's upset. Others are fighting the trustees' action. They hope you get a hearing, even though they won't publicly give you support. The choir—it feels it's been betrayed on finishing the organ."

Pat's eyes flitted with anger. "Has Straphe resigned yet?"

"No," Peter replied. Straphe had called several times threatening to turn in his letter, but so far there had been nothing. Peter surmised the market for used choir directors was more depressed than Straphe had anticipated.

"He's probably bluffing," Pat said. "He's sure a strange bedfellow, but we need everybody we can get." She drew a cigarette out of her cloth satchel purse. "Do you mind?"

Peter frowned. The heat already burned his eyes. He didn't need cigarette smoke to boot, but this was not the time to censure. Air sifting through the louvers bore yellow dust that swirled in shafts of sunlight. Outside, clouds of dirt billowed out from where the tractor chattered in the shallow trench it had dug. The operator raised the bucket bearing a round cylinder—a rusted steel barrel from which leaked a stream of dark fluid. "What's that?" he asked distractedly. He went to the window. Pat came up behind him.

"A drum of something," she mumbled.

The tractor set the drum down, and Mr. Jackson and the ladies gathered around it. John Rhodes strode up and cast it a wary glance. The tractor operator stepped down from his throbbing machine to have a look.

Suddenly the tractor started to move. So quick was the slip of the clutch that engine vibrations did not alter their pitch. The audience around the drum was unaware the tractor was moving down the hill — toward the window at which Peter and Pat stood. Involuntarily, Peter shouted. But his voice merely bounced off the glass unheard by the party at the leaking drum.

He whirled toward Pat. She stood like a statue, cigarette in hand, lips still round from exhaling a cloud of smoke, eyes bulging. "My God!" she gasped.

Peter pounded on the glass until he thought it would break. Slowly the tractor operator's head came around. But he was too late. The tractor bobbed backward across ruts and holes, still aimed at the office. It must stop, Peter thought. Surely the blade on the back end would catch on the window frame and the engine stall. He and Pat shrank toward the door.

The control arm of the blade struck the window like a boulder. For milliseconds the glass held, then it exploded. Fragments rained into the office. Peter grabbed Pat's hand and opened the door. They paused.

The blade had jammed against his desk, the large rubber tires could not get traction on the window sill. The engine stammered as if about to die. Suddenly the tires caught, the tractor bounded through the window and thrust the desk toward where Peter and Pat were standing. Through the gaping hole in the window, Peter could see the operator running down the hill. He was wringing his hands.

Peter pushed Pat into the outer office. Miss Hensley looked up with alarm. Her body froze at the fright she saw on Pat and Peter's faces. "Out," Peter shouted. He realized he must look like a madman. His voice came back high and sharp. Blood pulsated in his ears. He was moving with involuntary jerks.

Miss Hensley's fright turned to defiance. Was that her only defense against the unexpected? "The tractor!" Peter shouted. His desk crashed through the wall separating the offices, shattering opaque rectangles of glass, and staggered toward Miss Hensley. She had the look of one stricken with palsy. Her eyes were vacant, the voltage from her brain must have blown all her fuses. Peter started toward her. Behind his desk came the tractor, a yellow bull huffing and wheezing: his desk lamp dangling from the dozer blade.

His desk crashed into Miss Hensley's, shoving hers against her concave stomach, propelling her, firmly mounted in her castored swivel chair, toward the outer office door. Having gained some mobility, Pat shouted and ran ahead as Peter jumped in order not to be crushed between Miss Hensley and the outer wall.

With a lurch, the desks and Miss Hensley changed direction so that she passed unscathed through the doorway into the outer lobby. Her body was as stiff as the chair in which she was riding. Her desk crashed into the doorjamb and halted. The building trembled, groaned. The tractor's heaving tires clawed at the tile floor. The office section shuddered, glass shattered, the doorjambs burst loose. Once again Miss Hensley led the parade of two desks and el toro tractor.

Now get her! a voice shouted at Peter from within. But there was no time to jump in front of the desks and pull her away. In seconds, she would be crushed against the main entrance doors leading to the parking lot. "Open the doors. Let her out!" he shouted to Pat. They both swung open the double doors. Miss Hensley's arms made a strange swimming motion as if she were drowning in the din of tractor engine concussions and the groans of the building swaying overhead.

She emerged unscathed through the door. Peter grabbed the chair and hurled it and its pale cargo toward the parking lot.

The doorjambs gave way. The dozer blade crashed into a vertical beam supporting the tension ring encircling the building. The arms of the bucket-loader wedged under the lintel, the tractor strained as if at last it would quit. For a moment, everything held.

The engine coughed. Suddenly the lintel broke loose from its supporting jambs, the blade tore out the beam angling to the tension ring, and the tractor jumped through the doors like a rodeo bull released from its stall. The structure trembled as if besieged by an earthquake. The tension ring parted, a roar of shattering glass rose like a thousand timpani. Pane after pane of the lower wall crashed onto surrounding walkways. Air gushed out like the sigh of a ruptured dirigible; the upper walls and dome started to sink. Pat and Peter jumped back to avoid being crushed. The sound of breaking glass was like an unending explosion. Blue light flickered where wires and connectors shorted out. The entire structure was metamorphosed into an immense circle of bent beams and splintered shards; the one piece clear dome settled onto the wreckage and tilted to one side like the skull cap of a rebellious priest.

Silence fell like a curtain, except for the receding chug of the tractor as it pushed Mr. Jackson's pick-up truck, which it had gored through the cab door, toward the line of evergreen trees that would block its egress onto Valley Road.

Peter turned toward Miss Hensley and cried out her name. She sat rigidly in the swivel chair at the edge of the parking lot. Her face was deathly pale, her eyes devoid of expression. He ran toward her, paused at her gaunt look, and then, seeing that she was breathing, bent toward her awkwardly. She was not the kind of woman one knew how to approach with charity. "Miss Hensley," he said, "are you all right?"

Her head slowly turned, her vacant eyes stared up at

him, her frail body shuddered as if trying to rise. She half left the chair, took one step, then another, spun to the side as if drunk, staggered onto the grass, and dropped like a puppet whose strings had been rudely severed. Pat rushed over and held up her head.

Suddenly, Peter remembered Mrs. Peck. He had last seen her sitting at her desk, but there was no sign of her in the pancake of broken glass and beams. He shouted her name and looked for a way to get through to where her desk had been. Then a head popped up into the bubble of the skullcap dome like an unseen fish rising from the sandy floor of an aquarium tank. It was Mrs. Peck, waving and smiling. The first time Peter had seen a live expression on her face.

Around the edge of the wreckage sprinted Mr. Jackson and the operator. Their faces were ashen. The operator headed for the machine goring the truck at the tree line. Mr. Jackson approached. "My God. My God," he muttered over and over. "The whole thing went. The whole thing. Is everybody all right? Did everyone get out?"

Peter pointed to where Mrs. Peck was smiling and waving as if such demeanor were required by her job.

"I think so," came Pat's voice from where she was kneeling beside Miss Hensley. "She's in shock."

Peter went over and helped raise the spurtle legs against the concrete base of a light standard. All color had drained from Miss Hensley's face.

The convulsions of the tractor stopped. Mr. Jackson sprinted toward his truck. "I'll call an ambulance," he shouted over his shoulder.

From up the hill next to the leaking drum gazed the garden club ladies and John Rhodes. The ladies' hands half covered their wrinkled faces; their eyes were rimmed wide with disbelief. John sagged to one side, shoulders hunched, head hanging forward, his face as blank as if he had not a thought on his mind. If he felt any grief at losing one of his glass buildings, it did not show.

A siren rose in the distance. Pat was trying mouth-to-mouth resuscitation on Miss Hensley. Mr. Jackson came up and nodded toward smiling Mrs. Peck. "Well, we'd better get her out of there," he said.

Peter responded without thinking. He felt no grief for the loss of the building. Miss Hensley lying there on the grass with her feet propped against the light pole was etched in his mind. He could not detect in himself even a wisp of compassion.

Approaching the wreckage, he saw above the garden scarp the sanctuary, through which he beheld Gottschalk's sparkling ball—lined up with the brass cross mocking from the communion table.

Suddenly a familiar sound filled the air. A helicopter thuckered above Valley Road heading toward Good Samaritan's latest disaster. "Channel 7's 'Eye in the Sky' bringing you the latest news from where it happens, when it happens." With a sigh, Peter followed Mr. Jackson into the tangle of beams and shards.

26

Jeff's voice called up from the family room. "Dad, come here quick. The church is on TV." Peter thought about shouting down from the bedroom that he was too tired for the eleven o'clock news, but then church members would see the broadcast, and he should know what was said.

He settled onto the sofa next to Brenda, dressed in leotards from her play rehearsal. The tall reporter with the praying mantis physique Peter had talked to was standing in front of the wreckage holding a microphone. "Some of you may recall a couple of months ago when Channel Seven covered a demonstration at the Church of the Good Samaritan here on Valley Road. Members were protesting an action by the Board of Trustees authorizing several thousand dollars for the construction of a rose garden.

"Well, today, disaster visited Good Samaritan Church . . "

"As if there were a connection," Peter snarled at the screen.

" . . . when a grading tractor brought in to work on the garden slipped into gear, crashed through the administration building, and destroyed it." The reporter turned; the camera panned the jumble of glass and steel. "The pastor, Reverend Peter Camden, two secretaries, and several members of the church were in the building at the time, but all escaped without injury. One secretary, a Miss Henby, shaken by the tragedy, remains hospitalized for observation."

The camera swept the parking lot and zoomed in on Mr. Jackson's gored truck. "We asked the Reverend Camden what happened."

The mantis reporter shoved a microphone into Peter's face. Peter saw himself looking at the camera with a vacant gaze.

"You look shell-shocked," Brenda moaned. "Your jacket's off . . . your tie's loose. What's that in your hair?"

"Glass," Peter replied dully. "We had just gotten Mrs. Peck out when this zero comes up and starts asking questions. I told him to buzz off, but then he accused me of hiding something."

On TV, Peter recited what had occurred.

"You overlooked the other secretary?" the reporter asked with a hint of intrigue.

Peter's protestations about how quickly things had happened sounded hollow. If they only knew, he chuckled to himself, I would've gladly left Miss Hensley behind.

Mr. Krohn's face sprang into view. The reporter continued: "This is Henry Krohn, chairman of the Board of Trustees. Mr. Krohn, how do you assess the damage?"

Mr. Krohn's eyes wobbled nervously; he spoke through clenched teeth. "It's hard to put a price on the building right now. As you can see, it's completely destroyed. We don't know if it can be replaced. We'll have to see what the insurance companies come up with."

The reporter stared at him as if on the trail of skulduggery. "And how do you anticipate the insurance companies will resolve the assignment of damages?"

Mr. Krohn stood mute, then his lips began to move. "I really don't know. The adjustor for the company insuring the church says he'll contact the contractor's carrier. We don't know what coverage the contractor has."

The reporter squinted in the sunlight. "Mr. Krohn, do you have any idea exactly what caused the accident?"

"Nothing more than what the pastor said. The tractor came down the hill without a driver, and this is the result." Mr. Krohn waved his arm toward the ruin.

The reporter leaned toward Mr. Krohn. "According to the contractor, Mr. Jackson, there's a safety catch on the tractor. He says it could not have slipped into gear without someone releasing that catch. Do you care to comment on that?"

"No," Mr. Krohn replied. "Unless Mr. Jackson has someone in mind who would've done such a thing."

The camera zoomed in on the reporter. "A morning of tragedy at Good Samaritan Church on Valley Road. These buildings were given to the church by the late Hermann Gottschalk, founder of the Gottschalk Glass Company, one of the oldest firms in Oakdale. According to Mr. Krohn, they are the only ones of their kind, and the one destroyed is irreplaceable. Insurance company adjustors have a long fight ahead to determine who is responsible for this disaster, estimated to be a loss of a million dollars. Perhaps the church's company will pay. Or the carrier for the contractor. Or, perhaps"—a smirk appeared on the reporter's face—"the destruction of Good Samaritan Church's administration building will be judged to be—an act of God. This is Bjorkland Smith, Channel Seven News."

Jeff turned to Peter, his chest swelling with admiration. "Boy, you're the best-known minister in town."

Peter nodded grudgingly. It was not an honor he sought.

"Miss Hensley?" Brenda asked. "How is she?"

Peter had gone to the mental floor of the hospital, but

had been refused admittance. One of the doctors had come out to see him. The diagnosis was early and therefore tentative. "She's out of commission," Peter said.

"For good?" Brenda's deep eyes stared at him as if she shared the hope that lifted weight from his shoulders.

"It's possible," he replied.

"Then you've done it."

"Done what?"

"Taken care of her like you said you would."

He had forgotten he told Brenda that morning he was going to make sure there were no more leaks, even if it meant getting rid of Miss Hensley. But he had not meant putting her in a mental hospital. He chided himself for not feeling a twinge of remorse. He did want her to get well, but far from Good Samaritan.

"And the drum?" Brenda asked. Her voice brought him back from his reverie.

"Acid," he replied.

"Acid?"

"From Gottschalk Glass. Years ago they used the church site for a dump."

"Is there much?"

Again Peter saw the drum leaking dark fluid. "The tractor operator said there were more drums. How many, he didn't know. They'll all have to be dug up and carted away. In which case even thirty thousand won't be enough."

For that, he felt no remorse either. He recalled the picture hanging in the Delaware Club of the man on the bluff and the city below. Only now it did not suggest Jesus starting his triumphal entry into Jerusalem. It was Jonah he saw, standing on the bluff above Nineveh — hoping the city would refuse to repent, because he wanted her to fall under the Lord's judgment. Did he share Jonah's contempt? It would be strange for a minister. Then again, Good Samaritan was a strange church. Or is it a church at all? he wondered.

Part Three

1

The mental hospital to which Miss Hensley had been sent lay atop a rounded grassy hill in the northern part of the county. Red brick of turn-of-the-century vintage, with peeling white paint on the stout pillars guarding its front entrance, it was always embroiled in political controversy as to whether it should be torn down.

Peter obtained Miss Hensley's room number at the reception desk and made his way through long corridors until he came to one with a green tile floor and faded green paint on the walls. Miss Hensley was standing outside her room. At first he did not recognize her: the bent body, the head hung forward like that of a gaunt bird scratching for something to eat. The disheveled black hair caught his attention, then eyes no longer glowing with power. Vacant, as if nothing lay behind them.

He slowed his pace. A pang of pity worked its way up into his throat, he groped for some apology he might stammer, some condolence that the destruction of the narthex had so unnerved her. But the pang died before he could give it birth.

Her broomstick arms shot out, her face twisted into a pained grimace, from her bloodless lips emitted a high-pitched shriek that brought from farther down the hall an enormous nurse whose bosom flowed toward him like the prow of a ship. There was a quick glance at poor Miss Hensley, then a sustained glare at Peter which contained in its fiery depths accusation, trial, sentencing, and execution.

"I'm . . . " he started.

"If you're Reverend Campbell," she said cutting him off, "then you should never come here again." Her glare burned without abating. She turned to Miss Hensley, put her arm around her waist, and gently ushered her back into her room. Miss Hensley shuffled like a compliant child without another glance at Peter.

Peter stood alone in the hall for a few moments, fuming, formulating lists of complaints he would make to the hospital administrator. But the tide quickly abated, and he turned to leave — and not come back.

2

"Hi, I'm Sheila. You must be Peter Campbell." The voice came from a tall blond with a smooth, smiling face perched on the corner of Miss Hensley's desk. The desk, along with the rest of the furniture from the wrecked narthex, had been moved into a temporary office in Assisi.

"Yes, I am Peter," Peter said trying to catch his breath. For a few moments, he was certain he had come to work at the wrong place. To gaze at this gorgeous creature in the blue pantsuit instead of Miss Hensley was something he had never anticipated.

"I'm the temporary you asked for," Sheila continued.

"Well, yes," Peter replied under her engaging blue eyes. He searched for something profound to say, but nothing came. "Have you worked in a church before?" he asked.

"I've volunteered at my church. Mormon. I know how an office is run."

"Mormon?" Peter said absently. He tried not to let his eyes flicker, but he was relieved that she came from the stricter side of the religious spectrum.

"Church of the Latter Day Saints."

"Oh yes," he said as if he were a naive student learning something for the first time.

"You'll give me a chance?"

"A chance?" Peter asked. Would she give Good Samaritan a chance? he wondered.

"To see if I can do the work."

Peter laughed. "We don't take chances. You're on."

Sheila smiled, slid down off the corner of the desk and sat in the chair. "By the way, the custodian?"

"John Rhodes?" Peter replied.

"He comes in and asks me a lot of questions I can't answer. Does he do that all the time?"

"No," Peter said. "He never comes in and asks the secretary questions. At least, he hasn't as long as I've been here."

"Then why me?" Sheila asked.

"I don't know," Peter replied facetiously. "I sure don't know."

3

The opening for Brenda's play fell on a drizzly fall night. Tiny droplets of mist floated in air so still not a leaf stirred in the maples and oaks under which Peter, Jackie, and Jeff walked on their way from the car to the theatre.

"I'll bet Mom's nervous," Jeff put in out of the damp darkness as if in his artist heart he shared the apprehension she must feel performing before several hundred people for the first time in years. Jeff plodded with his head down, his hands in his coat pockets. Since he had not worn a hat, drizzle beaded on his tousled hair. Without his coveralls and welding helmet, he looked to Peter almost a stranger.

Near the theatre entrance, a woman from the congregation caught Peter's eye. "My, that's some secretary you've got now. Are you sure you can keep your mind on church business?" She laughed, and he smiled back.

Inside the lobby, Peter watched Jackie's eyes flit nervously at the many faces. If the wrinkle in her brow was apprehension, he understood. There might be School Board members among the audience.

"I feel like I'm being watched when I'm out," she had said earlier.

"It's because you're winning," Peter said. The lawyer for Jackie and her friends had found the School Board's actions regarding her track team in clear violation of a new state statute.

"Campbell, I want that suit dropped," one of the church member School Board officials had said to Peter.

"There's nothing I can do," Peter replied. "I didn't file the suit."

"She's your daughter," came the accusing reply.

"And she's doing what's right," Peter retorted. "That's a few notches above the School Board's actions."

The board member's round fleshy face turned red. "Campbell, you haven't heard the last of this. One of these days you'll find out who runs this town—and this church."

"I'd be interested to know," Peter shouted sarcastically at the retreating rotund figure.

A trustee not on the School Board saw Peter. "Too bad about that litigation holding up the new narthex," he said.

The wreckage of the old narthex had not been touched since the disaster. Insurance adjustors came from time to time to take measurements and pictures. But so far neither company had offered to take responsibility, and the ruin had to be preserved as evidence. With the offices in Assisi quite comfortable—as comfortable as anywhere in Good Samaritan, considering the glaring sun and insufferable heat—Peter was not concerned when the wreckage went or the new brick building came. "No hurry," he said nonchalantly, drawing a strange stare from his blue suited interrogator.

Sitting in fourth row center, Peter heard in the buzz of conversation around him the excitement of first night. He imagined Brenda pacing back and forth, her face glowing red with apprehension that she could dance before such a large crowd.

The house lights lowered, a hush fell, the curtain

opened. High-pitched notes floated from an invisible violin. Peter's heart beat with expectancy. A nymph-like figure leaped into a brilliant circle of light, spun across the stage, and vanished. The first violin was joined by a second, then a third. Onto a platform above and at the back of the stage emerged a dancer clad in a yellow bodysuit, his face ringed by a circle of yellow flame.

Floodlights slowly dispelled the darkness enshrouding the stage; five people uncoiled from frozen stillness—a mother, father, older son, daughter, and younger son. Their faces wore smiles; they laughed and joked with one another. They were celebrating. The porcelain mother had been elected president of a prestigious board, the father's business had prospered, the eldest son had won a tennis match, the daughter had achieved the honor roll at the university, and the youngest son had been accepted into his father's alma mater.

While they celebrated their triumphs, on the platform, other dancers joined the sun. The white moon and seven stars. Five dancers in blue and brown suits portrayed rippling water, and then land rising from the deep. At the end of each choreographic section, a chorus emerged from stage right and left and bowed in praise and approval. Peter was moved—the Genesis account of the Creation came alive like an epic poem.

A man in a flesh-toned body suit with appropriate leaves popped out of swaying animal dancers. The animals filed by; as each passed, his head shot forward and turned away. Brenda, also in very realistic flesh tone and with leaves, jumped into view from the wings. When the man saw her, he spun and leaped.

Below, the mood of the family changed. The mother bitterly accused the rest of the family of not supporting her opinions. The father shouted into the telephone at a business associate, and the son and daughter were telling their mother she was only preoccupied with her own affairs and gave no heed to theirs.

Above, the serpent appeared as a shadow from stage left and slinked toward Brenda, who was spinning at center stage. She stopped and looked up, her hands caressing as if admiring fruit hanging from a tree, unaware of the beast inching closer behind her. She spun in joy, jumped back, turned again to the imaginary tree. The serpent slithered around her, beckoning, beguiling, the mouth twisted in a leer of seduction. They spun and pirouetted — she away, the serpent toward. She turned her back, he slunk around to her front; he dogged her steps, mimicked her moves. The effect gripped Peter. Brenda had never been so good.

Eve stopped and listened. The light changed. Her white turned from yellow to orange to crimson. The scene throbbed with passion; it would offend bloodless types. The director had sought to portray the spiritual seduction gripping the family as the father shouted into the phone and the mother and offspring screamed at each other. The power generated by the two stages cast the audience into a sustained gasp.

Jackie leaned over to Peter: "Mom's really good. I can't believe it's her."

Jeff shook his head. "Boy, she can really move for her age."

Peter stifled a laugh. "She's not that old," he said.

When the final curtain fell, the audience exploded into applause. Dancers alternated with dramatists bowing to deserved praise. Brenda smiled, she looked striking with her red hair and tight suit. Peter's eyes moistened, he pounded his hands with pleasure.

"Excellent, excellent," a man with white hair and a limp exclaimed as Peter inched up the aisle toward the stage. "Your wife has unusual talent."

Backstage, Peter grabbed Brenda and hugged her hard. "You were magnificent," he exclaimed. "Jackie said she didn't know you had it in you."

Brenda laughed and wiped beads of perspiration from her face. "I'm so glad it's over. I'd forgotten how terrible first nights are."

Dancers and actors were moving toward the exit. But the enthusiasm that had risen in Peter was still growing. "The evening's young," he said. "Why don't we go somewhere to celebrate?" He looked at Jackie and Jeff.

"If there's food, I'm game," Jackie said. Jeff nodded.

Peter pushed his way back through the theatre to get the car. "Your wife was something," someone shouted at him. He turned to a girl with bangs and big eyes he had never seen before. "And to think she's a minister's wife. Wow!"

Peter thanked her and smiled. He did not care if he ran into church people or School Board members — he would greet them all with a good word. He saw Brenda's lithe form resisting the tempter, then giving in. On the stage below, the family fought to the threshold of violence. It had been a great performance. But as the images interplayed in his head, he saw something else. What the play portrayed was true — of the family, of himself, of Good Samaritan, of everyone. No one could bypass Genesis, any more than they could bypass Nineveh, or he could bypass Jonah.

Out in the gentle drizzle and still air, he realized part of his joy was the release of humiliation, the reminder he was just an ordinary fallen person. He had no call to play a role just because Good Samaritan wanted a suburban saint. All he could give them was himself, inadequate though he might be in their eyes.

4

Bishop Stone's high-pitched voice drifted over the plywood partition separating Peter's office from the secretaries, but the phone had not buzzed indicating Wes was ready to come in.

The lack of privacy afforded by the partition dividing the large room in Assisi bothered Peter not at all. Since the room was away from the garden, he looked out on an expanse of grass browning under the approach of winter, instead of the horrendous excavating project under way in the garden. There was not one drum of acid buried there, but hundreds. The Environmental Protection Agency was requiring that all of them be dug up and disposed of—at church expense, since the church inherited the land from the man who had authorized the drums be interred there: Hermann Gottschalk.

The glowing ball at the top of the ridge made the back of Peter's neck burn with anger. Hermann's benevolence had tarnished beyond restoration. So extensive was the burial that the rear of the sanctuary had to be shored up from beneath so drums embedded under its foundation could be removed. Everyone now knew, but refused to voice, that it would have cost the church less if it had refused Hermann's useless greenhouses and built its own plant. Yet Hermann lay on top of the ridge, a smug smile on his face, his crystal ball glowing overhead, and everyone in Oakdale extolling him as one of the community's greatest saints—Oakdale's Gandhi, Oakdale's Schweitzer. Brass cross generosity, giving without sacrifice. It sent waves of nausea across Peter's stomach.

Wes had given no clue as to why he was coming to visit. Certainly it was not to scold; things were going too well. Brenda's play was performing before packed houses. The *Inquirer* had published a rave review. Brenda had gained a name independently of Good Samaritan, and neither she nor Peter could have been happier about that. Jeff's Trojan was in the final selection that could lead to the grand prize in the sculpture contest, and the *Inquirer* had reversed its stand and printed a strong editorial saying the School Board should admit its guilt immediately and equalize funding for girls' and boys' athletics.

Wes's cirrus laugh came over the wall. "Why, you must have Norwegian blood," he chortled. Peter could not make out Sheila's muffled reply. He looked at his watch. He had squeezed Wes's appointment in ahead of another, so they should get started. He rose and went to the partition door.

Sheila had draped herself on a corner of her desk like a model on a TV game show. Wes grovelled before her, his face glowing above the tight clerical collar, his arms gesturing with far more animation than he used when he preached a sermon. His eyes shone hungrily, his tongue wagged as if its control cords had been severed. "Quite a secretary you've got here," he said. "I don't see how you get anything done. Why if I were you, I'd move my desk out here and just sit and look at her."

Sheila provided an appropriate smile and laugh — polite, but without an invitation for Wes to linger. "You have to watch these bishops," she said with a wink at Mrs. Peck, who was watching from her desk piled with financial papers.

"I'd say so," Mrs. Peck replied. She demonstrated the broad smile that came frequently since Miss Hensley's demise.

Wes continued to dance before Sheila as if whatever he had come to see Peter about had fled from his mind. Peter looked at his watch. "I think we should get started."

"Oh yes," Wes mumbled. He jolted himself out of his awe at Sheila and followed Peter into his office. "She's a beauty," he added as Peter shut the partition door and latched it. "Where did you find her?"

Peter knew Wes hadn't come to talk about Sheila, but obviously it was going to take time to get him out of his rapture. "Powerpool. They sent her to fill in for Miss Hensley. But now that Miss Hensley won't be back, we've employed her ourselves."

Wes's eyes glanced longingly at the partition. "I can see why."

Peter waited a moment and then said, "You had something you wanted to talk about?" Since the last visit, Peter found his tolerance for Wes's circumlocutions had grown paper thin.

The shine on Wes's face faded to pious concern. "Well, it's been a few months since I was here . . ." Wes searched the floor as if he could not get his thoughts together. "I should get right to the root of things — 'root,' 'radical,' you remember from seminary."

Peter remained expressionless. The bishop's humor dissipated in the white light, leaving him untouched.

"I don't know if you're aware of it or not, but my phone's still ringing off the hook." Wes lifted his gaze to Peter. "I hate to say it, Peter, but there are problems. Bad problems."

Peter felt as if the early winter sun glowing white in the southern sky were drawing heat out of his body. His face burned at the sly way Wes was approaching whatever was on his mind.

"If it were just one thing, you know, something small that upset just a few people — we could handle that with no bother." Wes paused, his lips quivered as if he struggled with some inner tension.

"Well, what is it?" Peter asked, making no attempt to disguise the irritation welling up in his chest.

"Miss Hensley for one thing," Wes replied. "People claim you made her ill."

Peter recalled the arms flung out like a scarecrow, the high-pitched shriek. "Nonsense," he replied. "She was psychotic long before I got here . . ."

Wes's hand went up like that of a policeman stopping traffic. "She claims you threatened to fire her. Or, I should say, those who called me say you accused her of something she didn't do."

Peter told how he had asked her if she was responsible for leaking confidential information from the church office.

Wes nodded, only half listening. Peter wondered if the bishop's mind had gotten off Sheila. "But shortly after that," Wes said in an inquisitorial tone, "she was committed to the hospital?"

Peter wondered why Wes's callers omitted important details. "The day I talked to her was the same day the tractor crashed through the office. She's one of those over-wired types. When she'd surpassed her limit, she flipped out."

"And you had no concern about that?"

"Of course I did." Peter's voice rose in protest. "I went to visit her, but it only made her worse. The head nurse told me not to come back."

Wes tugged at the sleeves of his shirt as if it were too small and he was trying to stretch it to fit. "But you did accuse her?"

Peter frowned. "I didn't accuse her. I asked her. She said she had nothing to do with the leaks, and I left it at that."

Wes's eyes were dull with skepticism. "You can't believe the number of people who've called. It's hard to discount so many."

It wasn't just Wes that grated on Peter's nerves. It was this nameless phalanx of church members who sat like tombstones in the sanctuary each Sunday, greeted Peter with tight upper middle class smiles, and then knifed him in the back during the week. How could he deal with them when he had no idea who they were? "You've got to consider that Miss Hensley was behind those calls," he said. "She's got nothing to do at the hospital but cry to her grapevine how mean I've been to her. There are plenty of bleeding hearts in this congregation, plus people she could blackmail, plus a few others, who, now that they know I won't play their silly games, would like to see me pack up and leave."

Wes's brow wrinkled at the suggestion members of prestigious Good Samaritan might be persecuting their pastor. "You would give her job back to her?"

Peter groaned inwardly. "I don't think she could ever work with me again."

"To protect your integrity, I must have a direct answer. Would you have her back?"

"She freaks out. When she saw me at the hospital, she went off like a banshee. It would never work."

Wes leaned forward. "I talked to her psychiatrist. He says her disturbance centers on her relationship with Good Samaritan."

Peter found the arrogant gleam in Wes's eyes repulsive.

He despised Wes's practice of unloading an allegedly authoritative nugget of information just at the opportune moment. "I don't believe that," he shot back. "She may have been using Good Samaritan to resolve some inner conflict. But the conflict itself started a long time ago. She's a very tense woman."

Wes sighed as if Peter's answers had the weight of fluff.

"Look, Wes," Peter said. "You and I have known each other ever since I started the ministry. You've been a friend and a help." Peter conceded to Wes the benefit of the doubt—there was precious little evidence. "But I don't understand what you're doing now. You're putting me on trial before anonymous accusers who don't have the guts to tell me to my face what they think I'm doing wrong. Do you condone that?"

Wes turned squarely to Peter. "I'm responsible for the well-being of all the congregations in this Synod. I've got one here that's riddled with problems. It wasn't always that way. Why, in the year you've been here there's been that picketing that got on TV, a building destroyed, a secretary gone mad, a Board of Trustees besieged by dissident members, threats from all over that people will quit and join somewhere else. Now that may seem small to you, but more has happened since you came than in the entire previous fifty years."

"I understand that perfectly," Peter said. "This congregation takes pride in nothing happening. It's a sign of health." In the back of his mind, he noted that Wes skirted Gottschalk's illegal burial of acid beneath his generous donation of the Good Samaritan site.

The veins in Wes's forehead stood out like moleruns. "Now listen, Peter, I didn't come here to joke with you. I have to find out what's causing this congregation to fall apart."

Peter's eyes hurt from the sun glinting off the brass cross hanging around Wes's neck. He felt an urge to grab the icon and hurl it away. But there was no way he could convince Wes it wasn't his pastoral leadership that was the problem, but brass cross religion, religion that demanded some undefined perfection, but gave no solace.

"This is a great congregation," Wes added. "Dr. Strong did a fine job. But now people feel there's no leadership. They come to you for help, but they get no satisfaction. They're ready to work, like the ladies in the garden club, but you don't support them. There's conflict, but you sit here in your office as if everything were fine."

"They don't come to me," Peter shot back. "And if I don't honestly agree with what they want, no, I don't support them. Is there something wrong with being my own person rather than their flunky?"

Wes retorted, "Peter, your job is to be a servant of this congregation. You're to help people get what they want. Servant—it's embedded in our tradition. But when you pick and choose, help one person and not another, you're no longer a servant but a judge. People are getting mad."

"That's crazy," Peter said. "You mean I'm supposed to do everything people come in here and tell me to do? Is that what Strong did?"

"Of course." The words slipped from Wes's pale lips like quicksilver. "He knew how to keep harmony. More than that, Strong kept his personal life in line."

Peter was not sure he had heard Wes correctly. "Personal life?"

Wes's stubby hands chopped the hostile air. "Well, it's common knowledge that your wife has a major part in that play at the Playhouse. Your daughter is behind the lawsuit that's blackmailing the School Board. And you defend your son and that monstrosity he's building in the parsonage garage. Everyone knows that if it's left there it'll cost a fortune to get rid of."

Peter reeled as if Wes had punched him in the solar plexus. "Damn," he mumbled.

Wes leaned toward him. "Did you say something?"

"That's none of their business. The play is great . . ."

"Some thought it erotic. I think I heard the word 'risqué'

more than once. In any case, it sounds as if at best it could only be poor taste. Certainly it's an embarrassment to many upright people in this church."

"Dolts," Peter exclaimed. "They don't know anything about theatre. If they thought the ballet was erotic, then *they* ought to spend some time in the hospital. As for Jackie — she's right. The Board has been breaking the law. It's time someone blew the whistle. Nothing changes in this town unless someone takes a stand, and those kids have. I'm proud of them.

"And Jeff. The horse he's building is large, but we warned the church before we came that we didn't want the house. We knew his hobby needed space. But they wouldn't budge. Saint Gottschalk has eternally decreed that the minister of the church will live in that house. And while we're on the topic of Good Samaritan's patron saint, why don't you ever talk about how the old buzzard unloaded buildings he couldn't sell and took a hefty tax credit? Now that we know he's the phantom rose killer — why he's costing this church far more than he's donated . . ."

Wes's face burned so red Peter thought the bishop might be on the threshold of a stroke. His lips moved, but no words came forth.

"It's cheap," Peter went on. "How can you, a bishop, listen to anonymous people who do nothing but gossip? How can you put credence in rumors?"

"After listening to you, I'd say they're not rumors," Wes squeezed out through a crumbling bulwark of self-control. "And to me, they're not anonymous." His voice was ragged with rage. "I'll put it to you straight. The leaders of this church want rid of you. That's the gist of the calls. But I've refused to give in."

Peter wondered if such magnanimity was supposed to elicit an expression of gratitude.

"I asked for time," Wes went on. "I felt you should have a chance."

"What chance do I have?" Peter asked.

"The Synod runs a program for pastors with problems. You go to Pinetree Center for a week and concentrate on what's not going right. I couldn't promise your detractors that would bring you around, but they're willing to give you a chance. There's no question something has to change."

"But you didn't suggest my detractors go off on a retreat to see if there's something wrong with them?"

Wes found no humor in the comment. "There are too many," he said. "If you go there and get a clean bill of health, then I'll know the problem is not with you."

Peter leaned back in his chair. He could think of nothing to say.

"You'll give it a try?" Wes asked.

Peter searched the round watery eyes for compassion, but there was none. "Do I have any choice?"

"You could resign for the sake of peace and harmony."

Peter saw the picture on the wall in the Delaware Club. Like Jesus entering Jerusalem, he had taken on Good Samaritan as a gamble. Jesus had not turned back. Neither had Jonah. "I'll go on the retreat," Peter said. "But only to give my detractors the satisfaction that I'm not beyond self-examination. I just hope they're big enough to change their minds if they're wrong."

Wes stood up with a smile. "I'm sure they are," he said. "I'm sure they are."

5

It had snowed overnight. A glistening blanket covered the lawn, bent the branches of evergreens, lay humped around the trunks of oaks and maples. Wind whining around the corner of the house hurled tiny ice particles tinkling against the window.

Peter, staring out, pulled his robe tightly around himself and fought off a powerful urge to crawl back into bed. It would be fifty miles of icy roads to Pinetree Center. Brenda lay unstirring beneath the covers with her mouth open. She wouldn't care if they didn't go. But it would finish him with Good Samaritan. To do so without trying to show his detractors what they were doing to him and to themselves — he nudged Brenda and whispered it was time to get up.

On the highway, the tires drummed over packed snow, slid ominously on patches of ice. Where salt had been put down, spray from cars ahead turned the windshield into an opaque white sheet. Brenda was slumped over sound asleep.

It had been a long time since Peter had been on a retreat. He recalled the old songs, feature speakers who got everyone fired up so they were ready to go back home and stand their parishes on end. Of course, it never worked out that way, but the retreats themselves were a pleasant relief from the parish routine.

Snow-covered fields with island clusters of barns, sheds, and farm houses gave way to dense thickets of pine and hemlock. They were approaching resort country. Billboards beckoned honeymooners to heart-shaped rooms, heart-shaped bathtubs, heart-shaped swimming pools; Chippewa Island offered low cost homesites with easy access to golf, tennis, boating, swimming, skiing, and a wine glass.

Brenda stirred and opened her eyes. Clad in plaid wool slacks and a sweater, she already looked like a resort resident. "I hope Wes gets set on his ear," she said. "It burns me up that he blames you for everything that's gone wrong — and for things that haven't gone wrong like Jackie and track and Jeff and Trojan and the play."

"It sounds like you've already got your agenda for the week," Peter said.

She smiled. "I do. You're on trial. We're going to get you acquitted."

"That sounds pretty serious," he said in jest.

"All you have to do is get a good report. Then Wes will know it isn't you but that crazy church that's at fault."

Since Peter did not know what the program was, he had

no idea what a good report would look like. "Well, we'll see," he said.

A blue sign with yellow lettering — 'Pinetree Center' — came into view. Small craters pockmarked the one lane access road, but Peter kept on, confident fresh tracks in the snow had been left by other trouble-ridden pastors seeking light on whether they or their congregations were contaminating the sacred temples of Christendom.

Smoke trailed from the high stone chimney of the huge log mansion. The steps of the porch, which ran across the front of the structure, had been swept in anticipation of visitors. The oak door was swung open by a woman of about forty-five: salt and pepper hair pulled back in a ponytail, lean frame clad in a black turtleneck sweater and black chino slacks hanging from sharp hip bones to black hightop sneakers. She seemed out of place here in the woods; her smile and a gaze that shot over his head reminded Peter of the love-hate relationship that hung in the fetid air of substandard nursing homes. The hospitable grin that covered a multitude of bad practices.

At the back of the wide entry, broad stairs ascended to the second floor. To the left was the living room — chairs and sofas of rough-hewn wood, a fire blazing in the fireplace. To the right lay the dining room: long tables with benches set with paper plates and plastic cutlery for the evening meal. Apparently Pinetree had abandoned the old-fashioned discipline of dishwashing. The smell of woodsmoke hung in the air, people could be heard shuffling about overhead.

Having scanned the list of names posted on the bulletin board and convinced herself that Peter and Brenda were properly registered, the woman identified herself as Trudy. Through the thin lips in her leathery face, she said, "You're in room two. Up the stairs and to the right. Orientation is at five, dinner at six, and the evening program will start at seven."

Several pairs of cross-country skis leaned against the wall on the stair landing. Peter felt a twinge of regret that he and Brenda had not rented some and brought them along. It had been a long time since he had been deep in snow-covered woods.

The room was cramped for twin beds. Its one small window looked out on a milk delivery truck parked next to an iron trash bin. "Gad, what a view," Brenda groaned. "We come to the mountains to look at that?"

Peter stepped to the window to see for himself. Beyond the milk truck lay a rusted water heater, lengths of unused pipe, discarded beams and boards, empty paint cans. "I'll see what I can do," he said.

Trudy was not to be found guarding the front door. A couple in matching sweaters had drawn a sofa up to the fireplace and sat with stockinged feet on the hearth. Peter found Trudy in the kitchen talking to the chef and milkman.

"I . . . we were just wondering if there was another room . . . maybe something with a view . . ." he stammered.

Trudy shook her head. "Sorry. We assign everyone alphabetically starting with room one. It's the only fair way."

Peter paused. "The rest are taken?"

Trudy ignored him to talk to the milkman. The chef, a woman with a white apron wrapped around her wide girth, swirled a large spoon in a steaming pot on the stove.

Back at the room, Brenda's forehead was furrowed with frustration. "I can't get the bottom drawer of the dresser open. I thought the sweaters should go down there." She pointed to the lowest drawer. One of the dresser's front legs was missing, and the corner had been propped up on a pile of bricks.

Peter knelt on the hard wood floor, grasped the handles, and gave a good jerk. The dresser jolted forward, bricks crashed to the floor. He rose up quickly to throw a shoulder into the top drawer before it fell on him. After leveling the antique on its bricks, he placed one foot above the sticking drawer, the other beneath, and heaved backward. The brass ring on one of the pulls popped loose with a metallic ping and sent him hurling against the bed. "Like glue," he mumbled from the floor, rubbing the sore spot on his back. "It's no use."

There was a sharp knock on the door. Brenda opened it to find Trudy standing in the hall. "Everything all right?" she asked coldly. "I heard a noise. I thought . . ."

Peter stood up quickly and put a smile on his face. "Just fine. We had a little trouble with one of the drawers, but it's okay." He cupped his hand so as to hide the brass ring. "We don't need to use it." He feigned a casual shrug. Trudy's eyes searched the two of them with a hint of annoyance, and then she was gone.

Sitting on the stool in the bathroom at the far end of the hall, Peter trembled with cold. He searched for a source of heat, but there was none. Thick frost coating the window above the tub raised up on lions-paw legs made a bath most uninviting. Tacked to the wall over the dripping tap which had stained the porcelain orange was a sign which read, 'Please conserve hot water.'

Back in the room, Brenda had put on her flannel nightgown and a sweater and was climbing under the covers. Peter halted in astonishment. "Are you sick?"

"No. Cold." The pillow muffled her voice. "I can't keep my eyes open." She peered up like a redhaired gopher. "Why don't you do the same? You're more exhausted than you realize."

She was right. Now that he was away from Good Samaritan, he could feel his body relaxing; there were no blows against which he needed to brace himself, no criticism requiring a hasty defense. Yet there was a schedule to keep. "Five o'clock. Orientation."

Brenda yawned. "We'll make it. I never nap for very long." She snuggled beneath the blankets.

Peter sat down on the edge of the other bed. His mind drifted as if detached from his body. The bathroom had chilled him to the point where he could not get warm. He changed into his pajamas and crawled in with Brenda, holding up his watch so he could tell himself how much time he had to sleep.

6

Consciousness came slowly. The room was dark except for the blue mercury vapor glow coming in the window. Peter held up his watch — ten minutes after five.

Brenda stirred. "What's the matter?"

"Quick," Peter said. "We were supposed to be downstairs ten minutes ago."

Brenda pulled herself up and rubbed her eyes. The pillow had etched lines across her cheek. "I never sleep like this."

"Come on. Just throw on what you were wearing." Walking in late on the first meeting is no way to make the kind of impression that will give me a good report with Wes, Peter thought. He drew on his socks and gave Brenda a poke.

She groped about with stiff, arthritic movements. "I look a sight," she moaned. "Is there a mirror?"

"In the bathroom." Peter nodded down the hall. "Leave the door open so I can comb my hair."

They descended the stairs at twenty-five after. Peter almost slipped on the landing; he was not used to navigating uncarpeted stairs in moccasins. Jovial voices drifted up from the living room, the bracing odor of cooked cabbage hung in the air near the kitchen.

They stopped in the doorway to survey the thirty-five or so men and women running about, feverishly greeting one another, looking at each other's backs. Pinned to their backs were yellow cardboard silhouettes of animals: an elephant, a giraffe, a mouse. A man in a gray cardigan sported a kangaroo. Peter had no idea what they were doing.

"Oh, there you are." Trudy slinked up like a black salamander and smiled. "I knew we were missing someone, but I couldn't remember who."

Peter nodded to the compliment. "Sorry," he said. "Took

a nap and didn't have an alarm clock."

Trudy's cold eyes dismissed the excuse as if it were a lie. "Here, I'll put your animals on. Turn around so you won't know what you've got." Peter felt Trudy's bony fingers pinning something to his sweater. "This is an introduction game called 'animal-breaker.' It's to get us all to know each other's names and loosen things up." Peter felt loose already, from the nap. He wished he could have slept longer. "What you do is go up to someone and say, 'I'm John Doe,' and then you ask one question for a clue as to what animal you have on your back. You know, 'Do I live in water?' or something like that."

Peter stared in dumb compliance while Brenda glanced at his back and rolled her eyes playfully. He wished he could get into the spirit of things like this as easily as she did. Her dramatic training served her well. She leaned toward him. "Now just go along and make it fun."

Peter gave her an obedient nod and launched himself into the crowd. "Hello, I'm Peter Campbell." He shook hands with a short, baldheaded man with no neck to fill his turtleneck sweater. "Do I live on land or in water?"

The man stared at his face and then turned him so he could see his back. "The questions've got to be 'yes' or 'no.' No multiple choice."

Peter pursed his lips. Why did he have to start off with a legalist? "Do I live in water?"

The man looked again at his back. "My name is Morton Bing, and . . ." He looked again and said, " . . . sometimes."

Peter wrinkled his nose. "Sometimes? I thought you said . . ."

Morton Bing had turned away and was now approaching a young blond woman who smiled coquettishly at the men lined up before her.

"Hello. I'm Peter Campbell. Do I live on land?"

The grayhaired lady ignored his face to search his back. She nodded gravely.

"Your name?" Peter asked.

"Mrs. Waters," she replied with tight lips as if the revelation were a violation of her right to privacy.

"Hello. I'm Virginia Hightower. Do I lay eggs or bear my young?"

Peter stared up at a female four inches taller than he and then went around to her back. Her long neck reminded him of a giraffe, but pinned to her sweater was the outline of a turtle. "My name is Peter Campbell, and you lay eggs."

Virginia smiled sweetly and turned to the man next to her.

Peter felt sudden relief to find himself next to Brenda. "Hello, I'm Peter Campbell, and I think this game is damn silly."

"Now, Peter," she said, glancing about to make sure Trudy was not in earshot. "You slide on your belly and have a venomous bite."

He laughed. "You haven't seen anything yet."

A man near the fireplace raised his voice. "Okay. That's enough." The man had a small nose, rimless glasses, a head of stiff black hair, and a full beard. He reminded Peter of a character from a Russian novel. "We've given you enough time for everyone to become acquainted, and you should know what animal you are." The man stepped back and grasped Trudy's hand on one side and Brenda's on the other. "Now let's form a circle and each of us introduce ourselves and turn our backs and tell what animal we are."

The man paused to heighten the anticipation. "My name is Alvin Cross, and I'm not wearing an animal." He spoke only with his tongue and teeth, like a radio announcer Peter had listened to on a classical music station. Peter felt Alvin's not wearing an animal was a breach of the rules. Alvin turned to Brenda.

"I'm Brenda Campbell." She turned. "And I'm an ostrich."

"Hi, Brenda," Trudy rang out in a steely tone with a nod to everyone else to indicate this was to be the choral response to each introduction.

Names rang out, bodies turned, the crowd's programmed refrain inched steadily toward Peter. "I'm Peter Campbell." He turned. "And I'm a snake."

Everyone broke into laughter. Peter felt his face glowing red. Brenda snickered and pretended she had nothing to do with him. "Then I don't know what the hell I am," he scoffed. "Maybe a jackass."

An awkward silence ensued. Then Alvin stepped forward and said, "Now we're here to help each other. Will someone tell Peter what he is?"

"He's a bear," Virginia Hightower said with a wink.

"Oh," Peter said dumbly and turned to the man next to him. Names and animals swept along the line, flitted about in Peter's mind like a flock of frightened birds. Normally, he was good at remembering names, but somehow this game approach created more confusion than clarity.

"All right, you can sit down." Alvin dropped hands and stepped over to the fireplace. Clad in jeans, hiking boots, and a sweatshirt, he looked as if he had just stumbled out of the woods. "Fun, wasn't it?" His beady eyes searched those sitting on the floor in front of him. They nodded in approval. "That's a game you can use with any group where you want to mix people up and make them feel comfortable with each other. Good for social gatherings at the church."

Peter squirmed back in the wooden chair he had found near the door. The chair, made of dowel rods, was as comfortable as a torture rack. Didn't Alvin have any realization how badly the game had backfired in his case? He was a jackass and knew nobody.

"Well, we're going to have a great week." Alvin smiled like the activities director of a cruise ship. Trudy stood with her arms crossed against her flat chest and one foot swung back against the chimney stones—the same color as her flesh.

"It's going to take work, though." Alvin surveyed the group. "I know this is called a retreat, but that doesn't mean vacation. Some of you want to ski." He sneered at a pair of skis leaning against the end of the mantle. "Won't be much time unless you like doing it in moonlight." He officiously listed the meal hours and explained how everyone would be divided into two groups listed on the bulletin board. To free everyone up so they could work on problems in their relationships, husbands and wives would not be in the same group. Alvin's eyes surveyed the faces as if everyone were riddled with troubles.

Peter felt a twinge of regret at not being able to ski. Perhaps he and Brenda could go out after the evening session. On the old retreats, there had been time for real games and for socializing and just plain relaxing, but obviously Alvin and Trudy were a new breed. Serious. Almost hostile with their piercing gazes.

"You've come for a purpose." The voice was Trudy's. "You may not know it, but most of you are in the most difficult period of your lives—as bad as puberty, maybe worse. Mid-life. Mid-career. How well you get through it will affect everything you do from here on out." Her tone hinted at dire consequences for those who foundered in the rapids of mid-life waters.

Alvin said, "It's our job to help you deal with the issues you're facing. We aren't experts. We don't have answers. This isn't a seminary." Whatever blew through Alvin's mind at that moment caused him to snicker. "What happens will be because you put yourselves into the experience."

"Are there any questions?" Trudy asked.

"Is there a shower in the house?" a heavy man in a sports jacket asked.

Trudy said there was none. A half bath on the first floor, the full bath upstairs to be used only by those needing the tub. The water was heated by wood—very slow. Use as little as possible, and don't linger because there will be others waiting to wash up.

Peter asked if there was heat in the upstairs bathroom. There was none, just what came from the hot water and the hall. The door was to be left open as much as possible. There being no more questions, Trudy announced dinner in ten minutes.

Both bathrooms filled immediately, so Peter followed Brenda and lay down on his bed. "Great game," he mocked. "I can see the members of the garden club playing it with gusto. They could use roses instead of animals."

Brenda ignored him and rummaged through the top drawer of the dresser. "I thought I put a beret in here."

"Cool move on the snake," he said sarcastically.

Brenda turned. "I thought you knew what you were. What on earth were you doing when you were supposed to be getting clues?"

He turned toward her. "Talking to you — which I enjoyed, and listening to a legalist expound on the rules of the game — which I did not enjoy."

She laughed. "Now, Peter, you've got to get into this thing and give it all you've got. It was obvious you aren't taking it seriously."

"Oh, but I am," he protested. "Trudy and Alvin are real professionals." He didn't say at what, but he was certain one area they had mastered was manipulation. They didn't even ask if he wanted to play their stupid game.

"Now there you go. You've got to pull yourself together and make the best of it."

Peter changed the subject. "Boy, I can see why Wes hasn't come to one of these." He paused and raised the pitch of his voice. "Hello, I'm Bishop Wesley Stone. Do I lay eggs or bear my young?"

Brenda laughed. "Peter, you're terrible."

"Well, you have to admit this isn't Wes's bag. There's no money here either. They all look like line preachers from lean churches. Not the kind Wes cozies up to."

Brenda flopped on her bed and reached over to him. "What's gotten into you? Can't you take anything seriously any more?"

Peter thought for a moment. Being away from Good Samaritan released energy he seldom felt when he was in

Oakdale. He saw the picture at the Delaware Club. What would Jonah have done on a retreat like this? Having rebelled against God, there was no mistaking how he would have responded to Trudy and Alvin. "I don't think this is a place for revolutionaries," Peter mumbled.

"What's that?" Brenda asked sleepily.

"Nothing," Peter replied. "I was just thinking out loud."

7

At dinner, the tables were piled high with platters of wieners, cabbage, and baked beans. Peter asked for whole wheat bread, but the chef only glared at him as if he had no compassion for the starving of the world.

Next to Peter sat a short, round-faced man dressed in a light blue velour shirt and purple polyester slacks, who wheezed loudly between bites. He introduced himself to Peter and then chuckled when he realized Peter was the snake. "My wife put me up to it," Peter snickered.

The man rattled off a series of "Do you know who?" questions. Peter weighed each name, but they were all foreign. He had a fleeting fear that the life of the denomination was going on without him. Who were all these people?

The man listened with wheezing attentiveness as Peter answered his questions about Good Samaritan. He seemed awestruck at the congregation's size, Peter's subdued description of the buildings, the understated prosperity of the members.

Peter was buttering a slice of bread—white bread—and searching in vain for some place downwind where he could park the cabbage when the man looked at him with a gleam in his eyes. "Have you ever tried sleep therapy?" he asked.

"Sleep therapy? You mean to help people sleep better—like during sermons?"

The jocular tone sailed right over the man's serious expression. "No, this is something entirely new in group work. It's a way of getting through to the subconscious. It's like hypnosis. The groups are about eight or ten. We provide cots. Everyone lies down, and I speak in a very soothing voice." He demonstrated by slowing his pace and dropping his voice to a sensuous whisper. "Then, when everyone's asleep, I make positive suggestions — you know, like 'You're going to work much harder at your job.' 'You're going to get along with the boss, you're going to cut down on the length of your coffee breaks.' Things like that."

"How do you know they take too long on their coffee breaks?" Peter asked.

"Well, I don't, but most people do. In this particular program — we call it 'sleep-suggestion' — we're concentrating on work habits. It does wonders for people. They're thrilled at the way they become more productive, more positive about their employment. It's amazing."

Peter nodded without enthusiasm and talked briefly to the couple across the table, a hardy Grant Wood husband and wife with graying hair: lean, affable, shy, their faces weathered by sharing in work on the farms.

The man next to him was back at his ear like a mosquito. "How's your preaching going?"

Peter dipped a piece of wiener in the baked beans. "All right, I guess."

The man's green eyes held Peter in a glare of compassion. "Guess? Don't you know? Are the people responding?"

Peter shrugged. "It's hard to tell. Some, I suppose." He saw the sea of faces waiting for the corpse at a wake.

"No more than some?" the man asked.

"People make remarks once in a while. Beyond that . . . I don't know."

"Have you tried the dialogical approach?"

Peter stared at the green eyes in puzzlement. "You mean two people talking to each other?"

The man's face broadened into an omniscient grin. "Oh no, that's passé. Went out several years ago. I'm talking about dialogue with the congregation, speaking to their questions, their interests."

"In the worship service?" Peter asked. He envisioned a chaotic scene resembling a TV audience talk show.

"No. No. Nothing like that." The man shook his head at Peter's naiveté. "I have them write on cards we provide — 'wish cards' we call them — their dreams and fantasies. What they want to be and do. Then I center my sermons on those dreams. That way, I know I'm talking to them where they are. They love it. Never in my life have my sermons gotten such a tremendous response." The man's voice rose in pitch.

Peter forced down another bite of wiener and beans. He could feel the green eyes searching his face for some hint of recognition that dialogical sermons were the ground swell of a new homiletical wave. But Peter gave the man nothing. If he preached on the aspirations of Good Samaritan's members, he would speak of huge rose gardens, teeming fundamentalist temples, cold business efficiency, ill-thought-out political revolutions. It wasn't Jonah's job to give people their fantasies, but to point and warn.

The man was not finished. "Maybe you don't understand what I'm saying. Take, for instance, a wife. She writes on her card, 'I wish I could be more loving toward my husband and children.' That's pretty straight-forward. I called that sermon, 'Successful Wifery.' In it, I drew on all the material I had on how women could relate to their husbands and work effectively with children. It was simple, very simple — that's where people are. Afterward, a crowd of women came up to tell me how grateful they were that I had dealt with the problems they face."

Peter nodded to the cook that he wanted more bread. "And what did the husbands and children do?"

"Well, they listened too. It was good for them to hear what successful wiving is — helped them know how to cooperate with a woman who's working on a wiving program."

"Wiving program?" Peter asked. This man's church seemed increasingly more remote from anything he had heard of.

"Well, certainly," came the reply with a hint of astonishment. "How can you do anything without a program?"

"But for being a wife?"

The man forked a wad of cabbage into his maw. "I gave them principles: husband first, children second, God over all, quarterback instead of boss; then a schedule of development. My sermons are mimeographed so people can take them home. It's hard to remember everything."

"It would be," Peter acknowledged. He saw wives with their refrigerators papered with sermons, check marks where they had tucked away another homiletical tidbit.

The man's eyes bulged like those of a salesman reaching the climax of his pitch. "I brought some along. I'd like to show them to you. They're not long. There'll be time after the meeting tonight . . ."

Peter smiled kindly and demurred. "I'm terribly sorry, but we've made a commitment to do some moonlight cross-country skiing. Have you ever tried it?"

"Skiing? At night? Isn't it cold? Couldn't you get lost? Those are big woods out there."

"I suppose we could," Peter replied. With the way he felt about the retreat, it might not be a bad idea. "But since we'd leave tracks, I suppose somebody could come and find us."

The man blinked nervously, as if Peter's emotional imbalance posed a threat.

"Peter," Brenda said, placing her hand on his arm. "We're not going skiing. We didn't bring any equipment."

"Then we'll find some. Anything to get away from here."

8

According to the list on the bulletin board, Brenda's group would meet in the dining room with Alvin, and Peter's in the living room under Trudy. The wieners and beans grew heavy in his stomach at the thought of a week with Trudy's cold eyes and flat voice. If she were the one to report on his progress to Bishop Stone, what chance would he have?

"Oh, you've got the fire," Brenda complained. "It isn't fair. We should have the living room half time."

"How about trading you the fire for Alvin?"

"Peter, can't you hit it off with Trudy if you try?" Brenda asked.

Eschewing a reply, Peter led the way to the fireplace where they could sit for a few minutes before the evening program began. Feet scraped overhead, the crash of flushing toilets rumbled through the thin walls.

Suddenly Brenda flinched. Peter glanced at the back corner of the room to see the cause of the upset. He too flinched, then searched for a safe place to rest his eyes. Alvin and Virginia Hightower were standing locked in an embrace. Virginia's eyes were closed, her chin rested on top of Alvin's curly head. Alvin's bearded face was snuggled into her long white neck.

Brenda searched Peter for some indication of what to do. "You're going to have a lively group," he whispered.

Brenda's eyes grew cold with alarm. "Maybe we will trade Alvin for the fire."

"Oh, don't let us disturb you." The voice was Alvin's. His arms still encircled Virginia's totem-pole waist. "This is a form of therapy—touching, feeling. We all need it. Purely platonic."

Peter cast them a limp smile. Had Plato developed his theory by going around hugging tall women he hardly knew?

"Maybe you're new to these retreats," Virginia added. "You'll get used to it. Why, by the end of the week you'll be hugging everybody. We get real close." She smiled at Alvin; he released his grip and planted a platonic kiss on her forehead.

To Peter, a week felt like a month. Even an all-night tour on skis wouldn't give him the sense of distance he needed.

At the sound of the gong, Brenda got up to leave. "Now you be good," Peter warned her. There were tiny lines of anxiety etched around her eyes.

Trudy slinked in followed by the man who had sat next to Peter at dinner. He walked with mincing steps; his face flexed through a whole series of expressions as he kept a stream of words pouring into Trudy's ear. If she was listening, the stiff expression on her face showed no sign. She stood impassively by the fireplace and watched as the rest of the group sauntered in and dropped into the randomly scattered chairs.

"Let's stand and form a circle." She held out her hands to those next to her. "Since we're going to be together for the week, I want us to think of ourselves as a big family. We're here to have fun, but also to work. The more you put into the experience, the more you'll get out of it." She nodded to the smiles worn by veterans of past retreats. How many times have some of these people been here to get their problems worked out? Peter wondered. They were like a club.

"We need to get to know each other better," Trudy said. Peter thought that had already been covered, although as he scanned those around the circle, animals and names swirled in confusion through his head. "What I want you to do now is introduce yourself and then lead the rest of us in some physical action that expresses you."

Trying to think of something other than bolting for the window, Peter's nerves began to vibrate. Trudy said, "I'm Trudy Valone." She leaped into the circle like a black lizard and sank down into a full split. 'Oh's and 'Ah's greeted her performance. Everyone tried to imitate her. Groans rose over wobbling, falling bodies. Peter just bent one knee and leaned forward with a dumb smile smarting his face.

"I'm Fred White, pastor of the Rocking Hill . . ." the man who had sat next to Peter began.

"No titles," Trudy shot out. "Here, you're just Fred."

Fred accepted the rebuke with an embarrassed smile and started over. Then he took two steps into the circle, bent forward from the waist, and raised his hands in an attitude of prayer. He looked like a poorly choreographed pope greeting thousands after stepping off the papal plane. Peter and the others followed like programmed robots.

As Peter's turn approached, the window still looked like the best bet. A cacophony of voices rising in his head told him the exercise was dumb, silly. Then he wondered if he was too proud to let his hair down. "I'm Peter Campbell," he blurted with a glance at the clone-like expressions around the circle. He stepped forward, nodded politely, and returned to his place to observe the robots mimicking his imaginationless gesture.

Virginia Hightower forced on the group a complete somersault, a slim man demanded a jump with feet slapped together while in the air. The group's landing shook the floor as if the supporting timbers were giving way. Laughter rose from veterans, while Peter and the other plebes glanced about as if maybe they could still get their money back.

"Good. Good," Trudy said. She was long on positive reinforcement for short accomplishment. "We're going to have a great time this week." She sat down on the hearth and gestured for everyone to relax.

Her enthusiasm attacked Peter like a weapon. A whole week. Impossible. It dawned on him that if he needed this kind of thing, at much lower cost he could have joined Mr. Drissle's yoga-ing leprechauns at Good Samaritan.

"We're going to form diads." Trudy announced. For those of you who haven't been here before, a diad is two people."

That made sense to Peter—monad, diad, although he wondered why the term 'pairs' had vanished from the common vocabulary.

Trudy's tone became businesslike. "Now we're going to begin work on our problems." She directed everyone to pick out a problem and begin to discuss it with his partner. "This is an exercise in communication and listening. Those of you who are listening are not to attempt to solve the problem. Just make sure you understand what your partner is saying and help clarify what it is he or she is talking about. Any questions?"

People stirred about looking for partners. Seeing Fred White padding toward him with a determined look, Peter slunk quickly toward the windows. Virginia Hightower cast him an inviting grin, but he pretended not to notice. Beneath the window sat a man with a long narrow face. He was dressed in brown slacks and a blue wool cardigan. Peter had noticed him before: Jack something—not Wolf, which he had worn on his back. For his introductory action he had lain face down on the floor like a corpse. Peter pulled up a chair and introduced himself.

"Jack Longley," the man said.

"You been to one of these before?" Peter asked.

"Never. Bishop Stone told me it might help." Jack spoke in a funereal monotone. His eyes were sad, lifeless.

They had just started to share information on their respective churches when Trudy's rapier voice cut them off. "No trivia. Details about churches are meaningless. You share feelings only."

"Lots of rules around here," Peter groaned. If feelings were all that counted, then it was out the window and onto cross-country skis.

Jack's impassionate face did not betray if he had heard Peter's remark. Peter waited for him to speak, but pallid lips remained unmoving. Eyelids drooped as if Jack were about to fall asleep. Whoever had cut his brown hair must have been having an off day; the sides were tufted like grass chewed by a herd of goats.

"Well, maybe we should start dealing with our problems," Peter said tentatively.

Jack nodded mechanically and began: "I know she said we shouldn't talk about our churches, but I can't describe my problem otherwise."

Peter nodded for him to proceed. He was aware that he was being graded for being a good listener. His ears ached with effort.

"Well, we're in this little church in a rundown section of the city. A lot of urban renewal has been done nearby, but none directly around the church. The congregation is mostly white, but most of the people have moved out of the neighborhood. At one time there were eight hundred members; now there are seventy-eight." Sadness weighed down his voice; his lifeless eyes crawled to some random spot on the floor.

"My problem is that I'm depressed all the time and can't get anything done." His hound dog eyes checked to make sure Peter was listening. "I stare at the study wall instead of writing sermons. I get in the car in good weather and sit in the park instead of calling on people — not that there are that many to call on anyway. And when I'm at meetings, my mind wanders. People have to tell me what's being discussed because I've lapsed. My wife thinks I need a psychiatrist, but my friends say it's the church. They think that if I got out I'd feel a lot better." He paused. "I don't know, though. I've never been anyplace else. If there were more demands and all I did was stare at the wall and go to the park, well, things might be worse."

"Like you've got no confidence?" Peter asked.

Jack ignored his remark and continued. "I'm beginning to wonder if I should've been a minister in the first place. Yet I can't think of anything else I want to do. Nothing interests me. I know that sounds crazy, but that's the way it is." Jack pursed his lips as if his problem had already been judged unsolvable.

"Seventeen years I've been there. And all that time, it's been down hill: one family after another moving out, the budget dropping, a few blacks joining and then quitting because they weren't accepted. There was a riot there in the sixties — broke a lot of windows. That kept new people from coming. No one'll go where there's been a riot. The roof leaks, the furnace doesn't work right. I could go on indefinitely."

Whatever weighed down Jack's shoulders hung like a storm cloud over Peter. He could think of nothing meaningful to say. "You're depressed," he added limply.

Jack's head jerked up. "Acutely. My wife's afraid I'll do myself in. My parents can't understand why I went there in the first place; they think I'm just pouring my life down the drain." His gaze drifted over to the sheen of night at the windows. "What about you?" he asked.

Peter cocked his head in thought. He hadn't taken stock of his problems; there hadn't been time with all the meetings and programs. "Well, according to the bishop, I'm not doing the job my congregation needs done."

Jack impaled Peter with an enervating stare. "You don't agree with him?"

"No. I'm doing what the committee that called me said was to be done."

"Committees," Jack scoffed. "They don't know anything."

Jack's ability to state an opinion amazed Peter. "After getting there," he continued, "I discovered that everyone in the congregation wants something else. There are factions; I'm being pushed around by one, then another. There's no willingness to work together for one overall purpose. People are uptight because the church isn't bringing in new members and getting more money."

Jack's gaze intensified. "Who do you think is at fault?"

"Why them," Peter answered bluntly. "Not that I'm without some blame. But I have been sticking to my original commitment."

"So you've got the answers and they're not buying?"

Peter stared into Jack's accusing eyes. "I didn't say that. Bishop Stone wanted me to come here and find out. If I discover I'm wrong, I'm willing to reconsider. . ."

"Sounds to me like you're on an ego trip. You know. You snow the congregation with your intellect. They're impressed, but they don't know what the hell you're talking about."

Peter reeled. "I thought we were only supposed to talk and listen — no diagnosis."

"Actually, it's a form of neurosis: intellectual pride — you satisfy your needs for acceptance and love by impressing the congregation with your wisdom. They don't understand you, there's no communication, but they hold you in awe. It's very effective, but ultimately damaging. I'd say you'd best get out before the congregation discovers there's no real person there. If they do, they'll get angry. They'll feel betrayed because they've admired a nothing."

Again the window exit beckoned. The only betrayal Peter felt was Jack's total disregard for the rules. "I'm not sure I'm going over their heads intellectually. We're on different wavelengths. My way of thinking doesn't fit their . . ."

Jack leaned forward. "There must've been a deficiency of affection in your childhood. Maybe your mother and father were preoccupied or unable to bestow love. Leaves the child impoverished for life, a beggar for attention. Lots of ministers suffer from it."

Peter's muscles tightened. "I don't think you're really listening to what I'm saying. Trudy said we're . . ."

"Might be something oedipal there. You never know. That's a tough one." Jack's eyes shone as if he beheld Peter's troubles growing like a volcanic mountain. "Have you tried therapy?"

Peter's muscles stiffened with rage. "Look, Jack, the instructions were that we're just to state our problems. That's all. I don't think amateur psychology is what Trudy meant."

Jack stared coldly. "Trudy, Trudy, Trudy. Why are you always talking about Trudy? Is she your mother? Maybe you have a dependency problem — never cut the apron strings — mama's little boy. You know what I'm talking about?" Since Peter's mother had died when he was an infant, he did not. He found the remarks infuriating, but with Trudy's judicial eyes playing over the room, he didn't think this was the time for an outburst.

"This defensive anger you're displaying. Where does that come from?"

Without saying a word, Peter stared at Jack. Then he said, "It comes from the fact that in this exercise we're just supposed to talk and listen, and you're using it as an excuse to show off your prowess in pop psychology. Easy answers with no awareness of the problems. I'll tell you it's damn irritating."

For fleeting moments, Peter thought he saw a cynical smile starting to form on Jack's face. It was a miracle Jack had any members at all left in his church. "You really are defensive," Jack said. "I think I've put my finger on the problem. You'd better work on it this week, or things'll get worse."

Without responding, Peter slid his chair back and looked toward the other diads scattered about the room. "Thanks for listening," he said sarcastically.

"You've really got problems," Jack said with mock compassion. "I hope you get them worked out."

Trudy stood near the fire, her lips curled in satisfaction. "All right, that's enough. Bring your conversations to a close and then form a circle. We're going to share all the things we learned about ourselves in the diad experience. It's called group echo."

Like a dog responding to a threat from its master, Peter dragged himself to his feet and locked hands with those beside him. His muscles jerked with frustration. What had he learned about himself? Nothing but that when attacked he got upset. Would that fall in the acceptable column on Trudy's checklist? He eyed the skis leaning against the mantle and the window black with night. Away. Away. That was all he could think of.

9

Friday dawned with the patter of rain on the roof. Peter groped through the steely light coming in the window and stared out. The snow behind Pinetree had turned to gray slush. It was a good time to be leaving.

He reached over and jostled Brenda's shoulder. She

groaned, raised her head, and cast him a look of disbelief that morning had come already. "Come on," he said mockingly. "Time for celebration." On the schedule posted in the entry, that was the title of the morning's session.

Brenda's head dropped back to the pillow. "What are you mumbling about?"

"Nothing," Peter replied. "I'm just having psychotic hallucinations."

"You're still fighting. Can't you just go along?"

"No." He pulled on his shirt. "Boy, is a shower at home going to feel good. Two frozen baths all week — with savages pounding on the door to get into the bathroom. You'd think the sanitation department would shut this place down."

Brenda pulled herself up and wrapped the bedcovers around her shoulders. "Peter, you're not listening to me."

Peter paused. "I am. I've spent all week sharpening up my listening skills. My ears are fine-tuned. You say I'm fighting it: you're right. If I didn't, I'd have to admit I've got every psychological disorder known to man. Probably even some that aren't known because they haven't yet been discovered. I may be out of whack, but I'm not as far out as some of the experts on this retreat think I am." His record for the week was intact. Someone had attacked him at least once each day. He had had no light shed on his troubles other than to be told that he rebelled against rules and held some deep-seated hatred against authority figures. Trudy and Alvin, to be specific.

"I don't know why your group has been so different from ours," Brenda said. "There's been a lot of support. People are truly helping each other."

"Maybe Alvin is a better leader than Trudy. She doesn't exactly bubble over with warmth." Her eyes reminded Peter of a pond covered over with black ice. He tied his shoes and glanced out at the rain slanting down. "Our group is in a contest to see who can put down whom. Those with the largest psychology vocabularies are winning. And then there's Virginia Hightower and a couple of other gals who try to smooth things over with talk about love and their constant hugging."

"Did they get you?"

"Just once." He had thought Virginia was out of the room, so he lowered his guard. Suddenly a bony hand spun him around and long octopus arms wrapped around him. He froze like a statue, trying to think of how he could get away without bruising her maternal instinct. "She was right next to me."

"Did you like it?"

He looked over at Brenda. "What are you playing now? Jealous wife?"

Brenda slid out of bed. "I just want to know. It isn't often you embrace other women." She put her arms around him as he was pulling on his sweater, so he could not see.

"It was part of Virginia's political campaign. She's running for mother figure of the group."

"That's not a feeling answer. Remember — feelings only." Brenda thrust her face in front of his.

"I know. I'm giving you an analytical response that's designed to evade the question. Quotation from Chairman Trudy. If I do answer it, then you've got to tell me how much you enjoy Alvin's platonic gymnastics."

Brenda laughed. "Jealous husband?"

The gong rang, and Peter finished putting on his sweater. "Another gourmet breakfast," he chortled. "Corn flakes soufflé."

The breakfast turned out to be sandstorm pancakes with molasses. When it was finished, both groups filed into the living room. Alvin and Trudy waited by the blazing fire. Suddenly, Trudy threw up her arms. "Celebration!" Her look remained as cold and distant as ever. Peter surmised this act came automatically every Friday no matter how the week had gone. "Form a big circle." Her arms and hands gestured like snakes. "For the whole morning, we'll share the progress we've made. After each one speaks, show your love and support by cheering." She reached into a cardboard box next to the chimney and passed out noisemakers and hats tattered and wrinkled from heavy use. Balloons came next, and for a few moments everyone was occupied blowing and tying. Peter's popped with a bang, drawing laughter.

The recitations of progress became dull with repetition: problems between ministers and congregations had been resolved, personal relationships were patched, struggles would be tackled with new resolve. And over everything like thick gumbo icing on a bad cake was love, love, love. A wave of nausea swept across Peter's stomach when Jack Longley reported he had never felt such affection for others. Peter sank down in a chair near the door where he hoped to be overlooked. But Trudy's radar eyes ferreted him out. "Peter Campbell, we haven't heard from you."

Peter rose slowly in the chair. His brain whirred. Faces waited eagerly for his response. "I'm afraid I'm a bit short on words," he said. "I guess I display a number of mental abnormalities . . ." A hush fell as the group waited for more. But there was nothing in Peter's mind but sarcasm that would sink his case before Trudy and Alvin for sure. "And that's about it."

"Let's hear it for Peter," Trudy shouted. Horns blew, hats bobbed, balloons bounced into the air. Smiles surrounded Peter as if he had just won an election to public office. The wave of levity ebbed, and the expectant hush waited for another victim to speak.

At lunch, boiled cabbage made its third appearance for the week. When Peter had eaten four slices of bread and nothing else and Brenda was finished, he said quick goodbyes to those round about and towed Brenda out of the lodge. "What a relief," he gasped. He did not even turn around for a last glance at the rustic building. He had no desire to stamp bad memories on his mind.

"I wanted to get some addresses," Brenda said mildly.

"What for?"

"I might write some letters," she said. Peter guided the

car carefully along the pitted lane now covered with rain-soaked mush resembling boiled cabbage. The wipers cleared ice from the windshield; by the time they pulled onto the highway, the heater had begun to make a dent in the damp cold.

Brenda turned to him. "Peter, did you have to say what you did?"

"It was the truth. I thought honesty was in at these conferences."

"Didn't you get anything from it? Didn't you learn anything about what to do at Good Samaritan?"

Peter paused. He hadn't been thinking about Good Samaritan, except for occasional glints that some of the people on the retreat resembled members of the church. "Yes," he replied confidently. "I should keep on with what I have been doing."

"You didn't come up with any new ideas? There's no way you can get people to work together?"

"Not if they don't want to. Did the people up here work together?"

"In our group they did." She snuggled up to him.

"Well, they didn't in ours. With all the jockeying for position, it was as if I hadn't left Good Samaritan. Do you think maybe I just don't hit it off with church people anymore?" That had occurred to him. Maybe there were people outside the church who were different. Since he spent so much time in the church, he had no way of knowing.

Brenda said, "I just don't understand it. I had hoped this retreat would make things better."

Peter slowed the car so as not to slide on the glistening pavement. Forest trees and open fields blurred past the rain-streaked windows. He too had hoped, but not overly much.

Brenda asked, "Will Wes get a report?"

Peter envisioned the bishop interrogating Trudy by phone. The report would be bad. He just didn't take to manipulators. "Yes," he replied in the monotone of a criminal court defendant.

Brenda faced the front of the car and did not reply.

"I have an idea," Peter said. "Since I'm not preaching Sunday, and Jackie and Jeff are in good shape, why don't we stop overnight at a cabin?"

Brenda's look brightened. "A real retreat?" she asked mockingly.

"Right," he replied. "Then we can tell Wes what a good time we had."

10

It was snowing on Monday when Peter drove into the church parking lot. The car slithered back and forth, then the wheels regained traction as he headed toward the parking place still marked, 'Dr. Strong.' On the radio, a jovial announcer reported the weather bureau had just issued a blizzard warning. "There will be falling temperatures, up to a foot of snow by nightfall accompanied by strong winds."

A small drift lay against the temporary door leading into the brick shell of the new narthex. Inside hung the reek of kerosene. Peter nodded to the workmen as he passed through to the freezing walkway leading to Assisi.

In Assisi's large meeting area, Mr. Drissle, his head pressed against the tile floor and his legs raised like an inverted statue, cast him a reserved nod. Mr. Drissle's charges, untouched by the diet program, strained and groaned like they were on torture racks. The lack of privacy Assisi afforded inhibited neither their gyrations nor their grunts.

John Rhodes' cup of coffee sat on the corner of Sheila's desk; John himself, perched on a chair nearby, stared at Sheila with the look of a hungry dog. Sorting through a pile of papers, she ignored Mr. Rhodes' trivialities about the storm, how lousy the roads were, and how he could run the road department better than the jerk who had been appointed by the mayor.

Sheila welcomed Peter with a smile, but then her blue eyes flickered with uncertainty: "I hate to have you start with a schedule conflict your first day back from the retreat, but that's what we've got. Last Monday Mary Jones called to set a date for her wedding. She said she followed your advice, found a great guy, and wanted to get married this afternoon at five o'clock at the park."

"The park!" Peter exclaimed with a glance at the snow mounding on the glass panes overhead. The wind could be felt through chinks in the frames.

"Her fiancé is a ski instructor," Sheila said. "They met on skis, so they want to get married on skis."

Peter nodded. He would go skiing after all. But the cold — he paused, then told himself he shouldn't complain. Mary had done what he suggested. She needed to have her marriage go well.

"And then," Sheila added, "Mr. Krohn called on Wednesday saying there would be a very important meeting at five-thirty this afternoon. I told him about the conflict, but all he said was, 'If Reverend Campbell knows what's good for him, he'll be at that meeting.'"

The dull ache in the back of Peter's neck, the familiar hallmark when he was at Good Samaritan, returned.

"I'm sorry," Sheila said.

"It's all right," Peter replied. "Mr. Krohn has no right to do that."

"What will you do?"

"Perform the wedding — and then come back for the meeting. It's all I can do. The park is only fifteen minutes away. Mr. Krohn will just have to understand."

11

The shop Mary had arranged for ski rental was located on Main Street. Cars crawled by with their lights on and kept to deep ruts banked with ice. Streetlights glowed against the dark gray sky. Wind seared Peter's face, ice particles stung his eyes. He shuddered to think of what the wind would be like at the park.

The bald, amiable proprietor of the shop was expecting him. A yellow slip had already been made out with Peter's name on it. He gave his shoe size and weight and sat down to be fitted on a dusty chair that looked like a bent snowshoe.

The man returned with misshapen sweat socks and a pair of scuffed black boots. The laces were so knotted the man had trouble tying them tight.

Peter stood and walked about. His feet felt like they were in a vise. The man disappeared into the back and returned with another pair, equally decrepit, but they fit better. Then came skis and a brief lecture on how to tell right from left. Peter told the man he had been on skis before, but the man remained unconvinced. Both skis had to be put on while Peter was in the store. The man recited a litany of the frantic phone calls he got when he let people out without showing them how the equipment worked. Peter looked at his watch. With the storm, the roads would be slow. Finally he got the skis, a pair of bamboo poles, and the boots tucked under his arms and was about to leave.

The man held out the yellow slip. "Who's paying for this?"

Peter stopped. Mary had made all the arrangements. He assumed that meant rental too. "It's for the wedding."

The man continued to hold up the slip.

Peter shrugged. "I'm a minister. Pastor of Good Samaritan Church out on Valley Road."

The man's gaze was unwavering. "Sorry, Reverend. But I've got regulations. You never know who you're dealing with nowadays."

Peter quickly hauled out his wallet and handed the man a twenty.

He nodded approvingly. "This'll be fine. When you return the equipment, I'll just deduct the fee for the time you've used it."

By using back roads heavy with snow but light on traffic, Peter was able to get to the park by five to five. His heart raced at the thought of getting through the ceremony and then rushing back to the church. Mr. Krohn had never done anything like this before. He should get a book on business etiquette. Dark clouds raced overhead; windblown snow made it almost impossible to see. After parking in a drift, Peter bundled the equipment under his arms and staggered through knee-deep snow to the pavilion. Woodsmoke blew horizontally from the top of the stone chimney.

Inside the log shelter, a plastic cloth covered a rustic plank table with platters of sandwiches and cakes. Half a dozen figures huddled by the fire. A girl with a red round face approached him. "Reverend Campbell?"

Peter nodded. His joints were stiff with cold.

"My name's Pamela. I'm the maid of honor." She pointed to a bearded young man in a turtleneck sweater and woolen knickers. "That's Artie, the best man. And Tony's parents, Mr. and Mrs. Perrone." The short, stout couple smiled; Mr. Perrone shook Peter's hand. "The others are friends. There should be more, but the weather might have discouraged them."

Undoubtedly, Peter thought. He stood by the fire, the only source of warmth in the structure. Through cracks between the logs, he could see that daylight was on the wane. Like a rising ocean tide, cold from the concrete floor seeped into his boots and up his legs.

"It's time," Pamela said officiously. "We should go out to meet them."

Grudgingly pulling himself away from the fire, Peter followed the others to the lee side of the building, threw down his skis, and bent over to fasten the latches. When he had secured one, he was puzzled at the way his heel hung out over the side of the ski. It hadn't done that in the shop.

"You've got them backwards," Pamela shouted with a laugh.

He did. He took off the ski, reversed it, and then put on

the other. In spite of being sheltered from the wind, his fingers were numb, when he puffed his cheeks he felt the stiffness in his flesh. He buttoned the top button of his overcoat, drew his vinyl gloves from his pocket, pulled his hat down hard so the wind wouldn't blow it off. Mr. and Mrs. Perrone shouted how hard it was to walk on skis, but they obediently followed Pamela out to the windblown knob in front of the pavilion. Peter slid his skis forward gingerly, fearful that he might slip backward or rocket down the hill and into the dark woods.

Unable to think of anything else to do, he suggested everyone line up for the ceremony: Pamela to his right, Artie to the left, Mr. and Mrs. Perrone and the others behind.

From a distant wall of forest, a figure emerged and side-stepped toward them. Between the darkness and the snow blasting his eyes, Peter could not tell if it was Mary or Tony. The numbness in his feet had reached his knees; he could not feel the tips of his fingers in his gloves.

The figure arrived with a series of lunges through deep drifts. Beneath the yellow stocking hat was Mary Jones' baby face—bright red, crusted with ice. Thin tears dripped from her eyes. "Oh, it's good to see all of you," she gasped. "I never believed it would be this cold." She glanced at each one, then scanned the fading treeline. "Anyone seen Tony?"

Artie drew his head down into the neck of his parka like a turtle withdrawing into its shell. "I hope he knows what time it is," he said. "It's cold up here!" His voice quivered. He swung his arms in a circle to up his circulation.

"This is damn foolishness," Mr. Perrone mumbled from behind the scarf drawn up over his mouth and nose. Mrs. Perrone nudged him sharply.

Peter reached up to make sure his collar was raised against his neck. Cold air still poured in around his chest. At the forest edge from which Tony was expected to emerge, nothing moved. Peter glanced at his watch. Five ten. He thought of Mr. Krohn and whomever else it was that he was supposed to meet with. Had they gotten a report from Pinetree already?

"He'll be here any minute," Mary said reassuringly. "He's a real good skier. He just took one of the long trails." Peter clutched at her words to inject hope into his cold veins.

The cold suddenly uncorked his sinuses. Cold liquid gushed down his upper lip. Groping with a gloved hand, he located the handkerchief in his trouser pocket and brought it up quickly to stem the flow. Every part of him was locked in cold: his legs trembled, his hands were numb to the wrists. The treeline had been swallowed up by a pall of darkness and wind-driven snow. He had a premonition he would become deathly ill. Wasn't this the way pneumonia started? "Maybe we should go inside," he suggested to Mary.

"Oh, he'll be right here," she said brightly. "I want us to come together on skis. That's where we first met."

"That's what I heard," Peter said dryly as he poked at the snow with his poles so as not to lose the use of his arms.

"I've had it." The angry voice belonged to Mr. Perrone. "This is stupid. We'll all be sick."

"Now, Gustav," Mrs. Perrone said soothingly. "This is the way Tony wanted it. We're doing it for him."

"No," Mr. Perrone said defiantly. "I'm going inside. You tell me when that boy gets here, and I'll come out. Who knows where he could have gotten to?" Mr. Perrone swung one leg, then the other, and started for the pavilion. A moment later, an oath sliced through the howling wind.

"He's fallen!" Pamela shouted. Peter looked over and saw a small black ball thrashing in a drift. Pamela jump-turned her skis so quickly she cut down Mary like a scythed cornstalk. Mary pitched headfirst past Peter and came up with her face coated with snow.

Peter helped pick her up and the two of them joined the others rushing toward Mr. Perrone. He thrashed about more angry than injured, his tongue loosened with every oath he knew. "Now, Gustav," Mrs Perrone scolded, bending over his wriggling figure. "This is Tony's wedding. Do you want to remember forever acting like this?"

"Just help me out of these," he shouted.

Artie flicked off his skis and helped the stricken figure to his feet. As they trudged to the pavilion, Peter scanned the darkness from which Tony was to emerge. "It's no use," he said to Mary. "Even if he does come now, it's too dark for me to read the service."

Sadness shone in Mary's eyes. "There's a light by the door of the pavilion. Can we have it there?" Her pleading tone tugged at Peter.

Pain shot through his fingers pressing the levers to release his feet from the skis. Without caring where he left them, or even if the snow buried them, he staggered to the pavilion door and thrust himself inside. Chills rippled through his whole body. He stole a glance at his watch. Twenty after. Even with no storm, he could not make the church by five-thirty. Tony had to get there soon.

Peter joined the others rubbing themselves warm by the fire. "What a stupid idea," Mr. Perrone grumbled. "I can see this in the summer, but now? That son of mine. He does the craziest things."

Mrs. Perrone cast him an irritated glare. "Quiet, Gustav. You spoil everything."

Artie glanced about. "Well, what do we do now? Does anyone know where Tony might be?"

Mary smiled bravely. "He's just late. That trail was too long for a day like this."

Artie zipped up his parka and drew the collar around his bearded face. "I'm going to look for him."

"On skis?" Peter asked. "How can you find your way in the dark?"

"There's a road on the far side of the park. I'll ask if anyone's seen him." The wind slammed the door shut behind him.

Mr. Perrone's eyes rested hungrily on the small sandwiches, balls of cheese surrounded by circles of crackers, mounds of potato chips and dip. On a large cake with white icing were two miniature skiers on one pair of skis. "What's in the thermos?" Mr. Perrone asked.

"Coffee," Mrs. Perrone replied.

Mr. Perrone ambled away from the fire and stared down at the sandwiches. "Why don't we eat?"

"No," Mrs. Perrone said threateningly. "It's only proper to eat after a wedding, not before. What would Tony say?"

"But I'm hungry. It's dinner time. I didn't get any lunch at the shop today."

The lines on Mrs. Perrone's face softened slightly. "All right. One sandwich and a little coffee. Just to warm you up. But don't anybody tell Tony."

Mr. Perrone picked up a sandwich and bit into it. In a moment it was gone. "They're awful small," he said. "That didn't do anything."

"No." Mrs. Perrone knocked his hand away from the table. "It's Tony's wedding. You just wait." She poured coffee from the thermos and handed it to him. "Here. This'll warm you up. Now you keep quiet."

Peter turned his cold side toward the fire. Feeling was returning to his legs. He wanted to look at his watch, but he was afraid of what it would say. The meeting would be under way. What were they discussing? His feeling of pity for Mary that her wedding was delayed became mixed with twinges of anger that she never seemed to know what she was doing. But he couldn't take out his frustration on her.

"I saw you!" Mrs. Perrone's eyes burned with accusation at Mr. Perrone. "You just took another sandwich. You thought I wasn't watchin' you. I told you—no more!" Mr. Perrone's gaze fell to the floor like that of a dog after a whipping.

Mrs. Perrone took a menacing step forward. "Everything here is for Tony. If you eat his wedding food, you're a pig. The next thing, you'll want his cake." She turned to Peter. "You tell him. It's wrong to eat the food before the married couple are here. He's so dumb. When he gets hungry, he don't care what anybody says. You tell him." She gestured for Peter to set on Mr. Perrone the way someone might sic a guard dog on an intruder.

Suddenly the outside door flew open. Artie, his face grave, gestured for Peter to come outside.

Peter pulled his coat shut and followed Artie out the door. They stopped under the glow of a dim light bulb. Artie shook his head and pushed snow around with his boot. His voice was barely audible above the wind. "Soused," he said. "Drunker 'an a pig. I found him in the tavern next to the park. I figured that's where he'd be. I couldn't even talk to him. He must've skied down there and gone in to get warm. He just forgot to stop drinkin'."

The darkness around the tiny sphere of light seemed impenetrable. What warmth Peter had gained in the pavilion was gone. "What do you suggest we do?" he asked.

"Well, someone's got to tell Mary." Artie eyed Peter with no hint that he was volunteering his services.

Peter sighed. "Okay, I'll do it." He swung the door open, and all faces turned toward them. Artie quickly shrank into a corner.

Mary rushed up. "What is it? Is he hurt? Has something happened?"

"I'm afraid he's drunk," Peter said as gently as he could.

"Drunk?" Mary's eyes grew large with hurt. "He never touches booze. He's a teetotaler. He told me that himself." She looked at Artie, who confirmed with a nod what Peter had said. "I can't believe it." She started to sniffle; a howl escaped her lips. She covered her red face with her hands. "He's a liar!" she shrieked.

Mr. and Mrs. Perrone's faces were lined with desperation. Mr. Perrone looked over at the table. "Well, we might as well eat. We're all hungry. It's dinnertime. And there ain't gonna be no weddin'."

Mrs. Perrone's mouth opened as if she were about to scold, but then it closed. She rose, scanned the lines of sandwiches, picked one up, and took a big bite.

Peter's watch said quarter to six. He had no interest in eating. Mary had sunk down onto a wooden bench; Pamela and Artie were on either side consoling her. The gist of what they said was that Tony was basically a good guy, but maybe the wedding had done something to his nerves. Peter hoped they were right, but he had a hunch Mary would never stop lunging into disappointment. How could she read people so badly?

He pulled Mr. and Mrs. Perrone's attention away from the food they were ravenously eating to explain that he was sorry he had to run, but there was a meeting he was to attend. They seemed not to mind. Mary cast him a tearful farewell, to which he said he would be glad to talk to her later in the week.

12

It was after six when he arrived at the church. Good Samaritan's glowing domes were almost invisible through sheets of wind-driven snow. Peter kept his car to the parts of the parking lot where the snow was less deep. There were no other cars in sight; during a lull in the wind, he could see that no office lights were on in Assisi. The meeting was over.

Or had it even been held? He made a circle of the parking lot, scrutinizing under the high beams of his headlights the snow near the narthex entrance. There were shallow ridges kicked up by car tires, but had they just been made or were they from the staff and workmen that afternoon?

13

The quarter mile cinder track lay in a depression behind the high school. On the smooth grass infield, girls in warm-up suits — blue and gold for Oakdale and cardinal red for Dorchester — paced nervously awaiting their events. The gun puffed smoke, six girls started the half-mile run.

Peter lay on the raincoat he kept in the car, shielding his

eyes from the warm spring sun so he could keep track of Jackie. She was sitting near mid-field stretching out her arms to touch her toes.

The struggle to get the track team was fading. Peter recalled the night the local paper editorialized: WHY DOESN'T THE SCHOOL BOARD COMPLY WITH THE STATE LAW? It was the turning point.

"Campbell, I won't attend worship services here again until you're gone," said the tall member of the School Board and church. "You're a family of meddlers. In Oakdale, we don't like meddlers."

There had been the crank calls. "Are you a man or a woman?" a strange man with a raspy voice had asked Peter at two in the morning. Peter had restrained the unministerial retort that flashed in his mind.

"What's the matter, do you think girls will run faster than boys?" Jackie asked one caller. "Afraid you'll lose your masculinity?" They usually didn't call back after Jackie was through with them.

The court announced its verdict, the school let Jackie and her followers become the track team, silence fell. And the two Good Samaritan members of the School Board continued their strike.

A stout official with a megaphone shouted the third call for the mile run. Jackie stripped off her warmup suit, flicked her hands nervously, and walked onto the track. In her blue shorts with vertical gold stripes, she looked trim, but gangly. She resembled one of those long-legged birds sometimes seen in wildlife refuge swamps. She spoke a few words to her teammate—a girl with the physique of a grasshopper—and smiled at the two girls from Dorchester. One was round, a bit overweight. The other, tall, big-boned, strong. They toed the starting line, the gun rose, and they strode to the first turn—too fast, Peter thought.

For seven laps, the big Dorchester girl, with Jackie a stride behind, pulled away from their teammates. Jackie's arms flowed smoothly; her feet sprang from the cinders as if they had an energy of their own. At the sound of the gun for the last lap, both teams crowded up to the track cheering. A gaunt Oakdale long jumper paused to watch, a Dorchester javelin thrower shrieked at the big-boned girl: "Faster! Faster!" She ran like a machine, her feet and fists moving in circles that suggested the wheels of a locomotive. Her head cocked to one side, her face set in a grimace of determination, she looked unbeatable.

On the back stretch, Jackie pulled out to pass. The Dorchester girl upped her pace, forcing Jackie to drop back and follow her around the turn. Shouts from both teams rose to a crescendo. Parents on the grassy hillside rose to their feet and cheered.

Coming out of the turn, the Dorchester girl glanced back over her inside shoulder. Jackie was not there. She had pulled to the outside and gained a stride. Both girls broke into agonizing sprints toward the finish line. Peter was on his feet shouting. Every muscle strained as if he were the one thrashing to win. Time stopped; kicking legs and staccato arm movements flailed in slow motion.

Both heaving chests broke the string; Peter had no idea who was ahead. Jackie dropped to the ground as if she had passed out; the other girl doubled over in pain. Peter started toward his fallen daughter. She stirred, then was helped to her feet by teammates. She walked slowly down the track.

When she had cooled down, she came up the hill shaking her head. "Tie," she said with a glint in her eye. "That girl is a truck. She's got to be the best in the conference."

Peter could not find words. He threw his arms around Jackie, hugged her as if her run and the victory over the School Board and the victory over the strange people who harassed them on the phone had all come in this one moment.

14

As soon as Peter turned the corner, he saw it. Jackie let escape a gasp. As large as a locomotive, colored in blotches from dull gray to bright orange, his legs as thick as tree trunks, his head looming fifteen feet above the pavement on a long neck—Trojan had taken command of the neighborhood. Mr. Tazano, the junkyard owner who had supplied much of the iron and steel, sat in his wrecker idling at the curb; a police car was parked behind.

Peter and Jackie got out of the car speechless. A group of small girls and boys from the neighborhood stared up open-mouthed. Jeff, clad in jeans and a T-shirt, led a bearded photographer in brown corduroys about, pointing out suitable angles for pictures. Two uniformed policemen stood back on the lawn gazing incredulously as if Trojan had diminished the "How to Respond" section of their police training manual to mere scrap paper.

Jeff came loping over. "I won!" he shouted. His face glowed. "Remember the art contest the newspaper sponsored? Trojan took the sculpture prize." He nodded toward the man squatting down to get the effect of Trojan's full height in a head-on shot. "They're running a feature on Sunday."

Peter felt as if he had just grown six inches. He grabbed Jeff's hand and shook it hard. "Congratulations." In the sunlight, Peter could see clearly the fine detail of the curved plates covering the body and neck, the port doors along the flanks that actually opened.

Jackie gave Jeff a sisterly hug. "You're great," she said.

"How about you?" Jeff asked. "How'd the race go?"

Jackie's cheeks reddened with energy. "A tie—the other girl is the best in the conference. Our team won the meet."

"Darn," Jeff said. "Wish I'd been there. I just got word they wanted to see Trojan when I came home; we had to get him out here in a hurry." His eyes, large behind thick lenses, played proudly over his masterpiece.

The taller of the policemen ambled over to Peter. "Quite a job your son has done there." He nodded toward the iron horse.

Peter smiled uncertainly. He hadn't quite learned to feel at ease with policemen since his stay in jail. "It's taken a long time."

"Got a call." The policeman's tone was apologetic. "Some man wanted us to arrest your boy for this thing. Said he was in violation of the zoning code — running a manufacturing plant in a residential neighborhood." The policeman put his hands on his hips and looked up at Trojan's brontosaurs head. "I don't see any problem, though. It's just a piece of art. Why if we were to arrest everyone doing something creative in his home, we'd be hauling people in every day. But we did have to come out, just to show we responded to the call. In a few minutes we'll move on."

Peter thanked the policeman and looked at the house next door. The sun, hovering just above the roof, glared in his eyes, so he could not discern whether there was a shape in the window or if the drape was twitching. He felt like waving, but thought the better of it. There was no use rubbing salt into the wound.

The policemen drove off, then the photographer; the kids from the neighborhood trickled away in knots exclaiming how 'neat' Trojan was. Leaving Peter and Jeff and Jackie and Mr. Tazano and the towering horse. Peter sighed. "Well, what now?"

Jeff's eyebrows knitted in puzzlement. "There are a few more things I want to do on it . . ." He paused. "I asked my art teacher. She suggested maybe one of the parks could use it. If they set the legs in concrete, it'd be around for years."

Centuries, Peter almost mumbled. "And if the Park Board doesn't want it?"

Jeff shrugged his shoulders. "Maybe the high school. There are some places on the Maple Street side where it would look good. It would break up all that grass."

Something in Peter's head jolted. "Jeff, I'm not sure that would be too wise."

"Why?"

"After the lawsuit, I don't think the School Board would care to have another Campbell trying to get something approved."

Jackie stepped forward with a determined look, but, after a glance at Peter, refrained from uttering whatever was on her mind.

Jeff gazed admiringly at Trojan. "I'm not really too concerned about it. I know he's too big for most places. And there'd probably be a big argument about it. There usually is when it comes to large sculpture." He sighed with satisfaction. "I won the prize. That photographer will give me prints of everything he took, and it was a lot. If I can't put Trojan somewhere, I'll still have the pictures."

Peter put his hand on Jeff's shoulder. "It's a magnificent piece of work. But in the long run, it's talent that counts — you've learned a lot."

Jeff nodded. His shoulder felt strong under Peter's grasp. It would lift lots more iron and lots more plaster, and there would be many more prizes.

15

In the new brick narthex, gone were the glass ceiling, glass walls, and glass partitions between Peter's office and the secretaries. But not gone were the floor-to-ceiling windows he had fought against. They looked out on the garden and what lay beyond — the sanctuary with its sacrilegious cross and the ridge with Gottschalk's twinkling ball.

It had occurred to Peter that they should have sold the rare ball to help pay for the herculean job of unearthing all Gottschalk's illegal chemical drums, replacing the soil, and bringing in topsoil. Even the fountain had been replaced;

acid had eaten away the pipes beneath the sculpture. Peter had told the trustees that with all the expense they should forget it. Again he lost. The new plume was half the height of the old, the sculpture less massive—just a pyramid of circular basins. He sighed when he remembered this was the day the manure was to arrive—tons of it. The ladies were making absolutely certain their dear, beloved roses would have the best possible chance of flourishing. Seeing in his mind the ladies themselves—determined, cheeks puffed with self-righteousness, voices raised in triumph—ripples of nausea crossed his stomach. The God who had fashioned the universe out of nothing had become incarnate in a flower with a prickly stem. God the Father, God the Son, and God the Holy Rose. Thankfully, the new brick narthex had an efficient air-conditioning system; when the manure was fermenting in the sun and rain, he and his co-workers would be spared the heavenly effluvium of fertility.

16

Peter got off the elevator with a flock of business lunchers at the dining room floor of the Delaware Club knowing no more about why he was meeting with Henry Krohn and two others than he did when Henry's uninformative call came the day before. The lunchers headed for the bar, leaving Peter in the vestibule facing the lounge. Two old men sat in deep leather chairs, their heads thrown back, their mouths slacked open in sleep. The reward of lavish retirement, Peter surmised.

Henry Krohn materialized out of nowhere in his indefatigable gray suit—or did he own a closet-full of them?—and grasped Peter's arm. His face wore an effusive smile, the kind sported by maître d's approached by high-tipping customers. Henry steered Peter toward the corridor leading to the private dining rooms. "Everyone's waiting," he said, as if he were ushering Peter into a party—birthday, maybe, or the commemoration of fifty years of faithful service.

Peter recognized the room immediately. The two ancient entrepreneurs cast in oil still glared from the walls. Opposite the empty chair to which Henry pointed hung the painting of Jesus and Jerusalem cum Jonah and Nineveh: Jonah waiting hopefully for Nineveh to fall.

Ralph Ritter, whom Peter knew only distantly, pumped Peter's hand as if they were old friends who hadn't seen each other for a long time. He wore a loose Harris tweed jacket and striped tie. Peter noticed the tie conformed to the latest New Yorker standard for width. His own lagged by an inch or so, rendering his appearance as anachronistic as Good Samaritan people apparently deemed his faith.

Charlie Jarvis had tucked a large white napkin over the top of his shirt as if he were going to tangle with the jumbo lobster. With his girth and heavy jowls hanging over his shirt collar, he didn't need it. He gleamed at Peter as if it was a royal privilege to sit at the same table with him.

They mumbled about the status of the red snapper, and then the waiter — black as always — entered, circled the table for orders, and left. Awkward silence gave way to desultory ramblings about offspring. Peter was tempted to share his enthusiasm about Jackie's track exploits and Jeff's sculpture prize. But with School Board members in the church on ecclesiastical strike and the property committee approaching hysteria over Trojan's future, he figured no one at the table would get much of a kick out of it. He sat quietly through Ralph's lengthy narration of his daughter's cello recital.

The food having come and the well of family triumphs having run dry, Henry shakily groped toward whatever it was they were to talk about: "Well, we should get down to business. We're all working men. We can't take too much time on the lunch hour." It wasn't very profound, and it didn't get things moving much, but it was enough to gain approving nods from Charlie and Ralph. They seemed relieved they didn't have to throw out the first ball. Peter felt a twinge of embarrassment at the difficulty they were having.

Henry lowered his eyes. "As we all know, Good Samaritan has fallen on some bad luck. We've got a good church — make no bones about it. The plant's in good shape. We've still got an excellent reputation. But, in the past few months our performance hasn't been quite what it could be. We've had meetings to try to find out what's wrong, but we haven't come up with much." He paused in expectation that Ralph or Charlie would take it from there, but they were hunting through the snapper for errant bones.

Henry wobbled on: "Apart from these meetings, there have been other discussions. Informal ones on the golf course, here at the Club, wherever members meet. It seems there's a strong consensus as to where the center of our trouble lies."

Watching Henry's eyes flit around the top of the table, Peter wondered, consensus of whom? Certainly not the whole congregation played golf or belonged to the Delaware Club.

Henry proceeded: "It's a lack of leadership. We don't have direction." His gray eyes beseeched the others for support.

Charlie Jarvis nodded gravely. "That's what I've said all along. Somebody has to call the shots. It's just like in a business."

Ralph Ritter pursed his lips. "People respond when they know what the man at the helm is doing. They did with Dr. Strong. They do with that Fennel character Charlie keeps talking about."

Peter found no foothold for entering the discussion — if that was what it was. He would agree there was a dearth of leadership. All the boards did was try to please everybody and expect some invisible army for which they provided no funds to carry out their milksop decisions. Peter salted down his salad and began to munch.

Henry stumbled on. "People are upset we're not moving ahead. We need new members. With costs what they are, we've got to raise more money for the budget. There's a spirit . . . an atmosphere about the place that worries people. It's negative, depressed — as if we've got nothing to be proud of . . . like we've lost the prominence we once enjoyed in the community."

Ralph looked up as if on cue. "As I've said before, you have to look like success in order to be successful. You've got to project a positive image."

Henry started bone hunting in his own snapper, silence fell. If they were expecting Peter suddenly to confess incompetence and take responsibility for all the failures in Good Samaritan, they had misjudged. He chased an elusive cherry tomato around the wooden bowl with his fork.

"Peter, since you're the pastor, we'd like to have your opinion," Henry said.

Peter felt a trap. "I don't have anything to add," he said curtly and continued working on his salad.

Henry leaned forward and rested his arms on the table. "Maybe we need to level with you. The name that comes up most frequently in discussions about the lack of leadership is yours." He paused to observe Peter's reaction. Peter continued on his salad. "People feel the pastor should be more direct, exercise more control over the congregation. Now maybe that isn't your style, but that's what the people want. They're floundering without it. Unless things change drastically, Good Samaritan will fall apart. There's discontentment with everything from the worship service to fingerprints on the windows. It's getting worse every day."

Ralph's brow knit. "Every time I meet people from the church, they want to know what's being done, when we're going to get rolling again. They're looking for someone to give us a spark."

The waiter came in, asked if anything was needed, and retreated.

Peter looked up at his prosecutors. "I'm doing what I was asked to do. The committee wanted someone to help the congregation follow Jesus like the original disciples. Those are the words of the chairman of the committee."

Henry shook his head. "That isn't what the committee chairman told me. He said they had a candidate who could lead Good Samaritan back to the prominence it had in the old days. That's a quote."

"I was told you'd put new life in the church," Ralph Ritter said. "The committee knew we'd lost ground in the community. You were the one to get us back."

"It was the basics," Charlie added. "I told members of the committee we had to do the kinds of things Fennel was doing if we were going to have a growing congregation. They said you were a man of basics."

"It looks like the committee misrepresented me," Peter said matter-of-factly.

"And the big givers," Ralph put in as if Peter had not spoken. "Any pastor of a church this size has to pay close attention to the people who underwrite most of the budget. That's a real sore point, in case you haven't heard."

Of course he had heard. It was Bishop Strong's theme song. It brought a wave of nausea now as it did when he was with Wes. How had they gotten their notion of Jesus so twisted up? When he died he had no bank account, no real estate, no tax shelters — just one garment the soldiers quickly disposed of.

An awkward silence ensued until Charlie Jarvis said, "We're trying to be supportive."

Peter's nerves crackled. "Supportive? This is support?" He glanced at them with a gaze that hurt his eyes. "Telling me I'm at fault because Good Samaritan hasn't recovered its past glory?"

They blinked as if embarrassed. "We've talked to Bishop Stone," Henry said. "We needed guidance as to what to do. He understands our situation very well."

Certainly, Peter thought. The bishop also preaches the gospel according to the rich. Peter could see Henry, Ralph, and Charlie in consultation with Wes: heads nodding in strong affirmation that Peter wasn't licking the right boots.

Bishop Wesley Caiaphas Stone.

Henry's voice sounded as if he had rehearsed what he said next: "There's only one conclusion we can come to. It's joint—the boards, us, Bishop Stone. Good Samaritan isn't the best match for you." His hands fluttered in a gesture of helplessness, as if the conclusion had been delivered to him on stone tablets. "That isn't to say there's something wrong with you as a minister or as a person." The salve, the balm, but not from Gilead. A sop for the condemned. "It's the match we're talking about. Bishop Stone calls it a marriage. As in a marriage, sometimes the partners don't fit."

Anger burned the back of Peter's neck. Bishop Stone was no more competent to comment on marriage than he was on the church. "Then?" Peter asked.

"We need to wipe the slate clean," Ralph said in an upbeat tone.

"God knows we've tried to make this work," Charlie Jarvis added.

God's opinion always carries weight, Peter thought. He had learned to be suspicious of those too certain about where God stood on matters. God always seemed to side with their predilections. "What are you driving at?"

Henry's eyes glowed with gray compassion. "Bishop Stone says he'll assign you to another church. No problem."

"So I'm fired?" Peter asked.

Henry recoiled in horror. "No, no, that's not it. It's a mismatch." He tilted his head as if looking at Peter at an angle would make Peter see more clearly how everything was for his benefit. "There's the matter of your own choice. The denomination requires a letter of resignation from you before Bishop Stone can act. It's part of the autonomy granted to pastors."

Peter envisioned them and Wes scouring the church constitution to see if the autonomy rights could be bypassed. It was obviously awkward for them to have to ask him to participate in his own axing.

Charlie rested his beefy arms on the table. "Surely, Peter,

you must be aware. Maybe people haven't said as much to you as they should. But there hasn't been much enthusiasm. Problems have been piling up."

"I'm aware of the silence," Peter said. "But I've got my calling."

Ralph Ritter nodded approvingly. "Of course you have. But unfortunately things just haven't meshed. The bishop says there are dozens of churches that would respond to your style of leadership. But here, we've got to move ahead. Too much ground has been lost."

Peter gazed up at the painting where Jonah stared down at Nineveh. Surely Nineveh wanted the prophet swept from his perch there on the bluff. But did that mean Jonah should pack up and leave? Preach and run? "I'm not ready to sign anything," he said.

From the perplexity on their faces, he assumed he had deviated from the script. They glanced at one another to see who had the next line. Finally Henry sighed, "Bishop Stone wants to talk to you. He might be able to clarify the situation better than we have."

"Maybe so," Peter said. But he had no intention of going to Wes.

17

Peter was sitting on the family room sofa. Late afternoon sun slanted in the windows. Before him lay the cold fireplace. Except for occasional creaks, the house was silent. Jeff was out in the garage welding more iron onto overweight Trojan, Jackie had not returned from track practice, and Brenda was at the new ballet class at the university. It was the first time since coming to Good Samaritan Peter had found himself with nothing to do. Or had the luncheon conversation temporarily disarmed his sense of responsibility?

He put on old trousers and a shirt that had grown thin at the elbows and went down to the cellar. It had remained largely untouched since the move: boxes of miscellaneous scattered about, junk piled on top of cartons. He cleared the workbench of wilted plants, odd bolts of fabric, the broken waffle iron he had been going to fix, and then brushed it clean. He rummaged through sagging shelves of canned tomatoes, rags, paint cans, empty boxes, pieces of pipe, wood scraps, until he came upon the thick rectangular board hollowed out with the rough cross.

The oak had darkened since he had worked on it in his previous parish, but there were no cracks. He ran his fingers over the cross. He liked its splintery feel, but the arms weren't well-defined enough.

Grasping his electric carving tool, he planed away tiny fragments of wood. The tool shrieked like a dentist's drill; the smell of freshly cut oak mingled with mildew dampness. The one bare bulb hanging over the workbench cast shadows, so he had to twist around to make sure he didn't shave too much off the upright and crossarm. The cutter's whine was a form of silence, obliterating the lunch meeting.

When he turned off the machine to exchange the angular bit for the small, spherical one good for smoothing carved out depressions, he heard a foot on the stairs. Brenda stood like a lizard in her leotards watching him. He held up the cross for her to see. She smiled and descended hesitantly to the bottom step. "You haven't worked on that for years," she said. "Why now?"

He slipped down off the stool, went over, and kissed her. "You're suspicious?"

She smiled. "Well, you've got to admit that since we've been here you've done nothing but work for the church. This is a bit different."

"You're right," he said. "I was taken out to a sumptuous lunch today and asked to resign." It amazed him he could say it so easily, that he was not beset by inner pain.

Brenda stood silent for a moment, then said, "Good."

"Good?" He had speculated on how she might respond, but this was not one of the options.

"Yes."

"You like it when people tell your husband he's responsible for everything that's gone wrong? There's no leadership, the church has a tarnished reputation, it's not moving ahead, its rich members feel like hothouse plants the gardener refuses to water?"

She laughed. "Do you want pity?"

"A little," he replied.

She kissed him on the lips. "There, you have it."

"But why good?" he asked.

"Because it will get us away from this church and out of this town."

"But your ballet class?"

"I'll miss it. But you've got to realize the big reason I'm going is because without it I would go out of my mind. If I weren't here, I wouldn't so desperately need something to keep my sanity."

Peter shrugged. He had expected a much different response. Wounded wife defending persecuted husband against savages trying to run him out of town. Vengeful wife threatening to go directly to the boards and tell them how heathen they were. Self-pitying wife complaining to the Good Samaritan grapevine how miserable the church made life at the parsonage. But 'good?' It was so simple, and yet apt.

18

Wes paced in front of Peter's desk. Crimson patches checkered his face, his gestures consisted of small jerks. "It's been five days, Peter." Thus far Wes had refused to sit down. His shiny brass cross swung back and forth across his chest. "People are starting to talk. Somewhere there's a leak. I need your resignation now."

Peter leaned back in his chair and clasped his hands behind his neck. Outside the window, mounds of manure dried in the sun. He had already shut the louvers to reduce the stench. Above the garden, in the sanctuary, the brass cross proudly desecrated the communion table. "I haven't said anything to anybody. If word's getting out, it must be from someone else."

Wes rammed his chubby hands into his jacket pockets. "You can't keep something like this quiet forever." Lines furrowed his brow. "People sense when something's up."

"I suppose so," Peter said, amazed at how no one had offered to help him squelch leaks from the office when Miss Hensley was around and yet now there was such a brouhaha.

"Peter, you're so calm about this. Can't you see the mess you're making? We wanted it taken care of quickly."

Peter sighed. "I'm not the one making the mess. You should talk to others."

Wes strode to the window. "Can't you see we're trying to make it easy for you? If the Council has to vote, if this thing has to go to the Synod, then everyone will be up in arms. People will be hurt. It may take years for this church to recover."

An obligatory twinge of sympathy for poor Good Samaritan passed through Peter and quickly vanished. "I'm sure it might," he said.

Wes whirled from the window. "Don't you care? Are you saying you want this church torn up? Has something happened to your mind?" His eyes bulged; he spit words through tightly clenched teeth.

Peter gazed pensively out at the brown hills in the garden. "I'm not trying to tear anything up. I haven't done anything. You don't seem to realize that. You and those others started this thing."

Wes resumed pacing. His hands fluttered as if they would like to throttle Peter's neck, but Peter was sure the bishop was held in check by his *imago dei*. "Okay, okay. So you didn't start it. But what you don't realize is that we've done it this way for your benefit. If you resign, you save face.

I'll put you in another church. Your pastorate here was an unfortunate mismatch. People can understand that."

Revulsion rose in Peter's stomach. Wes's theology of the church had fallen to total ruin. He stared over Wes's bald head with the halo fringe of white hair without answering.

Wes leaned over the desk and breathed into Peter's face. His offensive cross dangled before Peter's eyes. "Why? Why won't you turn in your resignation?"

"I haven't chosen to," Peter said.

Wes's lower lip trembled, his eyeballs puffed as if they might burst. "Haven't chosen to? What does that mean?"

"Just what I said. It's my move. Thus far, I've chosen to make no move at all. That is one of my options."

Wes leaned over farther until he was inches from Peter's face. "Do you realize the consequences if I have to remove you?"

Peter smiled. "Siberia?"

Wes reared up and resumed pacing. "You have no idea what you're doing. I really wonder about your judgment . . . about . . . about your mind."

Peter flicked grains of erasure dust off his desk. "I'm learning a bit about how churches are run. They hire pastors with commitments no one intends to keep. They talk about Jesus, but the real messiah is the money boys . . ."

"I've heard it before," Wes interrupted. He stopped pacing. "Don't you realize the whole congregation is against you?" His arms swept over the barnyard née garden. "Your ministry is finished. The people don't follow you. You've no future here. Every minute you stay, you're working against the best interests of Good Samaritan." He trembled, his head jerked about as if he were on the verge of a seizure. "You weren't like this in your last parish."

Peter arched his head forward. "No," he conceded. "Those people were self-starters; all they needed was encouragement. I gave them ideas, just as I've given the boards here ideas. But they did something with them. Here, they're ignored."

"Because they don't understand what you're talking about," Wes retorted. "They're corporate people; they need to be told what to do. They feel you're not doing your job when you just give them ideas."

"So I'm a corporate executive?"

Wes turned his gaze to the garden scarp. "There's no use going back over what's wrong. No matter what's said now, you're finished. You've got no followers. Nothing is happening . . ."

"Out there it is." Peter nodded toward the garden.

Wes shook his head impatiently. "Not out there — with the congregation. They're not with you." He paced with his hands in his pockets. "I wonder if you ever knew what you were doing."

Peter tilted his chair back. "It's clear to me."

"Clear? What's clear?"

"Discipleship. Following Jesus. What they called me to do."

"All they want is to be good church members," Wes blurted.

Peter felt like spitting. "What's that?"

"Something they can understand. Belonging to a church . . . attending a church . . . supporting a church . . . that has meaning."

"And that's all they'll get," Peter said.

"Just what do you mean by that?"

"Just what I said."

"Dammit." Wes pounded his foot on the floor and glanced sheepishly toward the door to the outer office as if he were fearful the secretaries might notice the tarnishing of his *imago dei*. "You think people are theological geniuses. You think they're standing in line to be saints running around in robes. You're hopelessly out of touch. This is the twentieth century. Everything Jesus did is in institutions now. He didn't have a church. If he had, he would've run it for the sake of its members. Remember, he was a servant of the people."

Peter rested his elbows on the desk. "Have you ever thought that maybe he didn't want a church? That he was trying to save people from the kinds of religious institutions that nailed him to the cross? That he knew something we don't—how easy it is for institutions to become ends in themselves? I'm not against churches per se—or I'd resign the ministry. But I'm dead set against churches that serve the egotistical ravings of their members."

Wes turned his back as if he were studying the far wall. "I wish you would resign the ministry." He whirled about. "It would make my job a helluva lot simpler and save this congregation from the disaster you're bringing on it."

Peter pursed his lips in mock thoughtfulness. "I could be a double martyr then—once for Good Samaritan and once for you."

"Peter, I'm not kidding. Time has run out. We've got a congregation that's coming apart, and you're in here cracking jokes. If you care at all about Good Samaritan, then you'll have that resignation in my hands today. If you don't, then we'll convene the Council to petition the Synod to have you removed." He pressed his pudgy hands down on the desk. "I'm telling you, Peter, if we have to do that, you'll find yourself transferred to a church so far out in the sticks you'll have to ride horseback to get to town."

"Circuit rider?" Peter intoned.

"You don't think I have the power?"

"You do," Peter said lightly. "But I didn't think you would use it to wreak vengeance on someone who stood up for the principles in which he believes." He stared down at his desk. "But maybe I'm wrong."

Wes paced to the window and looked out. Fountain spray sparkled in sunlight among the manure mountains. "For the last time, Peter, are you going to submit that resignation or not?"

Peter met his glare without blinking. "No."

Wes's cheeks quivered, his eyes glared coldly. "You give me no choice," he said. "I never thought of you as a troublemaker. It might take some time to find you a new parish, quite a long time."

When Wes was gone, Peter went out into the entry to see if there were any cars left in the parking lot. Satisfying himself no one was around, he went back to his office, picked up the attaché case he had brought from home, and strode up to the sanctuary. He mounted the chancel steps, laid the case on the communion table next to the brass cross, opened it, and drew out the hacksaw.

19

The congregation sat devoid of expression watching Mr. Straphe gyrate the choir through some obscure and difficult anthem. Above the sanctuary hung clouds the shade of wash water. It was one of those days when the air seemed so weary of stagnation it could do nothing but break into violence. Heavy rain had fallen through the night, straight down humid large-drop rain that came and went without warning. But instead of bringing relief, it had only made the air heavier. It had also turned to a darker shade of brown the manure mountains covering the garden scarp visible beyond the back wall of the sanctuary.

The hymn expired, Peter rose and called on Mr. Krohn to step forward. Henry's discomfort was immediately evident. He wobbled up the center aisle and almost stumbled headlong climbing the stairs to the chancel. Entering the pulpit, his face was ashen, his hands trembled. The congregation stirred uneasily at his discomfort. Peter felt he was a spectator at an event that only vaguely affected him.

Henry smoothed out a small piece of paper on the pulpit desk, cleared his throat, swallowed hard, then said he had an announcement to make in behalf of the Council, the Synod, and the bishop. The multiple responsibility gave whatever was coming the brassy sound of officiousness.

Peter recalled Wes's campaign to get him out. When the

Council met, Wes told it there was only one decision it could make or Good Samaritan was finished. The decision took only half an hour. At the meeting of the Synod, Peter felt as if he had been thrown to the vultures. He expected some envy would be directed toward him because he was pastor of a prestigious church. But he had not anticipated that Good Samaritan's troubles would draw such hostility. It was a field day for pecking away at an ecclesiastical carcass. And peck they did. Peter stood before the Synod making a defense of his ministry, but apart from a few desultory remarks supposedly in his favor, he was overwhelmingly defeated. Of course there was compassion afterward—the stammering apologies of pious executioners.

Henry's voice droned: "I wish to announce that the Reverend Peter Campbell has been relieved of his pastoral duties at Good Samaritan as of today. The bishop and the Council will immediately prepare for the selection of a new pastor." The voice ended with a quaver. Henry folded the paper, tucked it in his pocket, and wobbled back to his seat.

The faces of the congregation lost none of their funereal somberness. The wake with the absent body. Perhaps they were mesmerized by the brass cross or by Gottschalk's glowing ball. Brenda and Jackie and Jeff looked down, their faces flushed with anger. Pat Andrews peered about as if to see if there might be a mass rush to the door as a sign of protest. But there was none. Peter got up, and with no reference to Mr. Krohn's announcement, called for the morning offering and then sat down to listen to another of Mr. Straphe's anthemological oddities.

20

At an air base a hundred miles from Oakdale, four swept wing jet fighter planes, their engines turning at a low whine, taxied single file to the downwind end of runway twenty-two. From the cockpit of Number Four, Lieutenant Alfred Smith took an anxious look at the overcast sky. His radio crackled: "Ceiling—two thousand, wind—forty-five degrees, five knots. Storm cells in the target area with a cold front expected through late in the day."

"Why can't it come through now?" Lieutenant Smith whispered to himself. Of all the days. The squadron commander's ultimatum rang ominously in his brain. "If you arrive at the target late just once more, you'll be relieved from flight duty." The threat cut like a knife, as if someone had threatened to take his life. Only when he was slashing through blue sky did he feel his life had any worth at all. During the week, squeezing greasy ointment into tiny tubes, counting pills into bottles, listening to endless complaints from runaway hemorrhoids to premature baldness as assistant pharmacist at Barney's Drug Store, he felt as expendable as a used candy wrapper. Up where the sun was white and the earth a tiny insignificance, there were no women with female problems or men with canes looking for a vitamin that would restore their virility. Up there, there was only the roar of thousands of pounds of thrust and freedom that he knew nowhere else.

Number One turned onto the runway and accelerated. Alfred reminded himself: if there are clouds on the run to the target, keep your hand off the throttle. Sweat broke out on his forehead as he recalled how many times he had failed; today he would not.

Number Two was up. Number Three pulled onto the runway, accelerated, climbed at a steep angle. The ground trembled. Alfred spooled up his engine, turned onto the broad swath of concrete lined with light stanchions, pushed the throttle forward. The engine screamed, light stanchions blurred past, acceleration g's pressed him back in the seat. A glance at the air speed indicator. He pulled back the stick, the nose came up, then the smooth lift of flight. Adrenalin pumped through his veins. He aimed steeply into the clouds, his eyes locked onto Number Three's T-shaped tail.

21

Deep into his sermon, Peter felt like Jonah walking the streets of Nineveh. Gold and silver adorning palaces and temples. Armored warriors marching down a broad street. In the temples: idols—Ishtar, Astarte—the fertility gods. Worshippers lacerating themselves with whips, the gut-wrenching sight of dismembered hands and feet thrown up onto sacrificial fires. Peter made the scene as gory as he could, but the congregation sat in solemn silence as if he were nothing more than a TV huckster extolling the virtues of toilet bowl cleaner.

Would the people of Nineveh listen to Jonah's warning that the city would be overthrown if he did not attack their idols, demonstrate in some tangible way that the gods the people believed in were not God at all? There could be no equivocation; if there were to be a turning to God, there had to be a turning away from the gods. Still vacant looks.

He moved on to Jesus marching on Jerusalem from the Mount of Olives: his followers showering him with praise. But when Jesus entered the temple and took stock of the moneychangers and the sellers of birds and animals, the festive mood vanished. Words gave way to action. Jesus grasped purses and sent coins skittering across plaza stones. He slashed open cages, clapped his hands, watched flocks of birds flutter to freedom. He unbound ropes holding lambs and goats and shooed them out into the street, refusing to heed the cries of their owners and the stiff, formal frowns on the faces of officials. Peter lowered his voice: "There is a time when, in order for the new to come, the old must go." Power rose in his chest; nothing could bring to a halt the chain of events he had unleashed.

22

At thirty thousand feet, the air was clear. Alfred leveled off and fell into formation behind Number Three, his eyes riveted on the silver wing. He would follow it into the ground if that's where it went. Below lay a tufted carpet of cloud from which rose towering columns of cumulus. Dark patches could be seen in the columns. Lightning discharges looked like the gun flashes of giant battleships. Alfred thought of the awesome power of cold air clashing with warm, violent winds that sent the pillars ten thousand feet above his hurtling plane.

Suddenly Number Three turned on his back and dove. Alfred jerked the stick over and grimaced as g forces pressed him down into the seat. The three T-shapes ahead were hurtling toward the cloud deck at Mach point eight, sixty miles per hour below the speed of sound. It was like riding the down slope of a roller coaster from six miles in the sky.

Number One headed directly toward the foot of a giant cumulus. Alfred's nerves twitched. Did Number One have to do that? What had radar told him? The cloud loomed larger and larger until, like a Himalayan peak, its summit could no longer be seen. They were diving toward an invisible tunnel at its base.

Suddenly the planes ahead plunged out of sight and Alfred was engulfed in darkness. He marked on his instruments the angle of descent. He had a vague notion that he was holding his breath. His right hand tightly grasped the stick; a glance at his instruments assured him he was at the same angle as when he had entered the cloud. Water streamed back on the canopy. A flash of lightning blinded him. Sharp currents of air buffeted his craft like heavy waves slapping a speed boat.

Then he saw it. He blinked his eyes, but it was still there. The T-shape of Number Three's tail. He couldn't be seeing right. The clouds were too dense. If he could see it that well, he would be flying up its tailpipe. But the shape would not leave. He felt his left hand groping for the throttle, his fingers wrapping around it, pressure on his thumb and fingers as he eased it back. He must not. The commander had warned him. But the T-shape — surely they would crash. They could not fly through clouds this close together. Sweat pouring from the hand grasping the throttle soaked his glove.

Suddenly the clouds vanished. Below lay patchwork patterns of farm fields, the lazy ribbon of a river, pale dual lanes of an expressway. And directly ahead, Number Three had shrunk to the size of a gnat. Alfred glanced at his speed indicator. Mach point seven. His heart raced. In minutes they would make the final turn over the glass church. He had to be in formation. The hand clutching the throttle tightened, his palm felt the push. The craft surged like a thoroughbred, the speed indicator crept upward.

23

Peter turned to the communion table. Keeping his eyes fixed on the blasphemous brass icon, he recited all the idolatry it represented. No sacrifice, no blood, no suffering, no self-denial for the sake of Christ, no giving of oneself for the sake of others. It was religion without God, religion based on ego and false assumptions about human goodness. Energy pulsated through his chest and head, he rose to his tiptoes, his arms flailed in defiance of all the lies the brass cross represented.

He strode over to the table, picked up the gleaming offender, held it high over his head, and faced the congregation. "It must go!" he shouted. Suddenly above his head, above the cross waving in his hand, three shapes in quick succession, then gone. Their roar drew the congregation's gray gazes upward. Peter waited. When their eyes came back to him, he brought down his arm, hurling the cross against the old piece of carpet he had placed on the chancel floor. The idol shattered along the incisions he had cut with the saw. He stooped down, picked up the pieces and held them up for all to see. The ache that stiffened the back of his neck eased.

Suddenly another shape overhead. But soundless, until the entire sanctuary reeled as if struck by a cosmic hammer. Every pane of glass and the large dome shattered. Fragments fell in a blizzard of hailstones. Framing beams shuddered, the chancel beneath Peter trembled. The blast of the soundwave blew every thought from his mind.

All eyes focused upward. Then all were down: pinstripes, silks, and furs cowering in their pews, covering their faces with their hands to ward off the shards showering upon them. Peter too bowed his head, keeping a tight grip on the fragments of the false god.

The sonic boom rumbled its way out across the countryside like a retreating roll of thunder. The building stopped swaying. Peter looked up. Benedict and Assisi and the walkways were just naked beams and supports. There was nothing left of Good Samaritan but skeletal bones. Up on the ridge where Gottschalk's eternal light had glowed, there was nothing but a mound of fragments encircling the base of an empty Bunyanesque golf tee.

In the sanctuary, the congregation began to recover from shock. The sight brought Peter up short. It was the first time he had seen Good Samaritan saints in intimate physical contact. With careful precision, they were tweezing glass fragments from each other's clothing, out of each other's hair. From curly hair, from flawless blond permanents, from gray hair, red hair, brown hair, white hair, from bald domes, from buns and ponytails and bouffants and bangs—hesitant fingers reached in, pincered shards, and flicked them to the floor. He had seen it before, at a zoo, monkeys hunting lice. And to see them doing it in their pinstripes and silks and furs—it was as if they were suddenly struck naked. What he saw was what was. No guile, no images, just a bunch of frightened people hunting for glass lice.

Then, from the garden came the wave. Teenagers near the back of the sanctuary started to snicker, broke into uncontrollable peals. Their parents cast them stern glances and broke down themselves, raucous laughter rang up to the open sky. Waves of levity rippled through the army of glass pickers as if they were at a party.

Finally the garden's gift hit Peter: the defecations of ten thousand horses ripened in warm overnight rain to the peak of effluvial perfection wafted gently up the slope by the first breeze of the arriving front. A cosmic flatus that no amount of designer perfume, deodorant, or air freshener could dispel.

On Peter's bulletin, it said he should pronounce the benediction. But how could he when no one was paying attention? The atmosphere was carnival. The gods had fallen. What was there left to say?

He descended the steps and headed for the main exit. His shoes were thick-soled, so he didn't have to worry about the fragments crackling underfoot. Dark-suited-jackets-buttoned ushers had found straw brooms. Sweeping down the aisles, they looked like Dickensian streetcleaners. Members of the congregation waited jovially in their pews for their aisles to be swept. They had that eager look of the snowed-in waiting for a plow to arrive.

They snickered and smiled their way toward Peter. Gone were the stiff backs, piercing gazes of holiness, jaws rigid with rectitude. Their arm and leg movements were animated, they joked with one another. When they came up to Peter with spontaneous handshakes, they said "Hi," instead of the formal, "Good morning, Pastor. Nice day, isn't it?" For the first time, he felt he and the congregation were on the same level — as if maybe they understood what he was trying to say.

Pat Andrews threw her arms around him and gave him a kiss. "Act of God!" she shrieked. Peter laughed. "And I thought you were a patsy," she added. "I sure misjudged. I tend to look at everything from one point of view." She glanced at the glass-pickers around her. "They sure look different now. But whether they'll ever really get concerned about other people? I don't know."

"You never do," Peter said. But he could not tell if she heard him because she had swept away.

Charlie Jarvis took Peter's hand for a long shake and worked his jowls as if he did not know what to say. "Maybe I've been wrong about you. I always thought you didn't preach the Bible. But maybe I haven't been listening. That was a humdinger today. And the cross. I have to hand it to you. It was like seeing one of the prophets of old." Charlie's jowls continued to work. "I wonder if we should reconsider," he said to himself as he ambled off on his thick, stubby legs.

Mrs. Clayton scooted up with a broad smile. "They may think the smell is awful," she said, "but to me it's like expensive perfume. To think that at last we're going to have the garden. I'll always remember you as the minister who helped us finish it. It's been such a hard struggle." She wobbled off muttering: "If only Miss Hayes were here to see it."

Henry Krohn nodded his head thoughtfully. His discomfort at being the executioner revealed itself in a flitting gaze that examined Peter's tie, jaw, ears, hair, and shoes, but could not stare into his eyes. "Must admit you made yourself clear this morning," he said. "I'd probably have to agree with a lot you said. Maybe we acted a bit hastily." He paused. "Bishop Stone will find you a good church. I'm sure he will."

24

The parsonage front bedroom window and a window in the garage door were broken. And the garage looked different. Peter got out of the car, with Jackie and Jeff and Brenda behind him, to take a look. He could see right through to the back—Trojan had blocked that view for months.

He grabbed the handle and rolled up the door. Trojan was gone! At least he wasn't where he had been. In the floor loomed a huge hole: all the pavement had caved in and was hidden in darkness. "The salt mine," Peter said in astonishment, remembering how people mistakenly had thought it was the culprit killing the roses. His heart slowed in anticipation of Jeff's anguish.

Jackie moved, letting in daylight that dispelled part of the shadow. In the glow loomed Trojan's massive head. He was reared back in the cavity so only his head was visible—at an angle from which Peter had never observed it before. There were the dark iron eyes, the hollow round nostrils, and the mouth—curved upward in a sly grin.

Jeff chuckled, broke into unrestrained laughter. Jackie bent double, tears rolling down her cheeks. Brenda giggled. The ache in Peter's neck eased.

"Well, that solves one problem," Jeff said. "Trojan has taken care of himself. The Park Board said it didn't want him."

"That's two problems," Peter said. "We've got a nice hole here where the church can dump itself."

Inside the house, Peter went to the back window to look down on the remains of Oakdale's prestigious church. Dark steel beams stood bare under gray clouds, but he felt no impulse to cover her nakedness. She didn't belong to him any more. The power that had kept him perched on that hill had been broken. He hadn't done what the committee had envisioned—whatever that was. He hadn't done the discipleship he thought he had come for. But he was finished and could leave—after he'd done something about the hunger growling in his stomach.